I0742547

HER SIDE *of* HISTORY

Finding My Foremothers' Footprints

CLAUDIA J. SEVERIN

DEDICATION

To the descendants of Ina, Mary, Nellie, and Katie. May you live long enough to appreciate and honor all of those who trod before.

"Our ancestors are totally essential to our every waking moment, although most of us don't even have the faintest idea about their lives, their trials, their hardships or challenges."
—Annie Lennox

CONTENTS

ACKNOWLEDGMENTS

I have enjoyed writing as long as I have been able to put pencil to paper, and many teachers and my parents have been supportive. Like many would-be writers, I found it necessary to earn a living for forty-odd years, restricting my writing to mostly business use.

As this anthology is about ancestors, many efforts to make the sources of information available are unknown to me: volunteers or workers who digitized newspaper articles or contributed family trees and other information to online genealogy sites or in genealogy libraries.

I wish to thank JustWrite Communications for their editing expertise. I appreciate the feedback and support from the Lincoln-Lancaster County Genealogical Society of Lincoln, Nebraska; particularly the writing group, Time Travelers.

My thanks to my daughters, Elizabeth Miller, Summer Cowman, and Melanie Severin, who read early drafts of these stories. The cover design is by Melanie Severin with appearances by Summer, Aaron, and Lincoln Cowman.

INA

PROLOGUE

CAMP FUNSTON, KANSAS, DECEMBER 16, 1918

CLINTON CLAUDE MCCRACKEN

My Darling Ina,

This is not what we expected, is it? Here I am, finally training for the war in Europe, in the middle of Kansas. It doesn't look much different than the rolling fields in Iowa or South Dakota, but this place has been transformed since the army got here, just like the recruits, with discipline and sweat. It has been steamrolled with tens of thousands of boot prints. It is a small town full of barracks and barren fields for practicing organized maneuvers. We are prepared and the general himself said the Tenth division is one of the best-trained units. Now we are on standby. The men around me are so young: just out of school or plucked from their farm chores. They have not yet really lived, while I feel like I have a whole lifetime behind me at thirty years old.

Maybe you are watching over me from afar because it doesn't look like I will be facing combat or going anywhere near the front lines. Since the armistice was announced last month, frustration has set in. If we aren't going overseas, we want to go home. But the army moves slowly and so we mark time.

Sometimes I close my eyes and picture you waiting patiently for me in our home on South Center Avenue, the baby cooing in your lap, and all of the grandparents hoping to spoil her at Christmas. Home. I don't even know where home is anymore. I do get letters from my sisters and my mother, and they keep me informed of what is happening in the family. I even got a nice letter from your sister, Natalie, the other day asking me to keep in touch.

I can still see you riding in our beautiful roadster, the summer wind whipping through your golden hair and gossamer dress. Sometimes I just want to go back in time. I wish we knew each other when we were younger. I dream about the first time we met.

He stopped. It was time to head to the mess tent. He wasn't sure when he would pick this up again. Maybe this was a waste of time. What was the point in writing after everything that happened?

CHAPTER ONE

SIOUX CITY, IOWA, JANUARY, 1912

INA HAZEL HALL

The middle-aged man sitting across the table had a stern look on his face, kind of like her father did when he wanted the girls to take him seriously. That hardly ever worked.

"Miss Hall, please tell me a little about yourself and why you are applying for a stenographer position at the gas and electric company."

"Well, Mr. Allen, I am not sure where to begin. I was born in Peiro. Most folks have never even heard of Peiro, but it is right here in Woodbury County. My father farmed, and there were a few neighbors nearby, and a school, and a cemetery. Then the school closed, and the neighbors left, until all that was left was our farm and the cemetery. Now they call it a ghost town, I guess because most of the residents are in the cemetery. Sorry, that was kind of a joke. Anyway, I grew up in Peiro, then we moved to Morningside. My father is the auditor for the city, you know. I have six sisters and a brother, and we are all pretty close, I guess. After secondary school, I went to Morningside College. I thought it was pretty great. I made some wonderful friends there. Then I got a teaching job for a year, but I am not sure teaching suits me. So I went to business school and learned shorthand and all the other office skills, and that is why I would like to be considered for your stenographer job."

"A pretty young thing like you must have a beau or a husband. What will he think about you getting a job?" Mr. Allen asked.

"No, no beau, no husband yet. I guess I will work it out when the time comes. This seems like a real fine place to work. Maybe I will meet the right man here."

Ina smiled sweetly at Mr. Allen, then hoped he would not get the wrong idea and think she meant she was interested in him. My goodness, she was twenty-three and had never been married. Most people would consider her in the spinster category. But she knew she still looked childlike and could pass for eighteen. She decided a few years ago that teaching was no place for a single girl; you were not very likely to meet single men there. The Sioux City Gas and Electric Company, on the other hand, employed many men and more were hired every day. Even Flossie and Hattie told her this place was a goldmine of strong young men, and maybe she wouldn't be marrying a farmer. There were nice farmers, but she wanted to be able to move to a big city and travel to exciting places. Farmers were not likely to do that.

Ina could have gotten married already. In a houseful of girls, the boys swarmed through like bees in a flower garden. There was Thomas in college. He told her he was in love with her, but he was in love with his image of her. He had their lives all planned out for them. He was going to help his father build houses in Ames, and she would be home with the children. Oh yes, he wanted a houseful of children. This was all very nice, but he never seemed to care about what she wanted. If she tried to question him or make a suggestion about anything, he dismissed it saying he knew what was best for them. He even had the nerve to tell her she should clean her room when he came to visit her at her parents' house. She finally told him he should marry himself because a modern educated woman wanted a partnership with her husband. This was what her father called "being difficult."

"Miss Hall?" Mr. Allen was saying. Oh no, she must have been lost in her daydream. "Please come this way and I will have Mrs. Kenton give you a shorthand test. If you receive a passing score, we will have you start work on the twentieth. We do seem to lose quite a few of our office ladies to marriage. You will find the turnover is pretty steady."

She grabbed her cloak and handbag and jumped up. "Oh thank you, Mr. Allen. You won't be sorry."

APRIL, 1912

Ina smoothed out her curly tresses and donned her hat and jacket before heading out to catch the streetcar to take her to work. She had been working at Sioux City Gas and Electric for three months now. She enjoyed the work, but she still had not met the man of her dreams. She was not despairing over this because she knew she was going to be successful on her own. She hoped to find a man who could recognize her value.

She had just hopped off the streetcar, bidding a good morning to Mr. Goodacre, the driver. She could smell the first blooms as spring staked its claim on the budding trees lining the avenue. She always left home early to catch the streetcar, and so she could have a little time to read her library book before starting the morning tasks at work. Even though she had finished school and quit teaching, she still enjoyed reading every day to keep her mind open to new ideas. This latest book was so intriguing, in fact—

"*Ooooh!*" Ina cried.

A sturdy young man walking backward slammed into her, knocking her bag to the ground. She nearly spilled onto the path herself, but the man caught her before her knees hit the ground. In the process of trying to keep them both upright, he lost his balance falling on his backside. Since he had his hand around her waist, she ended up sitting on his lap in the middle of the brick sidewalk.

"I am so sorry!" her assailant said. "I didn't see you there."

Ina smoothed her skirt over her shins, glad she didn't hike up her dress or skin her knees. She turned and tried to stand up, which was difficult with her long black skirt spread out underfoot. Then she saw those eyes. Those extraordinary dark-blue sapphire eyes seemed to pierce right into her soul. He was not strikingly handsome, but he had elegant features, and they all seemed to be focused on her welfare now.

"Are you all right?" He jumped to his feet in one swift move. He reached both his hands out to help her up. "I can't believe how clumsy I am, and now I've taken such a lovely girl down with me!"

He thinks I'm lovely? No one calls me lovely, she thought. At least not until now. I was the disheveled girl whose hair was always sticking out oddly in the group pictures. Whose mother was always wiping food or dirt off her face. Whose knees and elbows were forever scabbed. While other girls had disdain for the sun, hoping to keep ivory complexions, I was outdoors most of the day and have the freckles to show for it.

She noticed her bag was nearly in the street, and her comb, wallet, compact, and book were littering the damp and dirty walkway like leaves after a rain.

"Here, let me get those," he said grabbing her book and other belongings. "Hey, what is this?" he asked, holding up her copy of *The Science of Getting Rich* by Wallace D. Wattles.

"Oh never mind," she flushed, embarrassed he'd seen what she was reading. "I got it at the library, just for a lark."

"What do you think of it?" he asked, those probing deep-blue eyes again scanning her face intently. He brushed the dirt off his pants, and bent down to brush some off her skirt, and handed her bag back to her.

"Well," she stammered, "I mean, I haven't finished it yet, but it seems like he has some compelling ideas…" He probably thinks this is overly enterprising, especially for a young lady. Most men considered financial matters their domain.

"You won't believe this." He pulled a matching book from inside his jacket. "I asked you because I am reading the same thing. I just don't know what this means."

"Maybe it means we're both poor as church mice," she laughed, but it was a pleasant serendipity. She noticed then he was impeccably dressed in a three-piece suit and tie, and his shoes had a high shine. Even after taking a spill, he looked like he could be in a haberdashery advertisement. He didn't look like he was poor.

"Clinton!" she heard a young woman calling.

Drat, Ina thought. That must be his wife.

"Clinton, what on earth are you doing? Did I see you knock this poor lady over?" A tall dark-haired woman appeared at his side. She was about the same age as Clinton. Her hair was pulled back in a neat chignon and she was stylishly dressed down to her leather gloves.

As Ina looked closer, her face seemed vaguely familiar. Her eyes were very much like the man's. In fact, her whole face was so similar to his. Enough she could be his—

"Sister," he said, a little bit too quickly. "This is my sister, Vera McCracken, and I am Clinton McCracken. We were just in the shop there, but I thought I heard thunder and I ran out to check the sky. That's when I backed into you."

"And you're Ina, right? Ina Hall?" Vera asked. Ina nodded. She went on, "I remember you from Morningside College. You were in the Crescent Literary Society, and now your sister Flossie is a member. My sister Ethel and I are in Aesthesians."

"Of course. No wonder you look so familiar. It's been several years though. Wait, is this your brother who came to the spring picnic? I remember you had three brothers and they were all running around playing some game." Ina gestured toward Clinton. "As I recall, he had a little boy on his shoulders, and they were chasing around another little boy who was a few years older. I couldn't tell if they were father and sons or brothers." She smiled at the comical memory but noticed a dark look passed between brother and sister.

"The three Mc C's, they used to call themselves," Vera explained with a tight smile. "Clinton and his little brothers, Clay and Clifford. They practically drove our mother wild!"

"I'm sorry to say we lost Clifford when he was five years old. Infantile paralysis. He went just like that," Clinton said snapping his fingers.

Ina reached out and touched his arm, then realizing they would both be equally affected, slipped her other arm around Vera's back.

"I am so sorry to hear that. It is heartbreaking when a child dies." Suddenly she remembered the time. "Oh my goodness, I must run or I will be late for work."

"Wait, where do you work?" Clinton asked.

"Gas and Electric just down the street."

"I will come by and check on you later. Just to make sure you weren't injured from the fall. Oh, and to see how you like the book."

When Ina looked back, he was showing the book to Vera and she was laughing. Ina didn't see any storm clouds in the sky. She thought it was turning into a beautiful day.

When she got off work that afternoon, Clinton was waiting outside the building, talking to a man standing next to a horse-drawn wagon.

"Miss Hall," he called out. He ran over to meet her. "Will you let me make it up to you by allowing me the privilege of giving you a ride home this evening?" He helped her into the wagon, and that was how they began. Once at her parents' house, they sat on the porch and talked about the book until her mother, father, and sisters, Flossie and Natalie, came out to meet him. Somehow, he just seemed to fit into her life right away.

MARCH, 1913

A lot has happened in the last year, Ina thought, carefully adding a corner of the patchwork piece to her log cabin quilt top. Goodness, a year ago I didn't even know Clinton. I certainly did not think I would be trying to make a quilt for my marriage bed. She giggled and hoped Flossie and Natalie, who were also quilting across their room, wouldn't notice.

"What are you giggling about, Ina? Are you thinking about what is going to happen under that quilt of yours?" Flossie teased her.

She looked over at Flossie, who seemed to be glowing in the lamplight. She had her quilt nearly done now.

"I should say not!" But she was blushing all the same. "You're the one who is on the verge of becoming Mrs. Charles Phenis. I would think you'd be worried about your own wedding night."

"Oh, I'm not worried. Charley promised that is going to be the best part."

"Hush you two, what if Father comes in?" Natalie cried bopping Flossie with a pillow, and they all laughed.

Flossie, or Florence, who was two years younger than Ina, met Charley at Morningside College. Like Ina, Flossie joined the Crescents Society. Charley was in the Hawkeyes, who were their "brother" club, and they did social events together.

"You know if you hadn't accidentally run into Clinton, you probably would have met him at our wedding," Flossie said. "I mean, Ethel McCracken's beau is George Barrett. He and Charley met in the Hawkeyes, and he is an usher. And Clinton's sisters, Vera and Ethel, have been close friends of mine since we started college."

"Didn't Clinton go to Morningside, Ina?" Natalie asked.

"No, he likes to say he was smart enough without wasting all of his money on tuition. I think he was just anxious to start earning his own way."

"Tell me what you like about him," Natalie asked. Being the youngest child, she sometimes felt like she had missed out on some of the girl talk.

"I like everything about him," Ina sighed. "We discovered we are practically twins. I am three weeks older than he is, so I told him I plan to start ordering him around. I told you we were both reading the same book at the same time about how to get rich.

"And he has the same kind of values we have. He grew up on a farm and he has a bunch of sisters just like me. He has six sisters and a brother: Agnes, Elizabeth, Dora, Vera, Ethel, Sylvia, and Clay. He had two brothers and a baby sister who died. And I have six sisters and a brother: Lela, Marie, Margie, Hattie, Flossie, Natalie, and Tracy. Of course, our family lost Bryant and Nellie at a young age. It almost seems like destiny that we should be together.

"I can talk to him about anything, and he actually listens to me. I told Clinton I believed men and women had different opportunities in life. A wife's job is to help her husband achieve success which would lead to his own fulfillment and the well-being of the family. Likewise, the husband should ensure his wife is supported and happy in the home. When he said he agreed with that completely, I started to cry. I was a little embarrassed, but he seemed to understand."

She was still thinking about him when she went back to her sewing. He was ambitious. She liked that too. She didn't mind admitting she would not marry a man who wasn't trying to make the most of his opportunities. When they met, Clinton was working as a machinist at Bennett Auto Supply Company in Sioux City. Prior to that, he was a mechanic at Adams Auto Company, and he learned how to repair the new engines on the gas-powered tractors produced by the Henry Ford Motor Company. This had all led to his latest challenge: he had accepted a position of traveling salesman with the Avery Company in Sioux Falls, South Dakota, selling farm equipment. He was leaving Sioux City for Sioux Falls at the beginning of next month. They were getting married in June, and she would join him there. It was all happening so quickly and perfectly she could not quite believe it.

She had to quit her job since she would be moving away from Sioux City. Mr. Allen and Mrs. Kenton had been gracious when she told them she was quitting the second week in June.

"Will you need a letter of recommendation, Dear?" Mrs. Kenton asked her.

"She's getting married, Mrs. Kenton. She won't be working in an office again," Mr. Allen reminded her.

"I suppose it would be better to have one if you don't mind," Ina said. "I hope we will have children right away. But if that doesn't happen…"

She heard Mr. Allen muttering as he walked away, "These young girls have no idea how much work it is to run a household."

"I suppose he is right, Mrs. Kenton," Ina said, "but it seems a shame to waste all those years I spent in school, not to mention the experience I got working here for eighteen months. Here is my address in Sioux Falls where you can send the letter. Thank you for your kindness."

That brought her thoughts back to Clinton once more. He might be open to the idea of her working in Sioux Falls if it didn't keep her from getting his dinner on the table.

Ina smiled, remembering the first time he'd ever kissed her. Oh, she'd been kissed plenty of times before, but Clinton had such good manners, she was sure he would never kiss her in a public place. But it happened last summer after she begged him to take her on the Riverside Park roller coaster. She was quite familiar with Riverside Park, because one of her good friends, Bertha Falsburgh, had a cottage at Riverside. They visited her there every summer in college and the girls always went on the amusement park rides.

"Are you sure you are not scared to go on this? It's pretty high and fast. You will probably scream your head off," Clinton had told her while they waited in line.

"You're supposed to scream on a roller coaster," she said. "That's the fun. You feel like you are flying and hurling toward your death all at the same time. I have been on it before."

He steered her toward the last car, which seemed like a bold choice. The cars were ratcheting up the first big slope and he slipped his arms around her back and gripped the safety bar in front of her to brace her for the drop.

"Are you scared yet?" he said.

"Not yet," she said, watching as they were approaching the top.

"Then look at me." She turned her head and had to lean back on his shoulder to look him in the eyes, but she didn't see fear there either. When he moved in and kissed her as they went over the top, she couldn't have been more surprised, but she didn't scream. At least not until he pulled back. She screamed in his ear then, as they kept plummeting and turning. When the ride ended, she just looked at him.

"I want you to feel like that every time I kiss you."

"I will try not to scream next time."

JUNE 18, 1913

"Oh Natalie, I can't believe I am so nervous! When you are nearly twenty-five years old, you should not be nervous to walk down the aisle!"

Ina was just about ready for the big moment, getting dressed for the last time in the bedroom she once shared with one or two sisters. Hattie and Natalie were helping her into her gown and veil.

"Nonsense, Ina. Everyone is scared to get married. I'll bet C.C. is shaking in his boots too," Hattie assured her.

Ina smiled, "It sounds strange to hear you call him C.C. But I guess we will all get used to it. New job, new town, new wife, new name. That is what he said. There wasn't anything at all wrong with 'Clinton.' I guess using your initials makes you seem more professional."

"Are C.C.'s parents here yet?" Natalie asked. "I don't think I have ever met his father."

"Well, you won't be meeting him tonight, either," Ina said. "He refuses to attend weddings, C.C. said. It reminds him of funerals and makes him sad."

"Well, no one better die tonight! It is just happy thoughts from here on. Let's get your fancy veil pinned up with the Lilies of the Valley. It may take a little while to get that fountain look you wanted," Hattie said, grabbing the flowers and a knife, then trimming the flowers while Natalie picked up the hatpins.

Ten minutes later, Ina was standing at the top of the old staircase, a vision in white charmeuse and lace, holding her Lily of the Valley bouquet, and her father's arm. He started to whisper something to her but stopped himself, and Ina could see tears in his eyes.

She felt like everything was moving in slow motion like she was descending the stairs at a snail's pace. She could not believe how many people had crowded into the parlor and sitting room of Platt and Catherine Hall's house, a house she'd lived in for the past sixteen years. I will never live here again, she thought.

They were all looking at her. Ina Hazel, the plain little tomboy who was always getting muddy playing with the animals at the farm where she was born. She was the young girl who loved school and loved to beat the boys in her class at just about anything she could, whether it was spelling or arithmetic, or sometimes even a footrace. She was the girl who loved to read so much she would forget to come downstairs to dinner. Her mother would find her asleep on the corner of her bed with books and papers piled next to her. She was the girl who enjoyed writing stories in the Crescent Club at Morningside College, who went into teaching, because that is what you did when you graduated from college. She was the girl who decided she needed to learn about business, so she quit teaching and headed to business college. Some of these friends and relatives had thought that was a rash decision. But none of them questioned this decision. They all knew this decision— this man— was the right one for her.

It was like being in heaven when you could see all of your relatives parading before you. Only she was the one who was parading, and they were frozen in place. There was her beloved look-alike sister, Hattie, beaming right in front with her husband,

Fred, leaning close to her; Flossie and her new husband, Charley, with their arms around each other; and right behind them her youngest sister, Natalie, clasping her hands. She could see her older sister Marie, and husband Leroy back by the doorway, ready to welcome guests as they arrived. On the right, she saw her brother Tracy and his wife, Carrie, over by the dining room, ready to oversee the refreshments after the ceremony. Knowing Tracy, he wanted to make sure there was enough wedding cake. And Mother was right in the middle of things, ready to guide her and the guests into the parlor for the ceremony.

And of course, her new family was also excited to see her in her wedding gown. Why just last week, Vera and Ethel had given her a bridal shower. All of her new gifts were safely packed in the trunk. She looked down at C.C.'s youngest siblings, Sylvia and Clay, standing with their mother, Ellen. There was Lizzie with Ethel and George. She was happy George was such a close friend of her brother-in-law, Charley. And there was Dora, or "Dode" as they called her, in a big hat with her distinguished husband, Clifford Miller. But where was Vera? Ina knew she was coming. There she was, at the piano, playing her song! And so many other friends. They all looked so happy.

Once they were on the ground floor, still on her father's arm, she felt like she was moving on a cloud toward Reverend Keck and Clinton, who was waiting nervously in front of a table draped in white linen, holding lit candles and a vase full of peonies. She had pictured more candle glow when she imagined this moment, but when you pick one of the longest days of the year to be married, twilight creeps in late. Clinton had told her the date was perfect. He wanted the day they married to last forever.

The rest of the evening was a blissful blur. They pledged their love to each other, then hugged everyone in the crowded house. They ate cake and drank punch, then spilled out onto the porch to enjoy the cool breeze coming in from the north. The wind picked up her veil and loosened the flowers so carefully pinned in by her sisters, but it didn't matter now. She was Mrs. Clinton C. McCracken, tonight and for all time.

One of C.C.'s friends and former co-workers, Jerry Cross, asked how the two of them had met.

"Well it's kind of a funny story," C.C. said putting his hand around Ina's waist. "I was looking for a wife, and this one fell right in my lap." He pulled her toward him to show what he meant.

"What are you saying?" Ina blushed.

"Well, isn't that what happened?"

"Yes, but it sounds so scandalous when you say it like that! You see what he meant was he …" Ina started to explain, but C.C. cut her off with a kiss, which brought cheers from their guests.

"Don't explain, Sweet Pea, just let them wonder."

Soon it was time to take their leave, and they escaped their childhoods through a barrage of rice. They spent their first starry-eyed night together at the West Hotel downtown, then took the train to Spirit Lake for three days before moving to Sioux Falls. It was the farthest she had ever been from home, but it was all one big wonderful adventure.

SEPTEMBER 3, 1914

I'm just not sure I should be here, Ina thought, sitting in the fourth pew in the First Methodist Church next to Maybelline Jurgens, her middle-aged neighbor lady from across the street. Waiting for a program to start always gave her the jitters, even if she was not a participant in the show. She remembered how she had felt when she and three of her good friends, Agnes, Martha, and Madge from the Crescents, put on a play in college with five of the

Hawkeye boys. Everyone said their performance kept them in stitches, but it didn't stop her stage fright.

"We are lucky to have gotten these seats, Ina. I am so glad we came early. You betcha. Look how fast the sanctuary is filling up," May said. "My husband, Professor Jurgens, heard about this at the college, and he said his students, especially the young ladies, are ready to march in the streets! What does your husband say about all of this?"

"Well, he hasn't said much so far. I haven't exactly told him about it. He is out of town for a few days for work."

"Well, Honey, if I know him, he will be so proud of you for showing an interest in something political. This may seem a little dramatic to someone your age. But when you have watched your husband vote in ten elections or so, along with the other men in your town…Well I figure, the ladies can't mess it up any worse than the men have, don't cha know?" May laughed, which turned into a cough.

Ina still had mixed feelings. Just last April, she read about the convention of the Woman's Christian Temperance Union in Gettysburg, South Dakota, about 200 miles northwest of Sioux Falls. The way she understood it, this organization was trying to ban the consumption of liquor, including closing saloons, while at the same time supporting issues relating to women such as universal suffrage. Ina knew women had always been able to vote in school elections. She agreed women should be voting citizens if they educated themselves about the candidates or the bond issues on the ballots. It seemed pointless if they just automatically voted for who their husbands voted for.

She wasn't so sure about the temperance part. Why, in Minnesota, the WCTU had unions advocating demonstrations in front of saloons. She read in the paper there had been scuffles, and women who were praying outside saloons had been doused with beer by the owners or patrons. She and C.C. were not big drinkers, but he occasionally had some rye whiskey with his customers and she did not see why anyone should care.

But Ina was here to listen. Listen and learn. And maybe she could take what she learned back to C.C., and he could pass it onto his associates. Men would have to go along with this "women voting" thing for it to pass muster. Her attention was drawn to the front of the room where the guest speaker was being introduced.

"Her name was Dr. Anna Howard Shaw," Ina later explained to her husband. "And she was one of the most mesmerizing speakers I have ever heard."

"Was she one of those prohibition proponents?" C.C. sat back in the rocking chair, lighting his pipe.

"No, she didn't talk about temperance much. She was talking about organizing a branch of the Universal Suffrage League here in Sioux Falls. She said the men in the eastern states, and the states where they now have women's voting rights, are wondering what is wrong with the women in South Dakota. Like it reflects badly on the men in South Dakota that they don't respect the women here enough to give them the vote."

"Well, that there sounds a lot like a sales pitch, Sweetie," he smiled knowingly. "But don't you worry. I heard they are working on something in Washington, and you girls will get to vote one of these days. I mean, you know how fast Washington works. And they do have a few other matters to attend to with the tensions in Europe."

"Exactly. Why should we have to wait for the men in Congress? As you pointed out, they have other things to do. We can get to work locally to put this on the state ballot so women can vote in South Dakota. Let the other states take care of themselves. I want to see if I can attend some of the meetings of this suffrage league." She had been pacing around the room, but she stopped and sat to face him, placing her hands on his.

"Go ahead if that's what you want to do," he said. "You're not going on a hunger strike or chaining yourself to a lamppost, are you? God helps those who help themselves. Just don't expect miracles overnight." He picked up her hands and kissed her fingertips.

Maybelline was right, she thought. *He does seem to be supportive of me.*

"But tomorrow … tomorrow you're staying home to clean, right?" C.C. asked.

Ina knew they had different opinions on how orderly they needed to keep their spaces. She had seen his work office, where he kept everything neatly tucked away and spotless. Of course, he traveled most days. She considered herself organized if she could find where she'd left something. When things became too cluttered, she took time to tidy them up, but that wasn't a high priority.

"Oh, well, yes. I suppose I will have to do the dishes. But I have ten new books from the library calling my name. We still have plenty of room to walk around. You didn't marry me to be the maid, did you?" Ina asked defensively.

"Of course not." He was still holding onto her hands, and pulled her into his lap, rocking the chair. "You do have other redeeming talents, Mrs. McCracken. But do we really need to keep the newspapers for a month?"

"Have you read everything in those papers? Neither have I."

JANUARY 15, 1915

"Can you believe those turkeys in Congress?" Ina cried, reading the front page of the *Sioux Falls Argus-Leader*. "They had a chance to pass national legislation giving women the vote and they failed. Again."

"You weren't expecting them to pass it, were you?" her husband said over his scrambled eggs and banana bread. "Why, most of the men I talk to think women's suffrage is a waste of time or just a fad."

"You don't think that, do you?"

"No, I don't think that, Sweet Pea. Heck, you read and interpret the newspaper for me almost every day. I'm not sure some men should be voting, but there is no legitimate reason to deny women the right to vote. Some people seem to think by giving someone the right to vote they will be forced to vote, which is just ridiculous."

"Yeah, that is just what Teddy Roosevelt was talking about. He said no one should believe women would be forced to abandon their work at home just to vote. Men aren't doing that," she went on, picking up the newspaper and reading, the words leaping off the page.

"Dr. Anna Howard Shaw was one of the suffragettes there in the gallery, you know, the speaker I saw last year. She said the fight is far from over. Only one of our congressmen, Representative Martin, voted for the resolution. The other two dodos voted against it. But the worst was Representative Bowdle of Ohio. He said the women of Washington were beautiful but had no interest in affairs of the state. Can you imagine? It says here the speaker constantly had to pound his gavel because there was so much booing and hissing from the gallery!"

"So where does this leave your little union here in Sioux Falls?" C.C. asked, trying to cover a bemused smile by wiping his mouth with his napkin.

"Well you can bet those other two representatives, Burke and

Dillion will be getting plenty of letters from us. I think they are planning a march in the spring. We are still trying to get suffrage on the state ballot."

"A wise man once said, 'victory belongs to the most persevering.' Persevere, My Dear, persevere." He winked at her. "Just don't forget to come home to your loving husband after fighting Congress."

And that is how she found herself, three months later, handing out banners and signs at the Women's Rally in downtown Sioux Falls. She and about a dozen of the league members had been painting signs over the past week.

Maybelline was there too, and she walked over to Ina. "Honey, are you all right? You look a little pale."

"Oh, I think I am okay. Just haven't eaten much today, and I am kind of crampy…you know, a woman's thing…" Suddenly she felt dizzy and grabbed May's arm as she started to go down. Luckily, May's husband, Professor Jurgens, was approaching, and he grabbed onto Ina's other arm when he saw her collapse.

The Jurgens helped her home where she began having the worst cramps and bleeding she had ever had. C.C. called Dr. Mason to come, although Ina insisted it was unnecessary. The doctor's grim diagnosis was that she had undergone a spontaneous abortion.

"But how can that be? I was pregnant?" she stammered, suddenly feeling devastated. "I felt fine, I have been working on the rally preparations and … I didn't think …."

A minute later, she was in her husband's arms weeping for a child she hadn't even known existed until it was gone.

APRIL 7, 1916

She leaned her head against the train window, watching the scenery fly by. This time she knew she was pregnant. It wasn't like the last time. She started paying attention to what her body was telling her and eating a little more. She knew when her period did not come on time and her breasts started feeling sore, she might be pregnant. She wasn't vomiting, but she did feel a little sick in the morning. When those symptoms did not go away, she talked to her doctor. He confirmed she was again with child and urged her to lie down and rest several times a day for the next few months.

It seemed like it was taking a long time for them to be in a family way. Most of her sisters and other girls she knew were having babies within a year of getting married. Ina and C.C. had been married for almost three years now. They hadn't done anything to prevent pregnancy. She worried there was something wrong with her. Her oldest sister, Lela, had given birth to four children, but not one survived. I mean, that must have meant there was something wrong with Lela, right? Ina worried she had the same thing.

She thought about all of this while the train made another stop. She was coming back from a nice visit with her parents in Sioux City and had called on C.C.'s parents too. Ellen McCracken, C.C.'s mother, was a midwife, so she had talked to scores of expectant ladies. Ellen convinced her "living in worry invites death in a hurry."

"Besides," Ellen had said, "You will have enough to worry over once the baby comes."

Ellen also pointed out if Lela's children had survived birth then later died, it was more likely related to the children's health. Ellen had seen a number of children who were born dead or died shortly after birth, and no one knew why. It just was part of life. It happened whether the labor was long or short, whether the parents were well-off or poor, whether it was summer or winter; it just happened a certain percentage of the time. Ina hoped she had already gone through her "failure."

She liked traveling on the train, especially this time of year when it wasn't quite so cold and you could see spring announcing her intentions. It was too early for the full green carpet, but you could see the first signs if you look close enough.

She hoped she and C.C. would get a chance to travel more. They had been to visit Margie and Bill in Westfield, Iowa, and Flossie and Charles in Mapleton, but she was dying to go on a nice long vacation somewhere far away. C.C.'s oldest sister, Aggie had moved to the state of Washington and married Clarence Moore, who became the school superintendent where they both taught. But now he had enough money that they could move to the orchard he started. She imagined it was beautiful: an apple orchard in Wenatchee, Washington. She closed her eyes and saw children running through the apple orchard. It would have to be her children, she smiled to herself, as Aggie and Clarence did not have any of their own.

She hadn't been to visit C.C.'s sister Dode and her husband, Clifford, in Omaha either. C.C. went there every few months or so on business. Clifford was now manager of the Avery office in Omaha and was trying to get C.C. transferred there so they would work together. Ina was not sure if it would be better, although she did want to get to know Dode. Last Christmas, at her in-laws' house, Dode had kept them spellbound with her stories of how she'd worked as a telegraph operator for Western Union before she was married. She had to scare marauding intruders off with her shotgun. It reminded Ina of some of the silent film melodramas she and C.C. had seen at the movie house. Dode and Clifford didn't have children either.

She was starting to get a little uncomfortable due to her advancing pregnancy. She still had three more months to go, but she was anxious to get home, sit on the chaise, and put her feet up. She closed her eyes and tried to rest the last few miles before the Sioux Falls railway station came into view.

JULY 8, 1916

"You ladies are just so thoughtful," Ina gushed. The other ladies in her Kro-tat-em club watched her open a gift bag with hand-sewn baby gowns and a crocheted cap. "But aren't you supposed to wait until after the baby comes to give gifts?"

"We know, Honey, but we just couldn't wait," her friend Emma answered. She was the hostess of the day. "Besides, your baby is coming any day now."

Ina hoped that was true. She already had a beautiful cradle with painted roses C.C. had picked out and brought back from Omaha, along with one of Dode's special baby blankets. If the baby came according to her plan, it would arrive within the next two days. But not before five o'clock this evening, when C.C. would be back. He hadn't made any appointments to see clients after this one, just in case the baby came. Dr. Mason had checked her just last week, and he was pretty sure this baby would be making an appearance soon. She planned to have Dr. Mason attend the birth, but if he could not make it, she had her friend Christina, a midwife, lined up. Christina was also a member of the Kro-tat-em club and lived just a few doors down the street, so she could be summoned pretty quickly if necessary.

When people asked her, she never knew how to exactly describe the Kro-tat-ems. They were a women's social club, sort of like the literary clubs they had in college. They did sometimes talk about books they had read, but she would not describe it as a book club. They usually brought some piecework with them, like quilting, embroidering, crocheting, or knitting, but they weren't all working on the same thing. She joined because of Emma, whom she met while working on the suffrage campaign. Ina was just grateful the

Kro-tat-ems had been so welcoming to her and had given her some great advice on having a baby. Because although she was smiling and laughing with her friends, she was scared. She had never been so scared of anything.

Emma was nice enough to walk home with her. These days, it was hard to even get herself out of a chair, and the last few days were even worse because her lower legs seemed to have swollen to twice their size.

"How are you feeling, Ina? You don't look very well." Emma was helping her onto the chaise lounge and picking up her legs. "Can I get you something?"

"Oh my goodness, the light. It is giving me a headache. Would you turn it off? And maybe a cool compress for my head. I have been getting terrible headaches."

Emma turned down the gas lamp and got her a cool damp cloth. She helped Ina take off her shoes.

"Your feet are very swollen, don't they hurt?" Emma asked.

"I know my ankles look like they belong to an elephant," Ina sighed. "I am just going to try to take a little nap before C.C. gets here…"

"Do you want me to wait until he gets home?" Emma asked quietly but wasn't sure Ina heard her. While Emma waited for C.C., she washed the dishes in the sink and on the table. Afterward, she went out onto the porch so she could call out to her husband when he walked by on his way home.

When C.C. returned, Emma told him about Ina's headache and swollen legs. He found her sleeping on the chaise lounge, and let her rest. He was frying eggs when he heard her cry out.

"What? What's wrong?" He rushed to her side.

She couldn't answer, instead holding her oversized belly and gasping for breath. She started making a strange noise halfway between a groan and a scream, then suddenly stopped and gasped for breath. "The baby. I think the baby's coming. It must be labor, it couldn't be anything else."

"I'll go fetch Christina." The smell of scorched eggs turned him around. C.C. turned off the stove and turned on the gas lamp by the chaise.

"No, leave it off…please…oh my head, my head is pounding."

C.C. sat next to her and put his hand on Ina's forehead. "You feel like you are burning up. Just try to relax. I am getting the midwife."

Christina was home and came at once. C.C. and Christina were able to get Ina into the bed, but the headache continued, and she sometimes sounded delirious. The labor was hard and went on for hours.

"Maybe she should go to the hospital. Are you sure I shouldn't fetch Dr. Mason?" C.C. asked the midwife impatiently.

"No, there is no need. This is perfectly normal," Christina assured him. "Husbands are often in the way during childbirth. Why don't you have a wee cup of the sauce to calm down? I'll come for you when it is over."

"We don't have any liquor in the house. I don't think that would help." He spent most of the last few hours of labor pacing out on the porch, listening to the cicadas.

Just before midnight, Christina emerged from the bedroom and told C.C. to come in. Ina was propped up in the bed, holding a small bundle in a blanket.

"Come see your son," Ina smiled, looking exhausted, her damp hair plastered to her forehead. She kissed the top of the baby's head.

He crept over to the bedside as though he was afraid of waking the baby. "Did he cry? I didn't hear any crying."

"Oh, he cried a little, but then he went to sleep," Christina said. "Your wife had a hard time of it, but she should be okay once she has a chance to rest. I am pretty worn out too, so I will leave you two, no, you three, on your own now." She cleaned her utensils and took everything with her she had brought for the delivery.

"He is just so little," C.C. mused, putting his finger in the tiny hand. But he was talking to no one. Christina had slipped out while he was mesmerized with the baby, and Ina was falling asleep. "I'd better put him in his cradle so we can all get some shut-eye. It will soon be morning."

CHAPTER TWO

SIOUX FALLS, SOUTH DAKOTA, JULY 9, 1916

CATHERINE AMANDA HALL

Catherine Hall stood waiting at the train station, wondering what might have gone wrong. She checked with the telegraph office, which was located in the same building. They told her one of the messengers had delivered her telegram to Ina McCracken the previous day, saying she was expecting to arrive in Sioux Falls this morning at 10:45 a.m. She was coming for the birth of her grandchild. However, when neither Clinton nor Ina was there to meet the train, it made her wonder if today was the big day. Ina and Clinton didn't have a telephone. They were on a waiting list to get one installed. She sat on the bench and waited another thirty minutes. She had several pieces of baggage with her as she intended to stay for a few weeks to help with the child until Ina got stronger. She thought she could walk to the house, but she didn't believe she could do it with the bags.

Finally, Catherine inquired how to hire a buggy to take her to their house. When she arrived and the driver had unloaded her bags onto the porch, she found an unfamiliar young woman sitting in a rocker with her face buried in her hands.

"Oh, you mustn't go in there!" the young woman cried, jumping up when she saw her.

"Is this the McCracken house?" Catherine asked. "Or do I have the wrong place?"

"Oh my goodness. You're Ina's mother, aren't you? She told me you were coming. I'm sorry, I'm Emma Baylor, Ina's friend. I think we met last year," Emma said, grasping Catherine's wrists in her hands. "It's just so awful."

"What do you mean, Emma? What is going on?" Catherine demanded. "Why don't you want me to go in? Where is Ina?"

"*Shhhh*, she might be sleeping. I probably shouldn't be the one to tell you, but they will need your help. The baby—" Emma started but her voice broke. "The baby was born late last night. The midwife was here, Christina. She thought it was fine, and she went home. Then, sometime in the middle of the night, the baby started crying and wouldn't stop. They thought he was hungry, so Ina tried to feed him. He wouldn't nurse. He just cried like he was in terrible pain. C.C. went to get Christina and she tried to help with the nursing, but the baby just kept crying. He fell asleep a few times but he would wake and start crying all over again."

"Babies cry, it is what they do," Catherine said, wanting to go inside, but Emma kept a grip on her wrists.

"I know. I came over very early this morning to check on everyone. Finally, at about seven, C.C. went to get Dr. Mason and they came back in the doctor's Model T. By then the baby was purple and gasping and hardly making a sound; I've never seen anything like it. Dr. Mason took one look at the baby and he ordered Christina to wrap him up and put him in the cradle. Then the midwife and doctor took the baby in the car down the street to Dr. Mason's office."

"So where are they; the doctor's office, the hospital, where?"

"Oh no, after that, Ina got hysterical, and C.C. was just trying to calm her down. The doctor didn't say to come or stay here. They didn't know what to do." Emma started crying again, harder this time. "So we just waited."

"And you don't know what happened?"

"No, there's more. About an hour later, Christina came walking back. She had the blanket and the cradle, but no baby. She said the baby was dead before Dr. Mason could start his treatment. He asked if they wanted him to do an autopsy," Emma finished with a quivering lip.

Catherine gasped and wrenched her hands free to cover her mouth. "The baby died?" she asked. "The baby died at the doctor's office and they weren't even there? God in Heaven. Where is Ina now? Where is C.C.?"

"They are in the house. I'm sorry to hold you like this. I just wanted you to know what had happened before you went in there."

Catherine looked toward the house again. The windows were open; it was a warm summer day. They had probably heard everything Emma said. They probably knew Catherine was standing there. She left her bags on the porch and opened the front door. Although it was midday, it seemed dark inside. When her eyes adjusted to the dimness, she saw that C.C. was sitting on a kitchen chair on the far side of the room, staring into the cradle. The cradle and blanket must have been sitting there since the midwife brought them back. He didn't look up at her, he didn't seem to realize she was there.

The door to the bedroom was closed. When Catherine opened it, Ina was face down on the bed, tangled in her nightgown and dressings from the birth. Her curly hair was strewn across the pillow and her face, and she seemed to be asleep. The bedclothes were crumpled in a mess, as though she had been fighting with them.

Before Catherine could step toward the bed, she heard the back-door slam. She went back into the main living room of the house. C.C. was gone. Emma crept through the front door uncertainly. Catherine noticed the cradle and blanket were gone too. She looked at Emma questioningly, but Emma's expression was blank.

Then they both heard a terrible whack, like firewood being hit with an ax, and a loud grunt. Catherine and Emma made it to the back door in time to see the cradle in two pieces, engulfed in flames. C.C. was standing in front of the fire, his back to them. Catherine could tell from the way his shoulders were shaking that he was sobbing. He dropped to his knees before the burning cradle. A strange cry filled the air, like a banshee's wail. At first, she thought C.C. was making the noise, but she saw him turn toward the house. He had heard it too.

Catherine bolted back to the bedroom and saw Ina was making that godawful sound and looking out the window, her hands braced against the window frame, her unruly mop of hair silhouetted against sun-streaked smoke from the fire.

"I'm sorry, ma'am. Dr. Mason was called away on an emergency and he isn't here right now," the nurse told Catherine Hall, who had barged into Dr. Mason's office with young Emma Baylor trailing behind. "Good morning to you, Mrs. Baylor."

"My name is Catherine Hall. I am the mother of Ina McCracken, one of his patients. I came for the baby."

The nurse looked concerned. "I'm sorry, maybe no one told you, but her baby died. He was waiting to see if they wanted an autopsy done before contacting the funeral home."

"And what is the funeral home here?" Catherine asked.

"Well, it's Clancy's, that's the closest one anyway," the nurse answered.

"Thank you, and where is the baby?" Catherine said moving around the desk toward the examination area.

"He's in the exam room, but you can't go back there. Not without Dr. Mason here." But Catherine was already ahead of her, opening the closed doors. When she found a room with a padded table in it, she went in to look for the baby. She found him wrapped in a white cloth.

"Is this the right one?"

"Yes of course, but Dr. Mason won't be back for a while. Old Mr. Thomas is having one of his heart spells out on the farm, which may take hours," the nurse explained.

"Come along, Emma dear," Catherine called as she picked up the sheet-draped newborn. "Just tell Dr. Mason we will let him know if there is to be an autopsy. Otherwise, we will take the baby to Clancy's ourselves. But first, his parents need to see him."

"But, no, you can't, not unless Dr. Mason says—"

It was too late. Catherine and Emma were already walking out of the office.

"Mrs. Hall, do you think that was wise? What will Dr. Mason think?" Emma asked.

"I don't care. Dr. Mason let this poor child die without either of his parents with him. Have you ever lost a child, Emma?"

"Well, no…"

"Well, I have. And his parents need to be with him right now."

Emma jumped into the street and waved her hand at a milk truck. "Henry, stop!"

The truck stopped and the driver smiled at Emma. "Good morning, Sis. What are you doing?"

"Mrs. Hall, this is my brother, Henry Gibbons. Henry, would you take Ina's mother in your truck to the McCrackens' right away? You don't have room for me, so I will walk."

"I don't think I am supposed to take passengers, Emma," Henry said.

"Just do it, Henry. It is a life and death thing," Emma cried.

Henry spotted the bundle in Catherine's arms but didn't ask any questions. Emma helped Catherine onto the seat next to him.

"Could you go to that Clancy's place and ask them to come by in an hour or so, Emma, or when they are able?" Catherine asked.

Emma nodded and Henry raised his eyebrows but didn't say a word.

When Catherine got back to the house, the fire was out, and the smell of smoke had dissipated. She found both Ina and C.C. huddled on the bed, which had been made. Ina had brushed her hair and pulled it back into a bun. Their mouths dropped open when they saw the bundle in her arms.

"Mother, what…?" Ina croaked.

"I'm afraid he is gone, my dears. But you need a chance to look at him. He is a beautiful gift from God. An angel who came to visit you just for a few short hours. You have to be able to hold him and cherish him, and most of all, to be able to say good-bye." She handed the swaddled infant over to Ina. Then, for the first time that day, Catherine began to cry, so she left the room quickly.

Catherine was sitting on the porch drinking cold tea when Emma came back.

"A man from Clancy's Mortuary will be here in a little bit after he has his lunch," Emma said. "What you did was so brave, Mrs. Hall. I mean how did you even think of that?"

"Losing an innocent little child is the worst thing I think can happen to you, Dear. It tears your heart out. I lost little Bryant, my first child when he was less than a year old. And after my oldest daughter, Lela was born, sweet Nellie came along. She was always sickly, and we lost her to consumption before she was four. You wait so long for the child to grow in your belly and come into the world, and then to lose them … well it just makes you so sick, and so angry. You are angry at everyone, I guess that is part of your grief. But mostly you are angry at God. How could God take a child who is loved so much?" She stopped for a minute, wiping at her eyes.

"I didn't want it to happen to Ina, or Clinton, for that matter. You saw how angry he was, and I knew exactly what he was feeling. I have felt that rage. They needed to see the child. To hold him, to kiss his face, and tell him they are glad he was born, even if it didn't last. A baby is a blessing. It always has to be a blessing," she trailed off. "I will talk to them about taking the baby's body back to Sioux City with me if the undertaker can get him ready. We have a section reserved in the new cemetery there. I can take him right away tomorrow if they want me to."

Three days later, Baby McCracken was laid to rest in the Graceland Park Cemetery in Sioux City, Iowa, in a plot his grandfather had purchased a few months earlier.

CAMP FUNSTON, KANSAS, DECEMBER 16, 1918,

CLINTON CLAUDE MCCRACKEN

He picked up writing, but it wasn't getting any easier.

The other men in my barracks are busy writing letters to their wives and girlfriends. My sisters tell me, well mainly Vera tells me, I should write a letter to you. I should get out all of my unresolved feelings so I can face the future. I am not at all sure I want to open up my feelings. Why does anyone want to experience pain after all? What good does it do?

I still don't understand why anyone so young and innocent had to die. They think I was just in shock at the funeral; and in the aftermath, I just threw myself into work like I always do. But isn't that normal? There are no answers. You just have to put such things aside.

I am stuck here for the time being, and can't change that. So I guess I can go through the motions of writing a letter to you. At least it might keep the other men from asking questions. But I don't want to ruminate about the darkest day of my life.

CHAPTER THREE

SIOUX FALLS, SOUTH DAKOTA, OCTOBER, 1916

INA HAZEL MCCRACKEN

Ina knew it had been hard for both of them since the loss of their son. She was grateful to her mother, Catherine, and mother-in-law, Ellen. Even though they didn't want to talk about their heartache, both mothers had sat with C.C. and convinced him he needed to express his loss by talking to Ina about the dreams he'd had for his child. Of course, she had the same plans, but it was somehow more acceptable for women to cry and grieve and even act a little crazy. It got a little easier once her body started to return to normal.

Their mothers had also made her understand she was not eating properly. Food wasn't appealing to her for a long time after the baby died. She spent a few weeks in Sioux City at the end of the summer, and they made sure she was fed out of their abundant gardens. It was lovely being pampered and looked after, but she missed her husband. She was glad when they seemed to be able to get back into a routine, a little bit at a time.

Now she worried their relationship had been strained. Ina couldn't shake the feeling that she had somehow bungled her maternal role. Should she have summoned the doctor or gone to the hospital when she was in labor? She wondered if, deep down, C.C. might blame her for the baby's death. She was afraid things would never be the same between them again.

After her mother made a scene at Dr. Mason's office, Ina thought it might be best to switch doctors. Dr. James Clark had advertised in the newspaper that he specialized in women's health issues, so she decided to try him. When she had her initial visit, he went over her medical history in detail.

He was especially concerned when she told him about the

blinding headache, light sensitivity, and swollen ankles that had accompanied her last pregnancy. He said it sounded like she had been suffering from toxemia, which could have led to serious health problems for the baby, such as liver failure, fluid in the lungs, or seizures. Ina was scared as he described how deadly this could be for mothers and babies.

"Is it safe to have another child?" she asked Dr. Clark.

"Many mothers have successful pregnancies after going through similar experiences to yours. Now that we are aware, we can monitor your blood pressure and other signs once you are pregnant. I would recommend you wait at least six months before you try to conceive again, in order to get back to good health," Dr. Clark told her.

JUNE 1917

War was an unfamiliar concept to Ina. Her maternal great-grandfather, Grover Gillett, had fought in the Blackhawk War, and his father, Henry Gillett, had fought in the Revolutionary War. C.C.'s maternal grandfather, Henry Hotopp, had been in the Eighth Cavalry in the Civil War. But she had been reading the articles in the *Argus-Leader* and sometimes in the *Sioux City Journal* and *Sioux City News* about the recent war preparations. Clearly, something unprecedented was happening if the United States was going to organize two million men between volunteers and a draft to comprise a wartime militia.

To learn more, Ina and C.C. went to hear a speaker one evening at Morningside College when they were visiting Sioux City. Frank H. Garver, professor of history and politics, had been one of Ina's favorite teachers when she attended college. He summarized the events of the last few years that had led up to the current situation.

"The official beginning of the European War was in 1914 when

Archduke Ferdinand was assassinated in Sarajevo. The United States largely stayed out of direct involvement in the war. But a few months ago, German U-boats began sinking American merchant ships in the North Atlantic to cut off supplies to Great Britain.

"At about the same time, the Zimmerman Telegram was intercepted and decoded by British intelligence. In it, Germany proposed an alliance with Mexico, if the United States entered the conflict, promising to return Arizona, New Mexico, and Texas to Mexico, which had been lost by Mexico in the Mexican-American war. Mexico did not accept this proposed alliance with Germany, but when the scheme was exposed, it built sympathy among Americans to oppose German aggression.

"Congress declared the 'war to end all wars' on Germany in April, at the urging of President Woodrow Wilson," Professor Garver told the audience.

Nearly every night, she and C.C. talked about the war and wondered how it would affect them. Oddly, the talk of current events seemed to give them some common ground to have lively discussions again. She began to feel like they were getting back to normal. The thought he might be going to war was simultaneously frightening and thrilling. There was talk of sending soldiers to France or Belgium. Neither of them had ever been outside the United States, and couldn't even imagine being in a country where the people spoke another language.

C.C. heard his customers' concerns regarding the war every day. Would there be enough able young men left to do the farm work? Would boys have to be pulled out of school, or women pulled from their house chores to drive a team, to plow, or to care for the livestock? He could make a case for gas, diesel, or steam-powered machines that would save labor, but he always tried to give his customers the best information he had. Not all of his farm customers had the advantage of being able to read the papers. Ina was his ace in the hole, because she had the time, ability, and interest to read much more than he did, and her teaching experience proved invaluable.

"We may get an army camp right here in Sioux Falls if they can find enough land," Ina announced one day in May as they were finishing dinner. "The war department is also considering Fargo, Watertown, St. Paul, or Sioux City. Either here or Sioux City would be ideal if you ended up going. They say the training takes about six months, so that would keep you nearby."

"Well, I don't think they let you out to go home for supper, no matter where your residence is."

"Maybe not, but at least I would know you were close. They are saying they may draft nearly a million men in the first round to get enough after they make the exemptions. That would put the first ones in camp around the first of September. How could they build camps so fast?"

"I think building the camp is the first assignment of the new inductees. But it may not be so much fun to live there before the latrines and barracks are built. Maybe I will come home and sleep in my nice warm bed with you," he teased.

"Oh, you wish! They have not made it clear who might qualify for an exemption, only that they will all be personal, not categorical. I read there have been a record number of marriages in the past week, for men who are hoping they won't take married men."

"Well, the men I have talked to think there may be some exemption for married men, but it is even more likely for married men with dependent children." She was clearing away the dishes, but he grabbed her arm when she reached out for his plate and pulled her toward him. "If you want to improve our odds, should we try to have another child? Are you ready to risk that again?"

"I've been ready for months." She felt the flush creeping up her neck and face. "I was waiting for you."

"We can't be sure the outcome will be any different. You are the one whose body will be affected. It terrifies me to think that you could be putting your health at risk. You know what the doctor said about toxemia. How badly do you want to have a baby?" He stood and took her face in his hands to look her in the eyes.

"I have wanted to have our baby ever since we got married. You know that. I didn't realize it was going to be so hard, but in some ways, that has just made me more determined. We can't quit. I'm not afraid … maybe if I am honest, I am afraid, but there are times you just have to take a chance. It's like the roller coaster. You ride it despite your fear because you know it is a terrific thrill." She couldn't hide the tears that filled her eyes, belying her brave words.

"You're sure?" he asked again. She bit her lower lip, then nodded. He wrapped her in an embrace and walked her backward toward the bedroom.

On June 5, 1917, C.C. went to the Minnehaha County, Precinct Three office and registered for the draft. This ritual was duplicated by more than ten million men between the ages of twenty-one and thirty-one throughout the United States that day. He was number 1,939 of the 2,169 men registered in Sioux Falls that day. At that point, they didn't know what the numbers meant, or what his chances were of serving in the military. After he registered, a pretty young woman dressed in patriotic garb pinned a medal on his shirt, indicating he was willing to serve his country. At 3:00 p.m. there was a military parade through the downtown, with bands, current enlisted military personnel, and all the men who had just registered. There were political speeches at the auditorium. It was a national holiday of sorts from work, but it didn't erase anyone's anxiety.

JULY 23, 1917

"How can you stand this suspense?" Ina asked her husband. "I have read these lists they have published over and over and there is no sign of your name or number yet."

"That is a good thing. My number must not have been among the first group drawn. Relax, Darling. 'The sun doesn't shine on the same dog's back every day.' But it looks like it is shining on mine," C.C. answered, reading the sports section before she cut up the paper for the draft listings.

"Okay, I just want to be sure. Explain how you understand this silly double numbering system is supposed to work."

"From what I have been told, and what I have read in the same newspaper articles you have been memorizing, the war department plus some senators started drawing out numbers from a big glass bowl on July 20th. It took them all day and most of the night to draw out and record about ten thousand numbers. These numbers were associated with the numbers on the draft registrations they are now calling 'red-ink numbers.' My number was 1,939. That was the number the local draft board printed on my card before I filled it out. So that is your magic number within your draft board area.

"So what they did in the national drawing was to determine the order of those numbers, or each man's liability to be called to serve. Since 258 was the first number drawn, all the men in over four thousand draft board areas around the country with lucky number 258 are now the first in line. They will get a letter from their own draft board, report for the physical, and if they pass, then they will determine if they have exemptions. If they are good to go, they are off to army camp.

"Even though they have drawn all the numbers, they have only published the first forty-seven hundred or so in the Sioux Falls paper, and they skipped all of the numbers that didn't apply to men in South Dakota. I suppose they will get to the rest of the list in a few days. It is a lot of names. It takes up a lot of space in the paper, and they still need room for the other stories and ads. The war department said they thought the first men called would be in the first three thousand numbers, so it seems to me you are not going to be missing your charming spouse anytime soon."

"Are you sure? I would miss you, of course. But are you sure the fact your name is not listed means you are safe?"

"Believe me, my new boss is concerned about all of his salesmen too," C.C. answered. "He has a couple of men who have numbers that were published yesterday. And he has to keep anyone's job open if they are called to the service, so we might be working short. Lucky me, more sales in my bucket."

"I wish you wouldn't be so glib about it. I will just feel so much better when I see your name next to a number and it says 'not a chance he's going.'" She narrowed her eyes at him.

"Well, it is possible all of those other fellows might not be the fine physical specimen I am, and they will be forced to take me anyway. Now, I will bet you fifty cents my name will be in the paper tomorrow with the latest list. Then will you stop worrying?"

She should have taken the bet. His name was not in the paper for two more days, when the last portion of the list was published. C.C.'s draft liability number was 7,315 which he said assured he would not be asked to report for duty in the first wave, probably not even in a second wave, and after that, it all depended on the war's progression.

SIOUX CITY, IOWA, AUGUST 25, 1917

Ina was picking vegetables in her mother's garden in Sioux City when Catherine summoned her to the phone.

"Come quick, I think something happened over at the McCracken house!" her mother called to her.

When Ina got to the phone, Lizzie asked her if she knew how to reach Clinton.

"I believe I have his hotel information in my diary I brought along. I like to keep track of where he is staying when he makes overnight trips."

"I think you'd better try to send him a telegram. He doesn't need to come but I don't want him to be mad later if it turns out we should have notified him. You know he always thinks he should be here for the family in emergencies," Lizzie stammered breathlessly.

"Slow down, Lizzie. I don't understand. Is there an emergency?" Ina fished around on her parent's desk for a pencil, while holding the earpiece of the candlestick phone.

"They took Clay to the hospital. Mother called back here a little bit ago to say they think he will recover just fine, but it was so scary. He and his friend Orpheus were doing some target practice with a .22 rifle, and somehow Clay got shot!"

Ina dropped the pencil she had found and grabbed the base of the phone before it fell over. "Shot? Oh, my golly. Where was he shot?"

"That was the scary part. Blood was coming out around his chest and stomach, and by his shoulder blade. It must have missed his heart or he would have died for sure. Mr. Cushing was driving along and heard Orphy hollering, and they loaded Clay into the

Cushing car and brought him back here. Then the ambulance came to take him to Samaritan."

Ina told her she would notify C.C. by telegram. She wished tonight, and many other nights, that you could call outside your own town on the telephone. She knew it would happen someday, but she was afraid she would be old and gray first.

The message she sent to him at the hotel just said this:

"CLAY SHOT. EXPECT RECOVERY. ADVISE IF YOU ARE COMING TO S.C. I WILL WAIT AT HALLS."

The more words she used in the telegram, the more it would cost, so she tried to be brief. Even so, she knew he would get goosebumps when he read the word "shot" next to his only surviving brother's name.

The next morning, she received a reply that he would be arriving on the evening train. Before all of this happened, Ina had planned to go over to Ellen and John Robert's house that afternoon. She decided to go anyway and see if anyone was home or if they were all at the hospital.

Elizabeth was there with Sylvia and said her parents were still at the hospital with Clay. The girls had gone to see him earlier, but there weren't enough chairs in the room and they thought it would be better for him if he could rest and not have so much commotion. Sylvia was immersed in a book she'd just gotten from the library, so Lizzie and Ina went for a walk down the street.

"How was Clay this morning?" Ina asked. "And how are Ellen and John Robert doing?"

"Clay is better. Complaining, so that is a good sign. Mother and Father just look weary. It concerns me that one of these days they will be the ones in the hospital bed. This takes me back to when we lost my other brothers, Grover and Clifford, just like it was yesterday. It is funny how on the most horrible days of your life, you remember the small details," Lizzie said.

"Tell me what you remember. C.C. told me the stories, of course, but he doesn't talk about them much anymore."

They sat in the shade of an oak tree near the old stone wall.

"I think Clinton had nightmares after Grover died. He was two years younger than Grover. I remember the two of them went out to try to plow with our old horse, Goldie. Horses always seem to cause problems for us. Father was kicked by one back in '02 when he was trying to hitch up the team, and it broke his leg. That was right after Clay was born. Anyway, this time the plow was stuck in the mud, so Grover got up on Goldie to get her to pull the plow while Clinton pushed the plow from behind. They worked at this for maybe an hour that morning without any luck. Then it started raining. So they let it get slimy, and they tried it again, Clinton was pushing with all of his might and Grover was kicking Goldie in the ribs to get her to take off. I saw what they were doing, and started walking toward them to help Clinton push."

"Then Goldie lurched and the harness broke and she went stumbling forward with Grover on her back. But she was off-balance, and she catapulted Grover up in the air head over heels. It was hard to see exactly what happened, but he landed on his head. Both Clinton and I raced to where he landed, but his body was bent at an unnatural angle and he did not seem to be breathing. I started screaming his name, and Clinton jumped on Goldie and galloped to the other end of the farm where Father was tending cattle. I think I screamed at him too, as I was afraid he was going to be thrown off the horse next. Goldie was a good mare though and followed his lead.

"When Father got there, he knew at once Grover had broken his neck. There was nothing we could do. He wanted to shoot the horse, but we convinced him Goldie was not at fault. Clinton said it was his fault because he should have been on the horse since he was smaller. Neither of us will ever forget that day. I remember Grover's eyes were open like he was staring at the clouds, and a little trickle of sweat, or maybe rain, was running down his face," Lizzie said quietly.

"I have never heard so much of the story. Thank you for telling me. But Clifford must have been different. He was ill, wasn't he?" Ina asked, squeezing Lizzie's hand.

"Yes, also scary, but in a different way. We'd moved to Sioux City by then. Cliffy was running all over as five-year-olds do, but at dinner, he seemed tired. We had eaten a little late that night because the weather was so nice. It was about this time of year when you want to get the most out of the waning days of summer. We'd been outside most of the day. Anyway, he just didn't feel well, and Mother put him to bed early. He got a fever in the middle of the night.

"Mother had read in the paper about an epidemic of infantile paralysis in northern Iowa. The next morning, she sent for the doctor. He immediately quarantined the household. Clifford got worse. By the next day, he was having trouble moving his legs and he couldn't breathe. I can still see Mother trying to massage his little legs and arms, trying to restore the feeling. Doc tried giving him some medication, but nothing worked. I think they were afraid to take him to the hospital, thinking it might expose other patients. Infantile paralysis affects your spine and the nerves in your body, and the doctor said sometimes patients die before you can determine what they have."

"That must have been awful," Ina said. "And you were all at risk too?"

"Apparently it was more likely to strike children, but adults could get it too. It is a wonder Mother didn't get it. She was by his side all the time. Sylvia came down with some symptoms. This time, the doctor made her go to the hospital and they isolated her there. She recovered, but you can see how it affected her spine."

"Cliff died three days after he became sick, and we couldn't even have the funeral until the doctor lifted the house quarantine. We were all devastated, of course, and no one more than Clinton. This was two brothers he adored who died within seven years."

Ina thought about how losing his son probably had brought all this pain back again, but thankfully Lizzie did not mention it.

Ina said, "At least it sounds like Clay will be fine. It could have been so much worse."

"Thank you for being here, Ina. I feel better just talking to someone, and I don't want to burden Mother when she is already so upset," Lizzie responded.

"That's what sisters are for, aren't they?" Ina smiled faintly, and they headed back to the house.

OCTOBER 15, 1917

Ina never got tired of visiting her parents' house, or the McCracken house in Sioux City, especially when C.C. could come with her. Sometimes she just liked to look around the room at their parents and her siblings or his siblings, and all the young children gathered. She wished she could just hold this moment in her heart forever. She didn't want anything to change. Maybe she did want one thing to change. She thought she might be pregnant again. It was too soon to know anything for sure, she just had a feeling. Once she knew her husband wasn't going to be leaving anytime soon for military service, she'd begun to relax and was trying to remember to "gather ye rosebuds while ye may." That was what she was doing during this visit, gathering roses from the garden and cherishing the moments she had with their families.

C.C. surprised her earlier in the summer by buying their first car. He had been driving a Model T Ford for the Avery Company on some of his visits to various farms around Sioux Falls, but most of the time when he had to go on longer trips, he took the train. He bought the Ford Roadster from a garage in Sioux Falls. C.C. felt confident he understood how the car worked, having worked in a garage himself, and having trained on tractor engines. So when they got ready to go visit the folks in Sioux City, this time they drove the eighty-eight miles in the roadster. They splurged, and Ina bought one of the new "garden dresses," and C.C. bought a Panama straw hat, and they took to the highway in style.

"You know what you're always saying, Darling? The best is none too good." Ina stuck her nose in the air for effect, and they were soon laughing.

A little while later Ina asked, "Have you heard any more from Clifford about the two of you starting your own road equipment company?"

"He is still making plans. Cliff has some good contacts in the Omaha area, but we would have to raise capital, visit manufacturers, and learn about the bid process to get the company off the ground. He knows a few others who might want to invest in this."

"Does he still want to transfer you down to Omaha while you are working for Avery?" Ina was still hesitant about this part of the plan, but it would likely mean C.C. would be given a promotion and more salary, which they could use if their family was growing.

"Yeah, he does. I am not sure about that. I don't want working for him to ruin our relationship as brothers-in-law. How do you feel about moving to Omaha?"

"What is good for the gander is good for the goose, I guess."

"You are starting to sound like a true McCracken," he laughed and patted her leg affectionately.

SIOUX FALLS, SOUTH DAKOTA, NOVEMBER 2, 1917

"Oh golly, listen to this!" Ina exclaimed one evening. "It is an editorial in the *Argus-Leader* about women's suffrage. 'Should the women of America gain nation-wide suffrage in the near future, it is going to be in spite of many supposed ardent workers in the movement, who are at present going about the country in a futile attempt to work up sympathy for the handful of militants in Washington. The poorest excuse for an argument on the suffrage question is to try to stir up sympathy for these women who made themselves public nuisances and then sought to lessen their punishment by posing as martyrs to the cause.'"

"They are just saying you don't have to break the law to promote women's suffrage," her husband suggested. "That seems reasonable."

"Yes, but it goes on; 'The girl who remains quietly at *home knitting for the Red Cross* is doing more in promotion of the feminist movement than all the defenders of the Washington militants on the platform today. In fact, her work is doubly effective in that she is doing a great and humanitarian duty and at the same time offsetting by her efforts the destructive work of her militant sister. Americans are not in a mood now to listen to talk prejudicial to the best interests of the government. The country is at war and no issue can take precedence over the determination to win it.'"

Ina shook her head. "Should Patrick Henry have said, 'Give me liberty or I will stay home and knit'? Did our patriots not dump tea in the Boston Harbor to protest? Did Abraham Lincoln say, 'I am abolishing slavery, but I think it is best to wait until the civil war is over?' No! How do they think a cause ever got attention without a certain amount of public outrage?"

C.C. cautioned, "Sweetie, you know what Dr. Clark said about letting your blood pressure get too high since you are expecting. Maybe you should think about this after you have had a good night's sleep."

"I don't believe it; you are patronizing me just like this newspaper columnist! Why is it men can't get it? Is it because they haven't had to fight for anything in their lives?" She knew it was an exaggeration, but she stomped off to the bedroom just the same. Sometimes you had to get indignant, even if it was a little misdirected. Her exit would have been a little more dramatic had she not stubbed her toes on a stack of books in the hallway.

The women's suffrage cause has not been an easy road, she thought, sitting on the bed massaging her injured toes. Not for those who had been pushing for it back in the nineteenth century, and not in the past few months. Maybe the most militant was a little extreme, but it was not fair to assume those who were working within the government system were cut from the same cloth. Maybe it was on her mind more now because she was thinking of the next generation, including the person growing inside of her.

Ina had tried to get involved in her local organization again. When the state amendment did not pass the last time, the wind went out of their sails for a while. But she had been proud to be a part of some recent activity. Miss Jane Pincus had been in Sioux Falls in October, arranging meetings for the state committee members with some national representatives of the Congressional Union for Women's Suffrage. Ina's group had hosted a luncheon for Miss Pincus. A few weeks later, women representatives from around the state met with the national union in the Quaker Tea Room downtown. Ina had been on a committee that made sure they had everything they needed. She was not an official participant, but she was in the back of the room and heard what was discussed. It was time, time for women to have the right to vote in all elections. Time to insist on that. Not time to sit back and knit.

NOVEMBER 28, 1917

"There is some sort of deadly flu going around this year," Dr. Clark told her at her appointment. "Some are calling it the Spanish Flu. It has hit people hard in Spain, according to medical journals. Many of the soldiers in Western Europe have been afflicted, and they think they are picking it up after they land in the hospital with war injuries. I am telling all my patients to especially protect children, mothers-to-be, and the elderly. We don't want to start some sort of epidemic here with cold weather coming."

Ina had tried to take his advice, but she couldn't be a complete hermit. She went over to visit Emma about once a week to see her new baby. She also went to her Kro-tat-em meetings every month, which were at different members' homes on a rotating basis. Several of the meetings were across town and she had driven the roadster by herself. Most of the talk there was about the war, and whose husband or brother or neighbor was answering the questionnaire to determine his exemptions. By now, they all knew married men with a dependent wife or child were pretty far down the list of those who were likely to be called. No one from Sioux Falls had been called to serve in the first round. Between the current enlisted men and the National Guard members, the local board had filled its original quota. Until they called for another round of draftees, probably sometime next year, everyone could breathe easily.

Ina and C.C. went to Sioux City for Thanksgiving and spent the day with her parents. C.C.'s mother had not been feeling well the past couple of weeks, and the doctor was running some tests. Because of her pregnancy, Ina was reluctant to go see her until a diagnosis was made, but it seemed to be something digestive in nature. So C.C. went over to the McCrackens' several times while they were in Sioux City to check on his mother. After two days, he convinced his parents Ellen should go to the hospital, and it was lucky she did. Her appendix had nearly burst, and she needed surgery. Once Ina knew the source of her illness, she did go visit her with her husband, but she kept a woolen scarf wrapped around her face when she was in the hallway of the hospital.

"You look like a highway bandit, you know," C.C. teased her.

"Do you want me to follow my doctor's advice or not? But since I look the part, give me all of your money and your watch, Mister."

When they got to her hospital room, Ellen told them she was glad to know what the problem had been, but she was sorry to put anyone else out visiting her.

"Mom, you are always the one taking care of others. It is time we all took care of you until you are back on your feet," C.C. said.

"Don't worry Darling. I will be fit as a fiddle by Christmas. I am so excited that all of my children will be home."

"I am excited about meeting Aggie and Clarence finally," Ina added. "She sent me a lovely card when she heard I was pregnant this time."

SIOUX CITY, IOWA, DECEMBER 26, 1917

Ina couldn't have imagined a better Christmas holiday, and it made her more excited for the ones they would have in the future. Every one of C.C.'s brothers and sisters was there, and they had a big duckling feast with potatoes, yams, plum pudding, and more pies than they could count. It was crowded in the small kitchen trying to turn out that much food. They all took turns trying to get Ellen to take it easy and taking over the preparations themselves. It was no use, she would no sooner sit down to rest when she thought of something else that needed to be done, and she jumped right up instead of delegating the task. They laughed every time it happened, and Ina thought she had never laughed so much at a family gathering. She and C.C. had been married now for four-and-a-half years, and she finally felt like she belonged in this family.

The McCracken clan, as she called them, loved to recite funny little sayings, like this one: "Promises won't butter any bread."

"What does that even mean?" she asked when young Clay said it while buttering his bread.

"I dunno, ask Dad," Clay said.

"It just means if you want to be successful in life, you have to be accountable and follow through on your promises," John Robert answered.

"Or you won't get any bread!" Sylvia piped in.

"Or any butter!" Clay added.

Or another nugget: "The old forget the young don't know." This was a favorite of Vera's and Ethel's. They used on their parents whenever they disparaged them for something that seemed to be common sense to the older generation.

Or one that made her laugh aloud when John Robert said it one morning: "Bad breath is better than no breath at all." She wasn't sure if he was talking about his morning breath, but no one argued the point.

A few days after Christmas, C.C. had to go back to work and the other siblings needed to return home also, except for Aggie and Clarence. They ended up staying with Aggie's parents for a couple of months, knowing it might be years before they could make the journey again. Ina was able to spend several long days with Aggie. They enjoyed talking about teaching, since they both had that in common, and Aggie talked about their adventures in trying to get the orchards up and working. Ina was a little envious of how much Aggie had been able to travel. They had been to California several times, along the Pacific coast, and to Vancouver, Canada, to promote their apple orchards. She had been to Alaska, and Lake Louise, both of which she said were breathtaking. Ina thought she and C.C. should have done more traveling before they started a family.

SIOUX FALLS, SOUTH DAKOTA, MARCH 24, 1918

Ina curled up on one end of the new couch, while C.C. read the newspaper on the other end. It had been a busy couple of weeks, and she was glad they had a day at home with no real commitments. She had just returned from spending the past two weeks in Sioux City with her parents. Ina and Catherine had worked out a schedule where she would come home about once a month, so Catherine could help monitor Ina's health during her pregnancy. She was pampered and spoiled, which her mother said would change drastically once the baby was born.

C.C. was traveling more than ever. The demand for motorized farm equipment was increasing. They tried to coordinate with his longer trips so she would be in Sioux City or her mother would be with her in Sioux Falls during his absence. Catherine usually made a point of cleaning their house from one end to the other, and her son-in-law was very appreciative. While Ina was engrossed in a book, Catherine even managed to throw out some of the old newspapers and other items her daughter had accumulated.

"Tell me more about this secret initiation you had the other night," Ina said.

"It's not secret," he protested. "There is nothing subversive about the Elks Club. It was nice that the district deputy grand exalted ruler came to visit on the same night we were initiated though. That felt special. And because of him, everything was cleaned up and the food was a little more elaborate than normal."

"So you didn't have to wear animal costumes or run around in the woods?"

"No. Seriously, I think it will be good for me to be in the Elks. It is a good way to meet men I might not run across dealing mostly with farmers. You just can't have enough contacts in sales. I picked up a new saying from the exalted ruler fellow. He used this in his address to the chapter: 'Reputation is what you are in the light, character is what you are in the dark.' I like that one."

"You just keep building your empire, Dearest. I am just growing a tiny human being, don't mind me," she said scooting down to put her head on the pillow. "And it gets a little harder every day."

He rubbed her feet, which had appeared in his lap. "It's a good thing your mother is coming while I am gone. I won't worry about you then."

APRIL 1, 1918

Spring again, my favorite season, Ina thought, as she sat in the south window in her rocking chair, the sun on her face like a promise of their future happiness. As she rocked, she felt the baby kicking beneath her ribs. Ina smiled to herself, because one day she was thinking of a precious girl to delight her father, and the next it was a strong boy to help with all the chores.

She thought about the Kro-tat-em club meeting she had just hosted. Mother would have been impressed at how well she had cleaned up the house before the ladies arrived. Of course, she did put a lot of papers and books which were stacked around the house in the spare bedroom. She'd have to clean up that room soon to prepare for the new baby. She still didn't have her platters all put away. Some of them went up on high shelves which were hard for her to reach now, and she didn't want to take any chances standing on a chair to put them away. She would wait until this afternoon when Emma came by and could help her.

Her friends had agreed this time not to surprise her with baby gifts until after the birth. She still had a couple of months to go, and she did not want to jinx anything. She had enjoyed seeing her friends, with their anecdotes about their children and grandchildren, and the news they had from men who were already in training camps preparing to depart for Europe within weeks. Of course, the newspaper made it sound like the Kaiser was whupped and it was only a matter of time before victory was claimed for the Allied Forces. She hoped now it was true and her husband would not have to go to war at all.

CHAPTER FOUR

SIOUX CITY, IOWA, APRIL 3, 1918,

CATHERINE AMANDA HALL

"COME AT ONCE. INA AND BABY GRAVELY ILL IN SIOUX FALLS HOSPITAL."

Catherine Hall reread the telegram from Emma, Ina's friend, over and over but the meaning did not change. What was happening? Where was C.C.? Why was Emma sending for her and not for C.C? She had so many questions and wished she could just call Emma. The only thing to do was to go at once, just like the telegram said. She had been planning to go to Sioux Falls three days ago, to stay with Ina while C.C. was at a conference. That's it, she realized. He must already be at the conference in Illinois, or was it a training session? Catherine had delayed her departure as her husband, Platt, had been feeling poorly for a few days. She wanted to make sure he didn't have anything serious. There had been a lot of flu going around. She arranged for Natalie to check in on her father, packed quickly, and headed to the train depot.

SIOUX FALLS, SOUTH DAKOTA, APRIL 3, 1918

Catherine spotted Emma in a waiting room in the maternity area of the Sioux Falls hospital. "Emma, thank God. There you are. What happened?"

Emma rushed to give Catherine a tearful embrace. "I'm so glad you got my message, Mrs. Hall. I didn't know what to do. My neighbor is watching my own little girl and I need to get back there."

"Sit down, my dear, and tell me what you know," Catherine said, pulling Emma into a chair.

"Ina called me yesterday afternoon. She had a terrible cough, and she said it came on suddenly. When she coughed, it felt like the baby was trying to come out, and it hurt her abdomen. It sounded like a labor pain. She wanted me to take her to the doctor. So I got my neighbor to watch my daughter and I took her to Dr. Clark's. He thought she had maternal pneumonia and told me to take her to the hospital. It is very dangerous for both mother and baby.

"I called the Avery office both yesterday and this morning, but no one answered the phone, so I have not been able to find C.C. Then I decided to send for you. I wasn't even sure I had your address right, but they helped me figure that out at the telegraph office. By the time I came here today, they told me to wait out here and said they would update me when they could. So I haven't seen her since last night. The last thing they told me was they thought they would have to deliver the baby today."

"It's too soon for the baby, isn't it? I thought she was only at about thirty-two weeks. How will the baby survive?" Catherine's question trailed off when she saw the answer in Emma's eyes.

"Mrs. Hall, I think they are trying to save Ina now."

While Emma's words sunk in, Catherine saw a young doctor approaching. Emma seemed to recognize him.

"Doctor Clark, this is Catherine Hall, she is Ina McCracken's mother. She is here to be with Ina," Emma said.

"I am sorry to tell you both, we had to take the baby," Dr. Clark reported. "She was having some irregular contractions and the pregnancy was making it hard for Ina to fight off pneumonia. I'm afraid she has been delirious. She is having trouble breathing and is in a lot of pain. These are all common with maternal pneumonia. We have given her some aspirin and salicin to try to reduce the fever and infection. You can go in to see her now, but she might not make much sense. She has been asking for her husband."

Catherine was torn: should she go in to be with Ina or try to figure out a way to contact C.C.? But she and Emma went into the hospital room. The doctor had not said as much, but she was beginning to feel like she might not have a chance to see Ina alive again. Ina's breathing was labored but she appeared to be sleeping or unconscious.

"Emma, did Ina bring her bag?"

Emma looked around but did not find it. "I don't remember her bringing a bag, but we could have left it at the doctor's office."

"I need to see her diary. She usually carries it in her bag, but it could still be at home," Catherine said, trying to remain calm and clear-headed. "She writes down where C.C. stays when he travels. Maybe we can figure out how to send him a telegram. Can you go to Ina's house and look for the diary?"

"Yes, I have her key, but then I really need to go home. I'm so sorry." Emma's eyes began overflowing.

"I understand, Emma. You have been an amazing friend. I can't begin to thank you. Let's see if the nurse's desk has a telephone number you can call if you find something in the diary."

Catherine stayed by her daughter's side throughout the rest of the day. The nurse gave Ina some more pain medication and some oxygen. They had a pot of water simmering on a device that looked like a one-burner stove. Ina slept for the most part, then lapsed into a coughing fit. When Catherine tried to talk to her, she didn't seem to know what was happening. Emma called the nurses' station a few hours after she left the hospital. She'd found the diary and gave the nurse the name and phone number for the hotel where C.C. was staying in Peoria, Illinois. Catherine was concerned he wasn't going to get a telegram in time.

The nurse directed her back to the telegraph office in the train depot, and she managed to get there before closing. Catherine closed her eyes and wished she did not have to send this message at all. She knew exactly how horrible it was to have been on the receiving end.

"COME HOME AT ONCE. INA CRITICAL IN S.F. HOSPITAL."

The telegraph dispatcher said Catherine could come back the next morning and they could tell her if it had been delivered, although that would only determine if the hotel had received it. Catherine wasn't sure how she would get a reply if C.C. wanted to let her know he was coming. She decided she had done what she could, and headed back to the hospital.

Later that night she went to Ina and C.C.'s house to try to sleep, but it was difficult. She was able to find some bread and jam, which was about all she was able to eat anyway. She called Emma to update her and told her to stay home with her baby.

Later, Catherine would only remember the next few days in a haze. She did go back to Ina's house to sleep when she could no longer stay awake. Often she fell asleep on the chair in Ina's hospital room. Ina seemed completely in oblivion, sometimes overcome with coughing and crying, but not necessarily speaking to her mother. Finally, on the third day after Catherine arrived, Ina seemed to be doing a little better. Her fever broke and she looked at Catherine like she knew her. Her hands covered her belly once she seemed to be aware of her surroundings.

"Baby?" Ina gasped.

Catherine just shook her head, unable to speak, eyes brimming with tears.

Ina stared at her for a moment, then began coughing and thrashing about, so Catherine called for the nurse. They asked Catherine to leave the room, and they gave Ina more oxygen and pain medication. She hasn't been out of that bed for days, Catherine thought. How can she get better like this? She had held herself together up to this point, but now she started to cry. For her daughter, for Ina's baby, and for C.C. too. Why has a merciful God let this happen to such a loving family? She knew she was exhausted and went to get some dinner and to sleep.

By the next morning, she still had not heard from C.C. and did not know if he had gotten the telegram. She called the Avery office herself, and a secretary informed her C.C. was out of town. After she explained the family emergency, the young lady said she would try to get a message to him through the Peoria plant. Catherine returned to the hospital, hoping she would find Ina had regained some strength.

Ina was awake when she arrived, but seemed listless and sometimes said things that did not make sense. Even her words were garbled. Dr. Clark had examined her, but he wasn't optimistic about her recovery. He told Catherine sometimes patients seem to be getting better right before the end, which allows them to tell their loved ones their final wishes.

"But can't you give her something to cure this? You're not just giving up, are you?" Catherine pleaded. "She's twenty-nine years old."

"We have pretty much done everything we can. The pneumonia gets into the lungs so deep it is very hard to expel it once the patient starts getting weaker. The next few days will determine if she makes it. But you need to prepare yourself."

Catherine knew she could not prepare herself for something like this. She considered sending a telegram to Platt, and Ellen and John Robert, but what could she say? It looked hopeless. She only wished C.C. were here to speak for his wife. All she could do now, she thought, was to pray. The hospital had a nice chapel, and she spent quite a bit of time in there. Ina had been in the hospital for nearly a week. Catherine wished she'd started praying sooner, but she couldn't change it now.

At dawn, a nurse came in to wake Catherine. She had fallen asleep in the chair with her head resting on Ina's hospital bed, trying to hold onto her hand.

"How…how is she?" Catherine stammered, trying to fight the sleep from her brain, and her neck felt stiff when she lifted her head.

"I'm so sorry, Mrs. Hall." the nurse answered quietly, touching her shoulder.

Catherine stumbled to her feet and peered at Ina, who seemed to be sleeping peacefully. She blinked, somewhat dumbfounded, and realized she didn't know what to do. It was too late now, too late to do anything, she thought. She had to get out of there, out of that room. If she went out and came back in, maybe it would be different, maybe it wouldn't be true.

She turned to leave and saw him silhouetted in the door frame. C.C. had made it at last. And those familiar dark-blue eyes were searching her face.

EPILOGUE

CAMP FUNSTON, KANSAS, DECEMBER 16, 1918

CLINTON CLAUDE MCCRACKEN

I didn't get her telegrams. I would have come sooner if I had, but the company changed my hotel reservation at the last minute. I will never forget the look on your mother's face when I got to the hospital room. She looked at me like she'd seen a ghost. Then I saw the pain and tears filling her eyes. She didn't hug me like she usually did. She didn't even speak to me. After a moment, she just pushed past me into the corridor. I know now that she had just lost another child. She didn't have room in her heart right then to deal with the agony she knew would be crashing down on me in seconds. Still, I didn't quite understand. It wasn't until I sat by your bedside and saw the stillness on your beautiful lips. I thought of all the times I had kissed those lips and realized that I never would again. It felt like all the blood was draining out of me and pooling on the floor. Like all my breath was being sucked away by some unseen cosmic vacuum and I couldn't move.

Was this happening because we wanted a baby? Then the second blow landed. The baby must have died too. It was all so unthinkable. So unreal. You hear about women dying in childbirth, but it seems so unlikely. Weren't we just trying to have what every married couple wanted? I would have given anything to have you there for just one more day, or even a minute, just to see the light back in your eyes.

I insisted the nurses who had tended to you tell me about the last days of your life. Whether you were in pain, whether you asked for me or if you were unaware of what was happening. I am ashamed to admit, I badgered them until they were in tears. They didn't want to tell me that you asked for me at least seven times and asked about the baby even after they told you she was gone. You probably didn't live long enough to forgive me for not being by your side. I don't think I will live long enough to forgive myself. It seems like it is too little too late to apologize now, but believe me, I have never been sorrier about anything in my life.

It's been eight months since that day. Sometimes it isn't the first thing I remember when I wake up. It doesn't get easier, but it does get less pervasive. Being stuck somewhere like this with too much time on my hands has not helped. But I will try to think about our wonderful life and the hopes we had for the future, and maybe that will allow me to live out those dreams someday. My sisters thought a letter would be a good way to say good-bye. But I am not ready to say good-bye just yet. I don't know if I ever will be. I think I will love you forever.

What could he do with a letter he couldn't mail? Ina's mother had offered to have her laid to rest in the Graceland Park Cemetery where their son had been buried. C.C. would have agreed to anything that day. Besides, he thought, what did it matter where someone is buried? Their soul, their life, their essence was not there in the ground. It was gone. Or maybe it wasn't. Maybe it went on in the wind, in the new life that came into the world. Maybe it resided in the memories of those they knew. People believed what they wanted to about eternal life.

C.C. kept going because he had no choice. He could never forget he wasn't there when she needed him the most, but there was no point in dwelling on that forever. If he did, his life would be over too. For months, he went on with his work and his life like he was numb. He got the news his brother-in-law had finally been able to arrange a transfer for him to Omaha. Then he got the notice he was called to the colors. This snapped him out of his emotional paralysis. His number had finally come up, and he now had no wife and no children depending on him for support. He sold that pretty little roadster he had loved. He could only picture her flying down the road in it. Cliff and Dode had wanted him to live with them in Omaha. None of that mattered anymore. He was off to Camp Funston and then to war. Or so it seemed at the time.

He kept the letter to Ina in his footlocker until he was discharged from Camp Funston. In February 1919, he returned to Sioux City to see his parents. While he was there, his mother gave him a beautiful photograph album with a picture of a steamship on the cover. Ellen had placed several family photographs inside, including photos of him and his father and sisters when they were children. She implied he was going to need these pictures when he had a family of his own. He didn't want to think about that yet, but he decided the album may be the perfect safekeeping spot for the letter he had been carrying around. Maybe if he could put the letter away, he could put the guilt away with it. He tucked the letter behind one of the photographs and took the album with him when he moved to Omaha.

Over the years, he remembered the letter and took it out a few times to read it. He found it was less depressing each time. C.C. did reinvent his life and, ironically, many things turned out just as he and Ina had discussed, at least for him. He realized how unfair that was. He got a chance to live the life they'd planned but he hoped he made her proud. C.C. met and married another wonderful woman and had four children. Women got the right to vote in 1920. He started a road equipment company with Cliff. He tried to appreciate the small victories in his life. And every time he bought something his second wife thought was extravagant, he could hear Ina's voice in his head: "The best is none too good."

Nearly sixty years after his death, and almost one hundred years after he first tucked that letter away, his grandchildren were cleaning out the home of his younger daughter after her passing. One of them found the letter in his album.

"What's this letter?" his granddaughter asked excitedly. "And who was Ina?"

HALL/ MCCRACKEN FAMILY

CATHERINE AMANDA GILLETT--------------------PLATT SMITH HALL

> CHILDREN:
> BRYAN ISAAC HALL
> LELA JANE HALL
> NELLIE L. HALL
> MARIE BEATRICE HALL
> TRACY GEORGE HALL
> MARGIE ETHEL HALL
> HARRIETT JULIA HALL
> **INA HAZEL HALL**
> FLORENCE ELLEN HALL
> NATALIE BERTHA HALL

ELEANORA HOTOPP--------------------JOHN ROBERT MCCRACKEN

> CHILDREN:
> AGNES M MCCRACKEN
> ELIZABETH "LIZZIE" MCCRACKEN
> DORA ELEANORA "DODE" MCCRACKEN
> GROVER WILLIAM MCCRACKEN
> **CLINTON CLAUDE MCCRACKEN**
> VERA CRUZ MCCRACKEN
> ETHEL PEARL MCCRACKEN
> FAY FRANCES MCCRACKEN
> SYLVIA B. MCCRACKEN
> JOHN CLAYTON "CLAY" MCCRACKEN
> CLIFFORD LANDON MCCRACKEN

INA HAZEL HALL--------------------CLINTON C. MCCRACKEN

> CHILDREN:
> TWO CHILDREN NOT NAMED

Left: Clinton Claude McCracken, taken sometime between 1913-1919

Below: Platt and Catherine Hall family taken about 1897
Back row: Marie, Tracy George, Harriett
Second row: Margie Ethel, Platt, Catherine, Lela
Front row: Flossie, Ina, Natalie

MARY

CHAPTER ONE

FORT WAYNE, INDIANA, SEPTEMBER 1865

Marya Maria Siedschlag sat like a statue on the hard wooden pew in the cool candlelit German church and tried to ignore the platitudes being spoken about her father by Reverend William Sibler. It had only been one day since her father, Herman Siedschlag, had died of *Nervenfieber*, a fever the doctor said was most likely typhoid. Many people in Fort Wayne, Indiana had been ill with it. But why Papa? And why would a merciful God have taken him from us? He was a healthy, hard-working, forty-nine-year-old man with a zest for life, and the energy of men half his age. Hadn't he led his wife and four children away from their lovely farm in Brandenburg, Germany, with a promise of a better life in America? Papa had found a good job managing a large farm for Mr. Dowd, but now he was dead, and his dream had died too.

When the tears fought their way to her cheeks, Marya sought to distract herself by thinking of anything other than what was happening in front of her. She stared at the painting of Jesus surrounded by heavenly cherubs and pictured her sweet little brother, Herman, her father's namesake. He was five years younger than Marya, and when he was born, she was sure he was a gift, *das Geschenk,* for her from her parents. She had doted on him and carried him around like a doll when he was a baby. When he was a plump, towheaded toddler, he'd followed her around like a duckling, and she had been better at entertaining him than their nanny. Marya would read him stories, like the *Children's and Household Tales* by the Brothers Grimm, and Herman was fascinated. Once he started school, she didn't see him as much. She never quite had the same bond with sister Gussie when she came along three years after Herman. He was her *kleiner Bruder.*

She loved him very much. But she had lost him too. It had been about a year and a half now, but she could still remember how sick and pale he had gotten on the three-week journey across the ocean.

The steamer *Tuisko* had brought them all to New York on October 14, 1862: her father Herman, her mother Auguste, her older brother August Wilhelm (then seventeen), her brother Herman (then nine), her sister Gussie (then six), and herself.

"We were six, and now we are only four," she thought.

The whole family had lost weight, by the time they finally set foot on land in the New York harbor. All but little Herman recovered within a month or so, after taking the train to Chicago and being settled into the north side of Chicago's predominantly German district. They found many a motherly *frau* waiting to prepare favorite pastries and meals from their homeland. That not only returned them to health, but it also made them feel welcome in strange surroundings.

They only traveled to Allen County, Indiana once Herman began getting a little better. He had gotten well enough to go to school that year, but Mama fussed over him more than the others.

Marya remembered the days when the winter storms painted their farmhouse with fairyland ice, and they all stayed home in front of the warm fireplace or cookstove. She would read to the younger children. She loved to watch how Herman's eyes would dance in the firelight. He especially loved the stories about bears coming to the cabins, although they had never seen a bear where they lived.

Herman's health never seemed to recover. When he came down with a bad cough, they sent for the closest doctor in Fort Wayne, who also treated some of the farm animals.

"I'm afraid it looks like consumption, Mr. Siedschlag," Marya heard the doctor tell her father. "There probably isn't anything we can treat it with. His system will either fight it off, or it won't. You should just try to make him comfortable."

Herman had not been strong enough to put up much of a fight, and he'd passed away. Marya had never seen anyone die before, and she couldn't understand why it had to happen to her sweet little brother. She knew she had to be strong for her parents and Gussie. If she had trouble understanding how this could happen, it must be worse for her younger sister. Her mother and father didn't say much in front of the children, but Marya heard them talking about an undertaker and a funeral.

Now she was at her father's funeral. One of the elders was reading scripture. She glanced over at her brother, Alexander, as August Wilhelm now called himself, who was sitting just to her left. He took her hand and squeezed it when she looked at him. She could see he was clenching his jaw and trying to keep his lips from trembling as the service continued.

He is my rock, she thought. Little Herman was my sunshine, but Alexander is my rock. I never would have survived here if Alexander had not been there every step of the way. He is amazing too. Always a top scholar in every subject back in Saxony, and now he is working for a pharmacist in Fort Wayne. Not just any pharmacist, but Colonel Hugh B. Reed, who had recently returned as a war hero, leading the Indiana Volunteers in battle. Dr. Reed let Alexander prepare potions and prescriptions, and sometimes they did their experiments with herbs they grew themselves. Alexander hoped to enroll in medical school, and would probably be leaving for Chicago to pursue that dream. What is it with these men and their high-fangled dreams? Don't they see how they are disrupting everyone else's lives?

She remembered the beautiful poem Alexander had written for her on her seventeenth birthday this past April. She had been feeling rather depressed because it was the first anniversary of her younger brother's death. The poem was written in Old German, a special reminder of their homeland.

> *If you look sister, back through the past year,*
> *You will see that joy has pushed sorrow away,*
> *But sorrow will return.*
>
> *In February, the days get longer*
> *I wish you luck that you will grow stronger*
> *To deal with grief for loved ones lost.*
>
> *Good health is a gift from these bygone times*
> *As good as gold I give to you*
> *I wish this for your future family as well.*
>
> *Now here at last, it is the best,*
> *I wish this for your birthday,*
> *Don't forget your brother, Alexander.*
>
> *Seventeen years of your life now added to eternity.*
> *You must, once again, give happiness a chance.*
> *Ask of him, this day, our Father in Heaven.*
>
> *Your brother, Alexander Siedschlag*

"Do you like it?" he had asked as the tears overflowed down her cheeks when she'd read it.

He got the answer when she flung herself into his arms. "Thank you, Alexander. I will treasure it forever. When you are a famous poet, I won't even sell it at an auction." She added more soberly, "Have I been awfully glum these past few weeks? It just seems like nothing is certain here if you can't protect your family from harm."

"We've all been sad over little Herman," Alexander had said.

"But he would have wanted us to find happiness. I want you to have hope on your birthday."

It had helped. She had begun to feel hopeful again, with spring beginning to bloom and the new baby animals being born on the farm. She loved to see how they delighted Gussie. In trying to be more American, Marya had started telling people her name was Mary. Part of her resented the fact they had changed their names, and they were now expected to speak English when German came so much more easily to them. But she had studied both languages in school, and she was getting better at becoming American.

Her reverie ended when the organ clanged a loud chord. Everyone stood and sang the final hymn in German before her beloved father was laid to rest. She dabbed tears from her face and took Alexander's arm before she had to join her family at the back of the church to thank the others for coming. Her mother was lucky to have her brother, Ferdinand Tapp, and his wife, Wilhelmina, who was also Herman Siedschlag's sister, at her side to support her. They had come to Fort Wayne from Germany a few years before Mary's family.

The day after his father's funeral, Alexander received a letter saying he was accepted at Rush Medical School in Chicago. Colonel Reed had written him a glowing recommendation.

"I won't be leaving for nearly a year. I still have work to do with Colonel Reed, so I will probably move to Chicago in the fall," Alexander told her. "I think you should come with me."

"I shouldn't leave Mama," she said, "with all she is going through. I should be here to look after Gussie, especially with you leaving."

"Maybe I need you to look after me. I don't need an answer now, just think about it. You liked Chicago when we were there before."

Mr. Dowd and his wife had been very generous with the Siedschlag family. As part of the farm manager's job, the Siedschlags lived in a farmhouse with three bedrooms, a kitchen, and a dining room. Mr. Dowd seemed to regret having to call on Auguste, at the caretaker's cottage, in mid-October, just a month after Herman's funeral.

"You know, Mrs. Siedschlag," Mr. Dowd cleared his throat, "I would really like to let you continue to stay here, with your two young daughters and all. I understand Alex has taken a room in town and hasn't lived with you for some months."

"That's right, Mr. Dowd," Auguste replied. "He moved out in June."

"I am going to have to hire another man to take your husband's job as overseer. You understand, don't you? And when I find someone, he is going to want to move in here with his own family."

"I do understand, Mr. Dowd. You have been most kind. When do we need to move out? I will start looking for a place in town," she said stoically.

They agreed the Siedschlags would begin preparations for the move, and Mr. Dowd would keep her informed about his progress in hiring the replacement. Auguste announced to Mary and Gussie that they would need to start packing their few belongings they had brought with them, and she would have Alexander help her find a house in Fort Wayne near him, if possible.

So Mary wasn't completely surprised a week later when she saw Mr. Dowd riding up with his two-horse team and wagon, along with a younger man she didn't recognize. She was saddling *das Ross,* who had been her father's horse, in the riding ring. Even though working on the farm was not her job, the family was still living there rent-free, so she had tried to help out where she could. She had wrapped her long black hair around her head and stuffed it into her father's wide-brimmed hat, put on a shirt, and a pair of her father's work pants and cinched them in with a belt, and decided to give *das Ross* some exercise. She had planned to go out to the meadow to see if she could find any of the new calves.

Mary's attention had been focused on the horse. She didn't realize the newcomer was approaching her until he was a few yards away. He was taller than she was by just a few inches, with thick medium brown hair and a beard that was just beginning to fill in. He was lean but strong and had a commanding presence in the way he moved. With those light blue eyes, he surely hailed from either Germany or Scandinavia. She cast him a cool stare but didn't speak.

"Herr Siedschlag, is it?" he called out.

"No, that was *mein Vater,* my father," she answered, speaking German, as she often did. "I don't know where you came from, but you will never fill his shoes, *Honyock!*" She swung herself onto the saddle, and urged *das Ross* into a gallop, heading for the open pasture leaving her companion in the dust. As the horse took off, her father's hat flew away and her sleek black tresses came tumbling out behind her.

"Fräulein, wait!" he cried after her when he realized he had mistaken her for her brother.

Mary found a new calf and watched as he nursed from his mother. "Oh why Papa?" she railed at him looking skyward. "Why did you bring us here and set our family on this course and then leave? I know you thought working for Mr. Dowd was a way for you to learn how to farm, but now there is another young man ready to take your place. But where does it leave Mama, Gussie, and me? You taught me to ride and to care for the animals, but I don't know it all, Papa. And I am not a man, they will never give me a chance to farm even if I wanted to." Her anger abated, and she knew she had taken it out on the new overseer. Her emotional reaction had taken her by surprise.

By the time she returned to the stable, the men had left, but Auguste met her at the door.

"Were you rude to that nice Mr. Severin, Dear?" she asked.

"Who?" Mary sniffed, pouring herself some tea from the pot on the stove.

"Mr. Dowd brought by the new farm manager. I heard Mr. Dowd tell him when they were still on the porch that your father always said you can be a handful. And something about 'that you can speak English when you want to, but you'd rather scold someone in German.' That does sound like something your father might have said."

"They thought I was rude? It sounds like they were making fun of me. Who is this new man anyway?"

"He said his name is Christian Severin. He's been working as a machinist at Agricultural Works, you know, the place on Calhoun Street that Colonel Reed started. They mostly fix farm machinery. Anyway, that is how Mr. Dowd found out about Mr. Severin. He asked Colonel Reed if he knew of anyone he could recommend for the farm manager job, and he said he had a young machinist who had come over here a few years back as an apprentice and had helped his father start a farm in Iowa."

"*Hmmm*," Mary said still annoyed.

"They said he tried to speak with you, but you rode off in a huff."

Mary shrugged. "Maybe I did. I hate the idea that someone thinks he can just move in here and take over for Papa."

"*Mein Kind,* you can't blame anyone else. Your father has no more use for his job. It is *gut* he found someone who is young and strong and has experience who can do just what *dein Vater* would do if he was here. We will move into the nice house in Fort Wayne. I will find some work soon, you will see," Auguste assured her. "Tomorrow he will be back around, so be nice. Maybe you can show him the horses and the pigs. Make peace."

"I will try. That is all I can promise, Mama."

The next day, she was dressed in her dark blue calico dress and apron, with her dark hair neatly plaited down her back. She was feeding the chickens in the yard when Chris rode up on one of Mr. Dowd's white stallions. He dismounted and tied the horse's reins to the fence rail, before walking up to her extending his hand.

"I brought my horse today. I was afraid you might try to escape again. My name is Chris. Christian Severin. I am going to be working for Mr. Dowd as the caretaker of this place."

He does have nice eyes, she thought. And a very good jawline. And he said "caretaker," not overseer, not manager, not boss, but caretaker—someone who will take pride in the place and care for the animals we have raised. She looked him in the eye and reached out her hand slowly and deliberately.

"Marya Maria Siedschlag. Just call me Mary."

He didn't shake her hand, instead bringing it to his lips.

Mary was caught off guard. It took her instantly back to Fräulein Hummel's dancing class when she was twelve years old, in Brandenburg. Her assigned waltz partner was Austrian, and he'd surprised her by kissing the back of her hand when the dance ended, to the dismay of Fräulein Hummel. She remembered how it felt both exotic and electrifying to a wholesome young girl, and she had been disappointed that she never saw that Austrian boy again.

Those same feelings exploded on her face, as she pulled her hand back in mid-blush.

"I'm so sorry, I don't know why I did that. I have never done that before. I guess your hand was just so durn pretty and … you know you look different than you did yesterday," Chris stammered.

She struggled to hide her delight and confusion and make her tone reproachful. "Yesterday, I was working. Today you are going to do the work." It was much easier watching him squirm.

She led him to the barn and showed him where the bridles, blankets, and saddles were stored, plus the various types of feed and supplies they had for the livestock. After a tour of the buildings, she sat on a bale of hay on the outside of the ring. He sat on the fence, and pulled a couple of apples from his pocket, offering her one. She accepted it and took a bite.

"I have a confession to make," Chris said. "Mr. Dowd showed me what was in those buildings yesterday."

Her anger struck like a bolt of lightning. "So you just wanted to make a fool of me by going through it all again?"

"Not at all. I just like hearing you talk, and watching you walk. Much more inspiring than old Mr. Dowd."

She found embarrassment flood her face again, but she didn't know what to say.

"How old are you, Mary?" he asked.

"I'm seventeen. How old are you?"

"I am twenty-two. I have a brother, Fredrick Charles, we call F.C., who is your age, and he is still in school back in Iowa. My brother John Henry is twenty-one, my sister Wilhelmina, or Mina, is nineteen, and my second sister Johanna is fifteen. We were all born in Prussia. There are two more children, August, who is only five, and Amelia, who is three. They were born on the farm in Iowa. The second batch, *zweite Charge,* we call them," Chris told her. She noticed he tended to switch back and forth between German and English, and she was impressed he seemed comfortable with both languages.

"You have a pretty big family," she said and took another bite of her apple. "There are only four of us left now. I had a little brother, Herman, but he died a year ago last winter. So now, it is just Mama, Alexander, me, and my little sister, Gussie, who is nine. I didn't mean to be rude to you yesterday. It is just hard for me to get used to anyone but my father running things here."

"I understand. I was sorry to hear about your father. Mr. Dowd had only nice things to say about him."

"Thank you," she managed to say as the tears started forming. "He was the one who wanted to come here and it was just so unexpected and... we are just a little lost... I'm sorry, I have to ..."

She found she couldn't speak as she backed away and ran into the house.

She was embarrassed again and found solace in her room. What was it about this man that was throwing her off balance? It wasn't just that he exposed her grief over her father; she understood that. But what about what happened before, when he'd kissed her hand, and pretended like he hadn't meant to, and what he said about wanting to hear her talk and watch her—was he just flirting? Was he trying to find out if she was interested? Was she? She didn't know.

She didn't see Chris for a few days. He had come by when she was in school, and her mother had given him some apple pie. He seemed to be fond of apples. Her mother relayed that Chris was also fond of animals. He had ridden *Das Ross* and brushed him down thoroughly. Their dog, Aldo, had started following him around, and so had the chickens as he dropped corn out of his pockets.

On Friday, there was no school because the teacher had to take a trip out of town. When he knocked on the farmhouse door that morning, Mary opened it. She was rolling out pear tarts.

"Oh, Mary. I'm sorry to bother you, I thought your mother was in here," Chris said.

"Mama went to Fort Wayne to check on the new place. I guess we will be moving in a few days. Alexander is going to help us. Have you met my brother?" she said politely as she returned to the kitchen and the pear tarts she was making. He followed her inside.

"Alex? Yes, I met him through Colonel Reed. He came to Ag Works, and I also saw him at Reed Drugs. Are you and your brother close?" he asked.

" 'Two peas in a pod,' Papa used to say. We were very close, but I haven't seen him much since he moved to town last year. It will be nice to live nearby. Mama said she is going to feed him and fatten him up like a spring hog."

"So where is your sister, Gussie?"

"She went along with Mama since we don't have school today."

"So we're alone?" he said as he sat on one of the chairs at the kitchen table which was covered with flour and dough. "Why don't you sit here so we can visit?" He pulled her by the elbow to sit on the chair next to his, and moved his chair closer, so they were inches apart.

"You'd better be careful. I am covered with flour," she laughed.

"I don't care, I like flour."

She slapped her left palm on the table in the flour, then smashed it gently on his nose and smeared flour over his face. She laughed, surprised she could have fun with him.

"Now you are in for it!" He stuck his hand in the flour, as she jumped up and ran off.

He caught up with her just outside the bedroom door and tried to put his hand on her face as she had done. She kept squirming her face away though until he held it with his other hand. By then, the flour had gone on her hair, his clothes, and some of it on the wall she was leaning against. She forgot all about the flour when he moved in for a kiss. She knew she should push him back, but she didn't want to. She felt his arms wrap around her as she kissed him back. Ever since her father had died, maybe even since little Herman had died, she'd felt like she needed something, someone she could cling to, to console her. He felt good, and warm, and comforting. He smelled faintly of new-mown hay and leather. And then she couldn't breathe.

She finally broke his embrace. "Maybe we'd better go outside," she gasped, as she staggered toward the front door. She reached the small porch and sat on the sturdy railing, inhaling the fresh air. "Mama will be home soon, I think."

He followed her out to the porch, leaning on the door frame. "Then I'd better make this quick. I like you, Mary. I think I like you a lot." He sounded very serious suddenly. "How would your mother feel about you courting with a man of twenty-two?"

She sized him up before answering. She knew this was the kind of question one should not answer quickly.

"Only if he had good manners and good intentions." She smiled, "At least I think that's what she would say."

"Then she has nothing to worry about. Nothing at all."

As if to demonstrate his honor, he vaulted over the porch railing and headed toward the barn.

"Better get to work while the sun still shines," he called over his shoulder. He turned back and added, "Let me know when those tarts are ready, won't cha?"

"A charmer! That's what I got here, a real *charmeur*," Mary thought aloud. "What do you do with that?" But she realized she felt happier than she had in a good long time. In fact, she started singing as she finished making the pear tarts.

A few days later, Chris and Alexander helped the Siedschlag ladies move into their new house near the Wabash & Erie canals across from Van Buren Street. Alexander's place was a few blocks away across the canal.

Mary had learned Fort Wayne was at the intersection of the St. Mary's, Maumee, and St. Joseph's Rivers. At one point, the canal system went from Ohio to Lafayette, Indiana, southwest of Fort Wayne.

Mary had to admit, she found the canals an unusual attraction in a part of the country that was so landlocked. As autumn gave way to the winter chill, Mary and Chris began spending more time together when she wasn't busy with schoolwork and he wasn't busy on the farm. When the weather was nice they would often walk up and down the sides of the canals and watch the boats advance. She had read about the creation of the Erie Canal in school, and Alexander was always updating the family on the latest gossip he had picked up about what places had the best transport between Fort Wayne and Lafayette or Cincinnati.

As they were getting to know each other, Chris talked more about his family and his journey to America from Prussia in 1856.

"We were fortunate enough to have money to secure a better spot on the boat and didn't become as ill as many others. Once we arrived in New York, we took the train directly to Guttenberg, Iowa. My father bought sixty acres and set to work improving the small house that came with the farm. My brothers and I helped him work the land. It's just like what you said about your father: we left Germany for America to own more property."

Both Mary and Chris had also traveled to Chicago before they met. Chris had moved to Chicago in 1863 to work as a cooper, learning to make barrels and casks, but the company he'd worked for offered to train him as a machinist because he had worked on a farm and could repair drills, mowers, and plows.

"One day, I met one of the men who started the Fort Wayne Agricultural Works. He asked me to move to Fort Wayne. I thought it might be a good way to see another state. I figured if I didn't like it, I could always go back to Chicago. So I started working at the Ag Works, and Colonel Reed was the president. Since Colonel Reed knew everyone in town and had been at your father's funeral, he knew about the job at Dowd's farms." Chris told her.

Mary told him about how they had lived on the north side of Chicago when her family came there in 1862.

"I loved living there because it was a German encampment, and everyone not only spoke German, they ate German, danced German, and sang German songs. It was like the homeland. When we moved to Fort Wayne, my parents told me we're in America and I had to start speaking English in school."

She had met Colonel Reed too since her brother worked for him at the pharmacy. "Alexander has repeated some of the amazing civil war stories he heard from Colonel Reed," she told Chris. "You may have heard them yourself. It sounds like he was right in the thick of it."

"Apparently the war was won by the Colonel himself if you believe him. I had to register for the militia before I left Iowa too, but they didn't call me to serve. I think I was excused for being a farmer."

"You considered yourself a farmer then, back before you became a cooper or a machinist?" Mary asked. "What about now? What do you want your profession to be?"

"I still want to be a farmer. I just want to own the farm. That's a lot different."

They made it through the long winter of 1866. Living in Fort Wayne, it was much easier getting to school, since the girls could walk down the street. Chris was the one who had to deal with the farm in the winter now. Sometimes, when he came to the Siedschlag's house for dinner, he'd just spent the night on the living room floor, rather than trying to ride his horse home in the dark. He and Mary would sit under quilts in front of the fireplace and watch the flickering flames. When Auguste got tired and went to bed, he would try to steal a kiss or two, but Mary was careful not to make too much noise, as she didn't want her mother to catch them.

They had a good deal in common and, most of the time, they got along very well. He knew how to have fun and to be silly and she realized he rarely made her lose her temper. Until the incident with that girl. Her name was Annabelle, but Mary just thought of her as *Der Flirt*. Mary walked past the Fort Wayne Agricultural Works shop entrance on her way to school. It was a beehive of activity, mostly farmers and the men employed to fix or sell machinery.

When a young blonde woman was hired as a payroll clerk, she became the center of attention. When Mary walked by after school, Annabelle was often sitting on a wagon or another piece of equipment parked near the entrance. She was always laughing at the things the men were telling her. Regardless of whom she was talking to, she always seemed to hang on their words. As if men don't already have big enough heads, Mary thought. It just made her mad to see such foolishness. They should be working.

One day in June when she walked by, she spotted Chris sitting next to *Der Flirt*. Mary couldn't believe her eyes. He seemed captivated by Annabelle's allure, just like the rest of those dullards. Mary pictured herself walking straight up to him and pushing him backward off the chair, but she restrained herself, and just walked quickly past the shop trying to get to her house.

"Mary, there you are!" Chris jumped to his feet and called after her when he saw her walk by.

She didn't stop walking though. In fact, she increased her speed, which led to peals of laughter from the other men in the vicinity. She was running by the time she'd reached her front door about two blocks away, and she slammed the door behind her. Chris had almost caught up to her. Perplexed, he knocked on the door.

"Mary, open the door. Didn't you see me or hear me? Are you mad about something?"

She opened the door a crack, her face a mask of fury. "I saw you talking to *her*. All of those other men can make jackasses of themselves fawning over that cheap hussy, but I thought you had more sense!" Then switching to German, "*Geh weg ich hasse dich.*"

He pushed the door open farther, and stepped inside. "I am not leaving, and you don't hate me," he said trying to smooth things over. "You love me, and I love you too."

"So why were you talking to *Der Flirt* at the Ag Works? And who have you been writing all those secret letters to?" she demanded.

"Annabelle? She's just friendly. She is married to the foreman of the manufacturing plant. She is helping for a month or so until old Mrs. Swenson gets back to town. I am certainly not interested in her. I am only interested in you, *Mein Liebling*. You must know that by now."

She looked somewhat appeased, so he went on, "And I don't know what you think you know about my letters, but I have been writing to several employers back in Chicago about possible jobs. I think I have a lead machinist job lined up for the fall. I was waiting until I was sure before I told you."

"Wait, what? You are moving back to Chicago? When were you going to tell me that? You are leaving me. What about poor Mr. Dowd, are you leaving him in the lurch too?" Her anger catapulted as she asked questions in rapid succession without giving him a chance to answer.

"No, I am not leaving you. Of course not. I want you to come with me to Chicago. We will go at about the same time Alexander is going in October. He starts his studies at Rush College then, or so he told me. I know you don't want to see him leave, and this way he will be close by. Right before that, we'll get married."

"Married? You're proposing marriage right in the middle of an argument?" she cried, both amazed and indignant.

"I guess I am. It's one way to win an argument." He paused and smiled, then took her by the shoulders. "Marry me, Mary. Marry me. *Heirate mich*," he said, his voice growing softer as he moved in to kiss her forehead, her nose, and finally her mouth.

Mary thought she ought to smack him. But she felt her anger retreating out of her reach the longer the kiss lingered. By the time he pulled her into his arms, her consent was apparent.

"You'll have to ask Mama, you know." She called out, "Mama?

Are you here?"

When there was only silence, Mary sighed, "I guess there is no one home."

"Even better," he grinned and pulled her onto the sofa. They rarely had any time together in private and took advantage of the opportunity.

Mary had not met anyone in Chris's family yet, so she traveled with him back to Guttenberg, Iowa, in August of 1866. Chris's brother, John Henry, met them at the train station and took them to the farm by wagon. John Henry looked surprised to see her, but she just assumed it was because she was someone new. They rode through part of the Mississippi River valley and the roads were hilly and winding, and it made her remember the foothills in her beloved Germany where she'd played as a child. The farm had a beautiful view of the surrounding countryside and she could see why they'd chosen it.

When they disembarked the wagon in front of the big farmhouse on the hill, Chris's parents came out to greet them. They hugged Chris and looked at her expectantly.

"Mama, Papa, this here is Mary Siedschlag. We are getting married in October," he said proudly.

Mary looked at him in wonder and tried to keep her jaw from dropping. He hadn't told his parents about her yet? Before her anger rose to her lips, she was in the warm grasp of his mother, his father, and an assortment of brothers and sisters.

"You didn't know about me, did you? He didn't even tell you I was coming today?" she asked, looking at Chris suspiciously.

"It's a surprise," he said. "I didn't know what to say in a letter. They probably wouldn't have believed me if I'd told them how perfect you were."

She had to admit, that got him back in everyone's good graces. She learned his father was Johan Christian Severin, called John, and his mother was Elisabeth. She met his other younger brothers F.C., and August, and sisters Mina, Johanna, and Amelia. Mina had gotten married the previous year to Christel Rauch, who was both a carpenter and a farmer and he was also in attendance when they gathered around a bountiful table for dinner. She wondered how she would remember all their names. Little August and Amelia seemed to think she was there for their amusement and insisted on showing her all of the animals in the barn as soon as they had a chance.

Even though the house was crowded, she enjoyed the five-day visit. Since it was too far for his family to come to Indiana for the wedding, they insisted they take one of his mother's prized quilts and a silver mug they had brought from the old country as wedding gifts. The evening before they left, Mary went walking out on the path to the field with Chris.

"Don't you miss this place?" she asked, as the gentle breeze swept the heat and humidity from their faces.

"Of course, but my home is with you now, whether we are in Fort Wayne or Chicago, or anywhere else," he said, kissing the back of her hand entwined in his. "I am sure I will be back on the land someday, just wait and see."

The wedding took place on October 14, 1866, at Saint Paul Evangelical Lutheran Church in Fort Wayne, the same church where Mary's father had been buried a year before.

"Look at me, Mama. Do you think this is nice enough for a wedding? We are going to the photographer's studio first. I just don't know if it is dressy enough, but what else do I have?" Mary spun around in the main salon of their small house modeling a steel gray taffeta dress with bell sleeves and a white lace collar.

"Let's see how it looks with the hat," Auguste said. She placed a black straw hat she had topped with a mixture of dried strawflowers, daisies, and sea holly on Mary's head, then pinned it to her hair. Gussie held the long grey veil up and Auguste pinned it to the hat.

"You're going to have to be careful that you don't get this veil caught on anything, or it will pull the hat off too," Gussie said.

Chris showed up at the doorway just then in his charcoal three-piece suit and a frock coat with a military-style overlay. He wore a white shirt with a detachable standup collar and a black neck stock.

"And don't you look handsome?" Auguste said. "Just like a bridegroom."

"And what are you hiding behind your back?" Mary asked.

"A gift for my beautiful bride," he said, presenting a blue parasol.

"How perfect!" she cried. "But isn't that extravagant?" She knew this was a cherished gift among brides.

"Don't worry about that. But it is a bit chilly this morning. You'd better wear your shawl and gloves." Chris said.

"Just remember to take them off for the picture, Darling," Auguste told her. They strolled down the street to the portrait studio of Edward Fleischer, with Mary flaunting her new parasol.

Alexander walked Mary down the aisle, and F.C. had arrived in time to serve as Chris's best man, representing his side of the family. Young Gussie stood by her sister's side as a junior bridesmaid. It rained early in the morning, but by the time the festivities began, the sun had come out, and the guests enjoyed the weather as well as the refreshments.

The day after the wedding, Alexander, Mary, and Chris all took the train to Chicago to start their new adventures, and F.C. returned to Iowa. Alexander would begin shadowing doctors and taking classes. Mary worried it would be hard on her mother, especially with both of her older children leaving at once, but Auguste had assured them it was just a normal part of life.

"The train goes both directions, you know," Auguste had said. "I had to leave my mother and father in Germany, never to see them again. I had no one but Herman, my brother Ferdinand, and you children. It's hard, but it is part of growing up and finding your destiny. We can write often, as long as my fingers still function."

Chris and Mary found a nice flat near where he worked in Chicago's *Nordseite,* in the same neighborhood where the Siedschlags lived before. Alexander was just a few blocks away, but he soon became involved in his studies and spending time with his fellow interns. She was able to lure him to their apartment occasionally with a *Weinersnitchel* and sauerkraut dinner.

One day in November, Mary caught her brother looking at her in an odd way. "What's wrong? Did I spill something on my dress?" she asked.

"No, nothing like that," he said, continuing to scrutinize her. "It's just we have been studying obstetrics, and I think you are expecting— trächtig."

Mary was shocked he was talking to her about this. "You are saying that because we just got married. But I suppose I could be. How would I know?" This was not a subject discussed in her family, and not even taught in those renowned schools she attended in Germany.

"Are your clothes getting tighter? When was the last time you bled"? He tried to be delicate.

She couldn't believe he had asked that. But if he was going to be a doctor, he had to talk about uncomfortable subjects.

"I don't remember, it must have been sometime in the summer. Before we went to Guttenberg, I think. And yes, I think I have gained a little weight, but I have been cooking more since I have a husband."

"Have you been sick in the morning?" he asked.

"Well, not lately. I did have a touch of some stomach ailment around the first of August. I couldn't get rid of it for weeks. I remember because Chris and I went to a party and I didn't think I could stomach any coffee."

"My diagnosis is you are going to have a baby, and it will become more obvious soon. Eventually, you will start feeling a fluttering as the baby grows. You might want to talk to Mama about this. I'm sure she remembers how she felt."

A baby? How could she possibly have a baby? She thought it was unlikely. But she remembered a few romantic encounters before they wed. Most of the women she knew who were in such a condition never mentioned it, and the baby just appeared out of thin air.

It soon became more obvious she was with child. When she took off her corset in the evening, her abdomen exploded in relief. She thought she should quit wearing the corset, but her dresses wouldn't button without it, so she took to wearing aprons with full bib fronts. When the problem persisted despite her eating less, she had to make herself some new garments.

About the same time, Chris's brother F.C. came to Chicago, got a job as a mercantile clerk, and enrolled in night school. Sometimes both F.C. and Alexander came to dinner at the same time. Alexander, talked of science and medicine, while Frederick Charles loved to talk about people, and their ideas and ideals. Mary often thought he belonged in politics. Both of them were working and taking classes, and Mary worried neither was getting enough sleep or fun.

It did begin to affect F.C. after a few months. He came down with a chronic cough and decided to go back to the farm in Iowa to see if his mother's home remedies would cure what was ailing him. He did recover, but he did not move back to Chicago.

Alexander surprised Mary one evening when he brought a lady friend to dinner. He had met Julia Lubhart when she'd brought an older gentleman in for treatment. She was a teacher, and Mary liked her very much.

As Mary's nineteenth birthday approached, she began to have signs of labor, and her brother requested she come to his medical school. One of his instructors attended her, and Alexander managed to find Chris and get him to the hospital shortly after she delivered her firstborn, Henry, on March 27, 1867.

By the time Mary's second baby, Frank, was born on June 17, 1868, Alexander was ready to take the helm. Although he was still a student of medicine, he was advanced enough in his coursework and legally permitted to practice on patients. Dr. Siedschlag's first delivery was his second nephew, and both his parents and his physician were pleased when it was over.

"You know I would do anything to help your career as a doctor, Dear Brother. But I would prefer a female doctor, as I am sure most maternity patients would. It would just be more modest," Mary mused, as she held baby Frankie. She was sitting up in her hospital bed with its crisp white sheets and metal frame.

Alexander laughed at the suggestion. "There aren't any women doctors. That is just absurd, Mary. Women wouldn't want to go through all the schooling. Besides, women aren't suited to be analytical, they are much too emotional and erratic. It is a scientific fact."

"Ha!" she snickered. "That is the most unscientific thing I have ever heard you say. Some women would do very well as doctors. But until there are women doctors delivering babies here, you can expect the midwife trade will continue to flourish. Expectant mothers are not happy about men seeing them so exposed."

"You're not firing me as your doctor, surely?"

"No, of course not. You are still my brother, first and foremost."

"And I will always be there for little Frankie. Whenever he needs some kind of medical help, just send for me and I will come, wherever I am. It is the least I can do for my first patient," he offered.

"It is very generous; I hope it is possible."

"As long as it isn't in October. Julia and I are planning to get married in October and go to New York for our honeymoon."

"What? Are you staying in your cramped rooming house?" Mary asked excited about his news.

"No, she says we need to find something larger, but we will stay in the same area."

"You know, Chris and his family have been talking more about moving to Nebraska and taking advantage of the Homestead Act. If we can find the right spot, his parents, his brothers, and his brother-in-law could all get 160 acres in the same area. We'd have our own little community."

"But no house, no trees, no water, no garden, and no livestock. That doesn't concern you, with two baby boys?" he asked.

"Well, we do have some issues to figure out." she

admitted ruefully.

Just then, Chris showed up for visiting hours, having safely stowed little Henry with the neighbor lady. He gave Mary a quick kiss and sat on her bed to admire the infant.

"It sounds like you are talking about our grand adventure. You know all our parents uprooted their families and moved to a different continent halfway around the world. Moving a couple of states over isn't so radical. I mean, I think the climate and the growing conditions are very similar to Iowa. You should think about coming with us," Chris told Alex.

It took planning and strategizing, Mary realized. There was the question of who was going to move to Nebraska and establish a homestead. It was hard for Mary to imagine there was an unlimited supply of land where they were going. That was not true in Germany, and not even true in Indiana, although there were always farms for sale if you could pay the price.

The list of relatives from Chris's side of the family was long, and she didn't even know all of them. First, his parents, John, and Elisabeth were planning to homestead, and they still had Johanna, August, and Amelia at home. Elisabeth was staying at the Iowa farm with the two youngest children for now. Johanna would go ahead with her father to cook meals and help however she could. Chris's brother John Henry planned to stake a homestead. Mina and her husband, Christel Rausch were planning to move to Nebraska, but not for a few years. F.C. was ready and eager to go as quickly as possible and hinted he might strike out a month or two ahead of the rest to get the lay of the land.

In addition to everyone in Chris's immediate family, his mother's brother, Fred Lindekugel, was planning to join them. He had one son who was nearly twenty-one, August, and one who would soon be twenty, Otto, who were both planning to try to homestead nearby. Twenty-one was the minimum age requirement for homesteading. Fred also had his wife, Lisette, two younger daughters, and three younger sons.

Mary's mother, Auguste, was also thinking about relocating and bringing Gussie with her. Since Auguste was a widow and head of her family, she was eligible to homestead in her own right. Alexander was on the fence. He needed to finish medical school, but he wanted to be there for his mother and sisters if they were going on this grand exodus to the uncivilized world. Mary sensed his fiancé was less enthusiastic.

In February 1869, Mary was busy sewing clothing to prepare her husband, herself, and two little toddler boys for the overland trip. She was also mindful that she needed clothing to accommodate various stages of pregnancy. And all her men needed extra clothing to stay warm and clean. She didn't know how often she would have a chance to wash clothing.

She was busy with this task when her brother, Alexander dropped by for a visit. He liked to come and see his nephews when he could, and they delighted in seeing him.

"It looks like you are sewing up a storm, Sister," he said, trying to grab both giggling children at once.

"There is so much to do to get ready: clothes, food, supplies. I am thinking maybe you could send some of the furniture along on the train later. Not just my things, but Mama's too. I don't want to leave behind anything she brought from Germany."

"I hate the idea all of you are moving to Nebraska without me. And I feel like I should be doing something to help. How does this work exactly? You just go find a spot where no one else is living and you build a house, and that makes it yours?"

"Well, Chris got a letter from F.C. the other day, and he thought the first thing you have to do is to go to the land office in Lincoln. You have to sign some paperwork there, and they will show you what is available. Of course, the plan is to have everyone living as close together as we can. F.C. wants to go as soon as the snow is over for the season, but I think it will take us until the first of April to be ready. Maybe we will be on the way by my twenty-first birthday."

"What if I went ahead of you by train? Maybe F.C. would want to come too. We could just go to the land office and pick out a nice piece of land for you, and maybe one for Mama too. You have a while to get the house built don't you, under the Homestead Act?" Alexander asked.

"I don't know if that would work or not if Chris isn't there. I guess I could ask him."

But she forgot to ask him with all the work she had to do, plus the two small children in her care. About four days before the scheduled departure, on the first day of spring, Auguste and Gussie arrived on the train, having packed their goods from Fort Wayne. Auguste had already said her painful good-byes at the gravesites of her husband and younger son.

"Alexander tells me he has already been to Lincoln and found us a nice piece of land," Auguste said at dinner with Mary's family.

"What are you talking about?" Chris asked.

"He said he and F.C. took the train to Council Bluffs, then a ferry over the Missouri River, and I think he said they took a stagecoach to Lincoln, and they each signed up for eighty acres. They had to sign some sort of declaration stating their intent to homestead there. Apparently, this is somewhere south of Lincoln, closer to Kansas."

"You're saying Alexander is going to homestead now?"

Chris asked.

"No, I don't think so, I think he was just saving the space for me or your family. He should be here tomorrow, you can ask him more about it. Maybe he has some sort of papers for you," Auguste said. When Chris continued to look confused, she added, "That boy is always trying to look out for us, you know, Dear."

"He has to accept that I'll be looking out for this family now," Chris admonished. "Including you and Gussie."

Later when they were lying in bed, Chris asked Mary, "Does Alexander think we are rushing into this without any preparation? We've read every newspaper and guidebook account we can find. We've got some useful skills for making a home in the wilderness. My father is an expert wagon-maker, and he has a couple of wagons ready to go that should be waterproof for forging rivers. I am a trained cooper, and I have a supply of casks for storing our supplies, and I am also a machinist who can fix any kind of sod plow or threshing machine: anything we might want to take to work the land. John Henry has been running supplies back and forth over the Nebraska prairie with a team of oxen, so he has valuable experience with animals and the elements. Mina's husband Christel is a master carpenter, who has built many houses in Iowa and Minnesota, and he is coming with us for the first month or two to pick out all of the lumber we need and to get us started with all of the houses. We've got this well planned out."

"I wish you had told me all of this earlier. It makes me feel a little better about the trip. Of course, you didn't mention the work the women are doing, making clothes and quilts and featherbeds, and packing all the food in those lovely casks of yours. So how long do you reckon it will take before we have a house to live in; I mean after we get there?" She snuggled closer to him.

"It is hard to say. But we will have a cozy little sod house for the four of us before you know it." He closed his eyes and relaxed against her.

"Better make it for the five of us."

"You're kidding." He opened his eyes and rose on one elbow to look at her. "I wish you had told me that earlier. Are you sure? I mean my sister has been married for four years and they don't even have one child yet. This would be three children in three years for us."

She yawned. "I am hoping for a girl this time. Don't look at me, you only have yourself to blame."

"Me? You're probably right, I just hope the soil in Nebraska is half as fertile as I am," he sighed, as she gave him a gentle shove, and he fell back down next to her.

The next morning, Alexander arrived to help them pack up their belongings in Chicago. They would take the train to Guttenberg, where they would meet the others at the Severin farm and pack the wagons. When Chris asked Alex about the visit to the land office, he dismissed it as unimportant, saying Chris could take over his claim if that is where they decided to settle. After a tearful good-bye between Alexander and the rest of his family, they were bound for Iowa.

CHAPTER TWO

"As soon as we get to Nebraska, I am changing my name," Gussie announced, as they were riding along the rails and she was bouncing little Frankie on her knee. "It was Alexander's idea," she added when her mother and sister looked at her questioningly.

"He is still thinking of changing his name to Von Mansfelde? I thought maybe he'd gotten over that notion," Auguste said. "What are you changing your name to?"

"I think he already changed his name to Von Mansfelde in Chicago. He said his patients couldn't pronounce *Seeed-schlog* correctly. I am thinking of just Mansfeld. Eventually, I will change my name to my husband's anyway, so I don't want anything too complicated," Gussie said confidently. "That won't upset you, will it Mama?"

"*Hmmph*," Auguste murmured. "*Unsinn*. Nonsense. But I don't care. My maiden name was Tapp, and it was easier. You'd better decide before we start introducing you."

"So if he changes his name to Von Mansfelde, won't people who know Germany get the impression that he emigrated from Mansfeld in Saxony instead of Brandenburg?" Chris asked. "I mean, *Von* usually means from, so it would be like saying Alexander from Mansfelde."

"I wouldn't waste time trying to figure out why Alexander does these things," Mary laughed.

Once they all got to the Severin farm in Clayton County, they found controlled chaos. With so many people around, they had to set up the new tents in the yard to accommodate the extra guests. After a good night's sleep, Mary and Gussie went with Elisabeth to Guttenberg to get the last-minute food supplies. They packed big barrels of bacon with bran to keep it fresh and packed dozens of eggs in cornmeal. They would use up the cornmeal as they used the eggs. They bought coffee and tea to disguise the taste of whatever water they might have to drink on the journey. In addition, they packed barrels of lard, sugar, flour, then added some dried peaches, beans, and apples from Elisabeth's larder. They packed one cask with some biscuits and honey, which would be easy to munch on during the day. Mary brought a kettle and a big cast-iron skillet, and they purchased a camping stove in town.

Once they returned to the farm, they found Chris had almost finished packing their wagon, and some of the other wagons that would carry the machinery. Mary was surprised when he put a rifle and a revolver in the front of their wagon, as she had never seen him shoot anything.

"You don't think we will have to fight off an Indian attack, do you?" she asked anxiously.

"No. John Henry says most of the Indian tribes have moved on to Oklahoma or north. This is for hunting game. We might be lucky enough to find some turkeys or quail, maybe even elk."

"Will you teach me how to shoot?"

"Sure, if you'd like. I may not have time for a while, though, as I think we're going hell for leather if we let F.C. have his way." He smiled at her. "It's probably a good idea for you to learn to shoot. Who knows what varmints we'll find in Nebraska?"

Early the next morning, they all loaded the final items in the wagons and everyone headed southwest. John and John Henry Severin had the biggest custom-built wagons, strong and waterproof and ready for the eight rivers or creeks they'd have to cross. Chris and Mary followed them with another large wagon filled with furniture and supplies. F.C. took the next wagon, and Christel rode with him. Auguste rode with John and Johanna, and Gussie rode with John Henry. Each wagon was pulled by a team of oxen. Each man brought his own horse, and John brought three milk cows along. By the time they reached the Turkey River a few hours later, they met up with the Lindekugel wagons, with Fred driving one and Otto and August vying for the reins of the other.

As the wagons gathered on the bank of the river, Mary watched as Chris jumped off the seat and motioned to the other men to gather around for instructions. Mary wondered why they had come in the spring when the rivers were so full.

"I am going to need someone to go across first with the ropes and tie them to those trees on the far side. The ropes need to be far enough apart so the wagons fit between them, but close enough that we can hold the ropes from the wagons. August, are you game? We don't know how deep the channel is, you will probably be swimming," Chris said to the other men. August gathered a couple of thick long ropes and got ready to ford the river with his horse.

"Wait a minute, Christian. I thought we were going to send one of the waterproof wagons first, and use the poles to keep from going downstream," his father corrected.

"Pa, we talked about this. The river might be too deep. This way is more secure," Chris argued.

"What's the worry? We've crossed this river before with just regular wagons and horses. I say we should try it on horseback first," John Henry chimed in.

Mary got the little boys out of the wagon to play in the grass, but she could see Chris waving his hands trying to get his father and brothers to see things his way. It was the first time she had seen him act like the oldest son, trying to take charge, and it was entertaining.

"Goodness, I hope they don't pull those revolvers out," Mary said to herself.

The river crossing took longer than she expected, but she had to admit, it was impressive. The two waterproof wagons were used as boats and all the supplies that they wanted to keep dry were transported across the channel in those. The wagons were guided across with the ropes. The animals had to swim if it was too deep to walk and this was a daunting prospect for a cow. The men seemed to be more in the water than out, trying to make sure they didn't lose one of the animals or a wagon. Mary and the boys rode in the waterproof wagon on one of the last trips across, and she cried out in surprise when she was splashed by the moving current.

"What's wrong?" Chris asked when he saw the look of fear in her eyes. He was in the water next to the wagon trying to keep it steady.

"Can't swim" was all she could muster. He started to laugh but coughed when he inhaled some water.

Everything had to be repositioned once they got to the other side. After their wagon was reloaded, Chris started to get back onto the wagon seat.

"You are soaking wet. Let me get you some dry clothes and you can dress in the wagon," she said. He dutifully stripped off everything and climbed into the back of the wagon to warm up with clean garments, hanging his boots upside down on the back of the wagon to dry.

"Why don't you drive the team for a little while? Just follow John Henry. I am going to take a little nap with my boys," Chris laughed, pulling them into the featherbed amid their squeals.

The first day they traveled about eighteen miles, according to John Henry the self-proclaimed chief navigator. He said that was about what they should expect if they had to take time to cross a river. They made camp and cooked eggs, bacon, and cornbread on the small camp stove. Their wagon had a tight canvas covering stretched over an iron u-shaped framework, and a blanket tacked up in the back to keep the cold air out. Chris had devised a two-tiered arrangement where they could put their featherbed on top of a platform resting on the food barrels. Mary felt snug and tired as she clung to her babies and listened to the sounds of the night on the prairie. She had missed that in Chicago.

Mary was surprised how many rivers they had to cross in the state of Iowa, but she had never seen Iowa. After a few days, they camped earlier in the afternoon than usual in the valley of the Cedar River near Cedar Rapids. John Henry announced this was prime hunting ground, and Chris and his brothers took the horses out to try to find game for dinner. Mary was playing with the boys on the ground behind the wagon, hoping to let two-year-old Henry run around a bit. She saw a shadow and jumped to her feet.

An Indian man, who looked to be about forty years old, stood next to the wagon. If he came on a horse, she didn't see it. He held out his open hand and said in a deep voice, "White man take our hunting grounds. Hungry. Give food."

Mary had never seen an Indian before. She had seen photographs, but not in real life. She was terrified and didn't know what to do. Chris probably left the revolver in the wagon, but she would never get to it in time. "*Spreche kein englisch,*" she said in German, hoping he wouldn't understand her German, and just leave her alone. He didn't move. That didn't work, she thought.

He bent over slowly and picked up baby Frankie, who had been sitting quietly on the ground, shaking a small stick, like a rattle. "*Awee bits aal,*" he said in his native tongue.

"No, no, no," Mary cried, as she rushed over to try to take Frankie from his grasp. "I'll get you something to eat."

"Ahhh. English?" the man laughed, bouncing Frankie.

"Come back later. I cook food."

"Come back eat? Bring squaw?"

"Yes, bring squaw," she said still trying to wrench the baby from his arms. She thought if she could get him to leave, Chris and the other men should be back if he returned.

He let her take Frankie from him. "*Awee bits aal*," he said again and nodded. He turned and walked toward the woods. She picked up Henry, too, and marched over to John's wagon, when she remembered he had stayed behind to stand watch. She found him asleep, his daughter, Johanna curled up in the back of the wagon reading a book.

"Johanna, will you let the boys stay here with you for a little while? I need to get the fire going," she asked, not wanting to alarm her.

Mary found the revolver in the wagon and kept it close by while she started the fire and made skillet bread and beans. She had not yet had a shooting lesson, but she had seen men shoot guns before. She could figure it out if she had to. Chris and the other hunters returned with six quail and three rabbits, and he sat on the grass to begin dressing them. By this time, the other women smelled her cooking and began to make their own preparations. The rabbit meat was sizzling in the cast iron skillet when she saw the Indian man approach again, this time accompanied by two women and three young children. As soon as Chris caught sight of them, he grabbed his rifle from the grass and pointed it at them. Even from a distance, John Henry and F.C. noticed this movement and had their rifles at the ready almost as quickly.

"Just wait now. Don't panic." Mary stood and moved slowly toward the Indian group. "He came here this afternoon, and we agreed he could come back for dinner, and bring his squaw. Looks like it is two squaws. Maybe he didn't know the English word for children.

"Mary, what do you mean? He was here before? Was anyone hurt?" Chris asked in amazement.

Mary busied herself telling the Indians where to sit, or rather pointing and using gestures to try to communicate. She brought the Indian man a plate of beans, bread, and a piece of rabbit, and Chris was dumbstruck. He put his rifle back in his lap, not knowing what to expect.

"I think we will need more meat," Mary told him, her quivering voice revealing she was considerably more frightened than she was letting on. He butchered two of the quail, which were added to the feast. Once John saw what was happening, he instructed his daughter to keep the little boys in their wagon. The other men came over to their campsite with their rifles at their sides, just to keep an eye on the Indians, looking for any threatening behavior.

After a tense hour, the Indian family stood up. "*Awee bits aal,*" the man said once again, and one of his wives brought forth a sort of woven basket. "Baby," the man said in English. He shoved his fingers into the basket to demonstrate how you could place a baby in the contraption and carry him around on your back or chest. He held it out to Mary.

"It's one of those cradleboards the Indians use," John Henry explained.

"For me?" Mary asked, and pointed to herself, as he handed it to her.

The Indian nodded and put his hand up in a friendly gesture bidding them goodbye, and then his family followed him into the darkness toward the woods.

Once the other men thought the danger was past, they returned to the other campfire where Auguste and Gussie were cooking for a crowd, not even aware there was anything amiss.

When they were out of earshot, Chris swiftly picked Mary up and practically threw her onto the seat of their wagon, which fortunately was facing away from the rest of the group.

"Are you trying to get us all killed?" he screamed at her, then realizing they were too close to the others, lowered his voice somewhat, and pulled himself next to her. "What in God's name were you thinking, feeding those … savages? We'll be lucky if they don't come back and scalp us in our sleep as if anyone could sleep after that!"

Mary had never seen her husband this angry, and certainly not this angry at her. He had it all wrong. He hadn't seen what had happened earlier, how she had only been trying to make peace with the Indian, so he wouldn't steal her baby.

"Don't yell at me. You weren't here! That Indian had Frankie in his arms. He said he was hungry. I couldn't blame him for wanting food. You left us out here alone with your father standing guard. Well, he fell asleep! I couldn't even get to the revolver if I wanted to."

Chris glowered at her and stepped off the wagon, pacing back and forth with his hands laced behind his head. He looked tired, she thought. He put up a good front, but he'd spent hours hunting, and this journey had already been physically draining, riding for days on end, crossing one stream after another. She only had her children to worry about, and he was worried about the entire family's safety, she could tell by the way he checked on them. Maybe he was just as scared as she was. Maybe they both realized now how real the danger was traveling hundreds of miles into an unknown wilderness.

He climbed back up onto the seat with a sigh. "You're right. I left you to fend for yourself. Tomorrow I will show you how to shoot the revolver."

She figured this was as close to an apology as she was going to get.

"Why did we leave Chicago?" Her voice began to tremble. "We were safe and happy there." After holding her fear in check all afternoon, it suddenly overflowed in endless tears. She saw the guilt wash over his face when he enveloped her tightly in his arms, buried his face in her hair, and waited for her to let it all go.

The next day, they rode on their first ferry of the trip, across the Cedar River. They had to wait in line, and their group was behind the Lindekugels. Otto Lindekugel came riding back on horseback and spoke to the drivers of each of the wagons.

"The fare is ten cents a passenger, a buck and a quarter for a two-oxen-team wagon, plus fifteen cents for each additional cow, mule, oxen, or horse. The children count the same as adults," Otto Lindekugel told Chris. "It's going to take us maybe three trips to get everyone across, but I reckon it is faster than unloading the wagons."

"Can we afford that? How many ferries are there along the way?" Mary asked.

"Don't worry. We planned for this," Chris assured her.

When they got closer to the river, they watched a ferry cross with two horse-drawn wagons, and several cows and mules tethered to the back of the wagons. Once the ferry was in the middle of the river, one of the cows started panicking, and ran into the river, nearly pulling the loaded wagon with it. One of the men on the ferry jumped into the water to try to save the cow. He was able to cut her loose from the wagon, so the wagon stayed on the ferry, but the cow appeared to have drowned.

The Severin group had gotten down off their wagons watching

this drama unfold.

"One of my cows might do the same thing. Johanna, you'd better stand with them to keep the cows from trying to run," John said.

"I'm not doing that, Papa. They will knock me off the ferry, sure as God made little green apples," Johanna cried.

"I can do it," Mary said. "As long as Johanna will sit in the wagon and hang onto our boys. I was around cows back in Indiana." She started to walk over to where the cows were when Chris grabbed her arm and pulled her close.

"Mary, this is a bad idea. You said you can't swim."

"If I do it right, I won't have to swim."

"Well, I'd rather lose a cow than my wife." He took her by the shoulders, forcing her to look at him.

She backed away from her husband with a confident smile and walked up to John's wagon. "Give me a bucket with some oats in it," Mary said to John.

"I'll give you some of the mixtures they get at night. It's oats, hay, and barley. It is kind of fermented, so it don't smell so great," John told her. When they got close to the loading dock, he got out the bucket, which already had the feed in it.

After the attendants loaded both John's and Chris's wagons, the extra horses and cows were led on. The attendants did not want to tie the cows to the wagons because of what had happened on the previous trip. Mary took their leads and the bucket of grain, then had the three cows all face the center of the ferry. Chris was clearly not comfortable with this and kept a close eye on them. She spoke softly and sweetly to the cows, and they batted their eyes as though they understood. Once the ferry reached the opposite shore, she led the biggest one off the ferry and the other two followed.

When she led the cows back to John's wagon, he asked her, "Are you sure you have never done that before?"

"Never done ferries. But I've done cows."

"Missy," John said, "You're hired." She just laughed.

When she got back on the seat of her own wagon, she waited for her husband to tell her she'd done a good job.

"You smell like cow dung," was what he said instead. He was right.

Before the day was over, they had gone as far south as they planned to in Iowa. They found the main trail that crossed the state from east to west, and there were more wagons than Mary had ever seen, most of them heading west like they were. She hadn't seen so many people since they left Chicago, and it was a thrilling sight. When they camped, it wasn't just their family group, they were among a group of about eighty travelers, and there were others just around the bend from them.

The next day, they came upon a family who had stopped their wagon atop a grassy knoll. They were standing in a circle and they appeared to be praying, the man leaning on a shovel.

"Why would they stop in the middle of the day?" Mary wondered aloud.

"I think they are burying a child," Chris said somberly. "I heard one of the other men saying last night that one of the little girls in their group was dying and they were keeping an eye out for a good place to bury her. It is more common than you expect. It is hard to know where to bury someone so the Indians won't dig them up, or the wolves won't get to them. They should have put the grave right in the path so the oxen would trample down the dirt, but they would be blocking the trail."

Mary didn't say anything more about it, but tears filled her eyes. She couldn't imagine having to leave a child out here alone, and never even be able to mark the gravesite.

They had good weather for most of the journey. It rained a few nights when they were close to the Missouri River, and some of their supplies got wet, but almost everything dried out the next day. Most evenings, Mary would help John milk the cows, and she would bring a bucket of milk back to their wagon. After the milk sat in the wagon during the night, she would skim off the cream, and put it in her butter churn, which they'd hung off the back of the wagon. The motion of the wagon would churn the butter without even having to use the churning handle. So they usually had fresh butter for their biscuits or bread.

"Chris said there is another ferry ahead, that's what we are waiting for," Mary told her mother and Gussie after the wagons came to a halt, and they started forming a queue. The ladies had disembarked from the wagons to walk after a long ride.

"Just think. When we get over the Missouri River to Nebraska, Alexander will be two states away. I wish Herman and Herman Junior were with us," Auguste said.

"They are in our hearts, Mama," Gussie reminded her. "And Alexander has already been this way, and crossed the river right where we will."

When their wagon got near the Council Bluffs and Nebraska Ferry Company dock to wait for the steam-driven ferry, Mary climbed back up in the wagon next to her husband.

"I saw a sign saying this used to be called Kanesville," Mary said. "The Mormons settled here on their way to Utah. Did you know some of the Mormon men have ten or more wives?"

"They would have to be mad as a March hare. I can't imagine having even two wives. Especially if they didn't do what I told 'em."

"You're not still talking about the cows, are you? That worked out fine."

"You were just lucky. There are all sorts of dangers out here. I don't want you taking chances."

She studied him, trying to determine why he was becoming more controlling. He pulled her closer to him on the wagon seat and kissed the top of her head. Maybe he was just protecting her, she thought and leaned on his shoulder.

That evening, they camped on the eastern shore of the Platte River. Around a campfire, they discussed plans for the following day when they hoped to arrive in Lincoln. The men were debating their strategy for filing their homestead claims at the courthouse. Mary was putting the children to bed, but she could hear Chris arguing with his father, F.C., and John Henry.

"Alexander and I already put our claims in for Buda Township, which is where every one of us should be. A couple of months ago there were plenty of homesteads open," F.C. said.

"I don't understand why you didn't just wait for the rest of us. What did Alex say about his claim?" Chris asked F.C. "Did he say he wanted to move here or stay in Chicago?"

"He's your brother-in-law, what do you think?" F.C. answered.

"I vote we just take his claim. Unless of course, we can't find land close to it, then we should start over in some other spot," John Henry pronounced.

"But what about my claim? I already put my declaration in to start the five years. I don't want to start over," F.C. added.

Their father tried to settle the dispute. "Let's just wait to see what we find when we get to the land office."

A while later, Chris slipped in next to Mary in the featherbed, rearranging his sleeping boys in the process.

"I need to know what to do about Alexander's land claim tomorrow morning. If I decide to take over his claim, will he be agreeable? I don't know yet if we will use it for ourselves or your mother."

"He told you it was all right to take it. I heard him say that myself."

"Far be it from me to know what he wants. I don't want to start a family feud. But if you think it's okay, I might take his claim."

Our claim, Mary thought. But she knew her name would never be on it. Married women had no property rights. Still, she would know the land was first claimed by the Siedschlags.

They arrived in Lincoln late the next day and were fortunate to find hotel rooms to accommodate all of them for two nights. The next morning, Chris, John, John Henry, F.C., Fred Lindekugel, and his oldest son August all went to the land office. Mary, Gussie, and Johanna went with Christel Rausch and Otto Lindekugel to scout out stores to buy supplies. Christel had saved enough room on his wagon to get the first load of lumber, nails, and related supplies to start house construction, so they bought those. Auguste and Lisette stayed at the hotel to rest and watch the children.

Chris arrived at the hotel mid-afternoon, exhausted, but exhilarated.

"We got it, Mary. The plat that Alexander signed up for is going to be our new home."

"You think it looks good?" she asked, as he spread out a map on the table in their room.

"Look, see how this creek starts over here and crosses over to this spot? That is where my parents are going to be. We will be south and east, still near the creek. It seems like a perfect spot. All I have to do, they said, is to have Alex sign it over to me within the next five years," Chris said.

Mary was relieved to hear he liked the spot Alexander had chosen. Maybe her husband could overlook her brother's interference.

"We did have a land agent help us. He told us a Henry Dietz had already put in papers for the spot we wanted my parents to own, but Dietz already changed his mind and moved somewhere else. The land agent will track him down and get him to sign this parcel over to my father. I hope this goes through, or the whole kit and caboodle falls apart.

"F.C.'s land is just south of ours. We reserved acres for John Henry, Auguste, and Fred Lindekugel nearby. For every eighty acres we signed for, the land office reserved an adjacent eighty acres that would be our pre-empted claim once we fulfill the five-year proving requirement. Or, we can just purchase the first eighty acres after six months. Then we can use it as collateral for operating loans.

"Tomorrow morning, the land agent is going to take us to the parcels. I am so tired, but I don't think I can sleep a wink." He got up from the table and laid on the bed. Mary took his boots off for him. Despite what he'd said, he was asleep in minutes.

On April 19, 1869, it was five years to the day after the Congress of the United States authorized the people of the Nebraska territory to form a state government, and two years after Nebraska became a state. The Severin and Lindekugel wagons headed for their final destination, to find the homesteads they had claimed.

"This is it, Christian," Mary sighed. "God has led us through our journey. Today we are finally seeing the place we have been heading towards for the past few weeks. The place we will probably live for the rest of our lives, where our children will grow up, and we will die."

Chris beamed at her. "You're gonna go and get all sentimental on me, aren't you? I bet it looks just like what you see in front of you. Miles of prairie grass."

She linked her arm in his as he held the reins. "I can see you are excited too, don't try to hide it. And look how beautiful this is, all the blue flowers blooming just to welcome us, all that aquamarine grass. It looks like it could be painted on a canvas. This is different than Indiana, or Iowa. This is where we belong."

"You're right, *Mein Liebling*, today is a beautiful sunny day. Today we become homesteaders."

They followed the land agent on his black gelding along the trail south out of Lincoln. Late in the day, he signaled to the group and turned toward the setting sun, and went another mile, to the top of a hill.

"He's stopping," Chris said. "I think we're here."

CHAPTER THREE

By then they were all tired, and dusk was falling. They decided to camp where John's homestead was near the creek. The agent would take the others to their designated spots the following morning.

The women made a big breakfast the next morning, while the men saddled the horses and took off to survey the various locations they had chosen. There were very few trees, except for small ones along the creek. The agent had brought some markers so they could identify each location.

It was now time to transform this prairie land into home. They camped in a group like they did while traveling and began working on one house at a time. Until they had houses, they continued to sleep in or under the wagons.

Mary and the other women watched in wonder as they tried out the sod plow for the first time, first pushing it by hand, and then attaching it to a horse. The sod did not give easily, Mary could see that, and sod was essential for building the houses. When they finally successfully ripped a piece of sod with the plow, it cracked like a lightning strike. When the plow failed to cut as deep as they wanted, John Henry jumped up on the plow as added weight.

"Mary," John Henry called out to her, "come sit up here with me to push this thing down." Since the other men were busy guiding the horse and assessing the progress, she did as he asked, and they determined having two people weigh down the plow was successful. After variations, they eventually had the ox pull the plow so they could have it go slower and could control the length of the cuts.

"John, I think for your sod house, we should take advantage of the slope, and carve it into the hillside," Mary heard Christel telling his father-in-law, as they were eating dinner. "That will protect you from the wind coming over the hill and save some time in construction. You will also be using the earth to help heat and cool the sod house."

"As long as we can make it big enough. F.C. and John Henry will be staying here with Johanna and me until their houses are done. Elisabeth and the two younger ones will join us next spring," John replied.

Christel pulled out his Thoreau pencil and drew some lines and numbers on a piece of lumber to show how the house would be framed, the dimensions, and where the windows and doors would go. John and Christel went back and forth a few rounds until they agreed on the design.

A few weeks later, Christel called out to Mary, Johanna, and Gussie. "Ladies, we need your assistance. Would you let the older women mind the children and the cooking? We will be cutting lengths of sod about one-and-a-half-feet wide by six-feet long. We have built a travois out of sticks, to haul the sod from where we cut it. A horse will pull it uphill to the house. We need your help lifting both ends of the sod off the travois and carrying it to John and F.C. who will pack it onto the frame of the house. This way, most of us can stay in one place, and do the same job over and over. Otto will be on the horse with the travois, and the rest of us will cut the sod. We discovered the sod dries out pretty quick, so we need to get it packed into the house while it is still moist."

One hot June day when she was hauling sod, Mary slipped and sat down hard. She felt a little faint like she couldn't stand again. Chris came bounding up the hill to check on her.

"Mary, what is it, are you all right? Here, let me help you up."

"I think I am fine, maybe need to drink some water. I just slipped."

"Go back to the wagon and rest. I'll help the girls up here today. You shouldn't be doing such heavy work in your condition," Chris told her.

She heard Gussie and Johanna whisper to each other. No one else in the family knew she was pregnant, and it was indelicate to speak of such things. It was out in the open now.

The days and nights flew by quickly, full of hard work and exhausted sleep. Between helping with the construction, hoeing and planting a garden (so they would have fresh vegetables to eat), hauling water from the stream, and chasing two toddlers around, Mary was pushing her body and mind to the limits. In many ways, it was the best time she had known, working with her husband and his family, and everyone pulling together. Her belly was slowly growing along with the houses they were building.

The next sod house to be built would be theirs. It was over the hill to the south and east. The group felt like Chris and Mary should be on their own, especially with two young children and a baby coming soon. Mary suspected the real reason they agreed to build their house next, was no one else wanted to be awakened by a baby crying in the night.

Mary came over the hill one morning as the men were finishing some of the framings for their soddy.

"Chris, where is the rest of it?" she asked. "This looks smaller than John's."

Chris walked over to her and pointed to the framed walls. "You see over there will be a window, and the door here in front, and another window on that side. We are almost done framing, and then we will be ready to sod it."

"But it is smaller. Did you lay this out? You didn't even ask me what I thought."

"Ask you? You don't know anything about construction! Do you think we asked my mother what she thought about my father's house?"

"Your mother is back in Iowa. I am right here sleeping next to you every night. Don't you think I have an opinion? Isn't this our house?"

Mary noticed that Chris's father and younger brothers were watching them. None had wives living with them.

"Mary, go back to the camp. We can talk about this tonight. Privately."

Mary didn't like the way he was dismissing her like an errant child. She glared at him, turned on her heel, and walked quickly back over the hill. She was grateful that the tears stinging her eyes were gone by the time she reached the camp.

When he found her late in the day, she was sitting in John's nearly completed sod house, leaning on the cool earthen wall. The boys were playing next to her, and Auguste was resting in a chair they had fashioned from branches and reeds.

"Auguste, would you watch the boys for a few minutes so I can talk to my wife?" Chris asked. Mary took his outstretched hand and he pulled her to her feet. He kept her hand in his and guided her through the wild waist-high golden grass, blowing gently in the south wind.

"What was your problem this morning?" he asked when they had gone far enough away from the camp. "Don't you like the house we are building you?"

"Building me? You didn't consult me at all. You used to ask me what I thought about things that affected me. But ever since we left Chicago, it's like you no longer care or trust what I think."

"That's not true. It's just I have to come on a little stronger to show my brothers—I mean, I have always felt like I had to set an example."

She stopped and faced him. "So you are showing off for your brothers. You want them to treat women like they don't count?"

"No!" He sighed, "If it makes you feel any better, every one of them told me I should be kissing your feet. They said it would be hard to find a girl like you in the middle of nowhere. Heck, John Henry asked how I found a woman willing to share my bed at all. They goaded me about it all morning."

"That was decent of them. But when we talked about moving with your family, I didn't realize that they'd be with us all the time. We don't have any privacy."

"Why do you think we are getting the next house? You want privacy? All you have to do is..." He suddenly sat in the tall grass and pulled her on top of him.

She let out a little yelp in surprise. "What are you doing?"

He rolled her onto her back and laid next to her. "See? Very private."

She lifted her head but couldn't see anything beyond the grass all around them, and the reddening sky above.

"I guess this could be romantic."

"Romantic? Well, there is no candlelight or music. But we've got fireflies and cicadas and bullfrogs serenading us. Is that what you've been missing, *Meine Liebe*, romance?" He leaned over her to kiss her.

I guess I have missed this, she thought, running her hands through his sweat-dampened hair. Then she started laughing.

"It's the baby. As soon as you started kissing me, the baby started kicking."

He laid back on his side and put his hand on her belly.

"He's getting bigger and stronger every day, isn't he?" he teased her.

"She is getting bigger. She will have to be tough enough to handle two brothers." Mary sat up and started to get to her feet. "Speaking of her brothers, we'd better go check on them. They have been finding worms and bugs crawling out of the sod walls. Today Frankie tried to put a mouse in his mouth."

A few days later, the Lindekugel family split off to start work on their own homes and followed the same concept. They all worked on a bigger house for Fred Lindekugel, which they could all live in temporarily. Auguste and Gussie decided to go stay with them to help with the cooking because Lisette Lindekugel was not adjusting well to the harsh conditions.

Even while all of this was going on, they managed to dig wells for both Chris's and his father's places. Chris was lucky enough to only have to dig fifteen feet to reach the water table. His father's well was forty-four feet deep, due to his placement high on the hill. They also built fences and stables for the animals they kept on John's place.

At the end of summer, Mary realized she didn't know who was going to assist her in the birth. Her first two children had been born in the hospital, which was unusual. She didn't know if anyone in the family had ever served as a midwife. It soon became apparent Lisette would not be a good one to count on due to her diminishing strength, so Mary asked her mother for help.

"When do you think this baby is coming?" Auguste asked her.

"How would I know? I haven't been to a doctor."

"You remember how you felt the last time? *Meine Tochter*, you've had two babies. How did you feel when they were close to being born?"

"Like I was going to explode. Like my ankles were so big I couldn't walk by the end of the day. I know I am not there now."

"Okay, then, think back to when you felt like you feel now. Was it two months before the birth? Six weeks? What do you think?"

"I didn't pay much attention. I had Alexander looking out for me. This time I am getting less to eat and I'm on my feet much more. I remember the babies moving. They really started kicking my ribs and insides in the last two months. I am feeling that now."

Auguste said she would write a letter to Alexander asking him to send them information on how to deliver a baby without a midwife or a hospital. They agreed that might make them both feel better. Within a month, Christel came back from one of his supply runs with a package he'd retrieved from the post office. Alexander had sent some basic tools for obstetrics, clean sheets, and instructions written by midwives in both English and German.

After she opened the package, Mary started to cry. Chris came over from the sod wall the men were constructing to see what was happening.

"What's wrong now?" he asked.

"I am going to have this baby in a house made of dirt. How will we ever get anything clean again? How can we keep a baby clean with a dirt floor and dirt everywhere?" She wiped her eyes, and went on, "Before I have another baby, we have to have a house made of wood, with wooden floors for the baby to crawl on."

"Yes, ma'am, working on it." Under his breath, he mumbled, "Don't know why a baby has to be so gull-durned clean when none of the rest of us are." He wiped his dirt-covered hands on his pants.

They had been settled into their sod house for a week when Mary went into labor on a rainy afternoon in early October. The sod roof leaked, but just in a couple of spots and Chris was working to try to reinforce those areas. Auguste, Mary, and Gussie had all read the midwife instructions and felt like they were as ready as they could be. The labor was shorter than it had been in her previous pregnancies. By evening they had baby Anna Marie wrapped in a clean blanket and sleeping in her bassinet the ladies had woven using branches and grasses from the creek bed.

Six months later, Chris presented Mary with a pencil drawing.

"Here is your chance. This is the plan for the new house. It is twelve by twenty-two feet and has four windows and three doors, and yes, it will have wood floors. Is there anything you want to change? Since Christel went back to Iowa, it will take me longer to build, so I better get started before you are expecting again."

"I thought you were building a granary after you finished the stable. And you said the other day, you wanted to start planting fruit trees," Mary answered.

"We're going to plant the fruit trees. You and the boys can help. You will probably have to haul water to them if you want to keep them alive," Chris told her.

In addition to the house construction, Chris began to work with his father to cultivate the fields. They were running short of funds and needed cash crops. They also needed the crops to feed the growing number of cows, sheep, and swine they were raising. It was difficult work getting the sod broken down to plant corn, oats, and spring wheat, but working together, and using the oxen and horses, they started to see results. Mary used that Indian cradleboard when she was needed to help with the planting or other fieldwork. Sometimes, everyone in the family was working.

Mary wrote a letter to Alexander in July of 1873.

Dear Alexander,

I am sorry I haven't been better about writing letters. I'm sure Mama has told you some of this, but I wanted to keep you up to date. I can't wait for you to meet baby Alexander, your namesake. He is a handsome baby and tries to eat regular food without any teeth. Augusta Julia is just two now, and she is doting on him. Of course, Chris was happy to have another boy to help with the farm work.

I can see our decision to come here four years ago is finally paying off. We have our own community with so many of the Severins nearby. Chris worked so hard to till the land, but every year we have more crops! The Dear Lord has given us many blessings. I expect my mother-in-law Elisabeth and little August and Amelia will be coming any time now, as soon as they sell the farm in Iowa.

Let's see, what else happened. Oh, poor Lisette Lindekugel died, but that was a couple of years back. Christel went back to Iowa and he and Mina had a baby girl. Sorry to say the baby died after a little more than a year.

F.C. got married! Maybe you've heard from him. I like his wife, Gesine Albers, very much. Her family also lives near here. And Johanna married Fred Lucke. He homesteaded just east of us and has worked with all of the men. John Henry married Margaret Clausen in May, and they are building a school on their farm, so it will be easy for our children to get there.

Not all good news. There was a major drop in farm prices, which Chris thinks will continue this year. We had a terrible blizzard this spring which killed some of our livestock. We have seen a few locusts, but nothing to be concerned about so far.

Let me know when you plan to come back for a visit. We finally have a framed house, so there is room for guests.

Love, Mary

Of course, they had seen locusts before. They looked like grasshoppers. Chris talked about years in Iowa where there had been droughts and the grasshoppers had eaten some of their corn. Mary had seen some on the farm in Indiana too. But she would never forget the day in early August 1874 when she saw them swarm for the first time in Nebraska. She was about six months pregnant again, and hauling water for the apple and peach trees.

It was a calm day but she saw a shadow pass over, blocking the sun, and heard a strange noise like a train or a gust of wind. When she turned to look, she saw an ominous cloud moving toward her, but it didn't look like a rain cloud and the buzzing sound was getting louder. When she saw locusts dropping right in front of her in the cornfield, she was paralyzed for a moment with fear and shock. When they started dropping on her head and her clothing, she screamed and swatted them off. She thought of her young children, who were playing in the yard along with the animals. She dropped the bucket and ran for the house, stopping only to grab young Augusta and Anna in the yard and yelling for Frankie and Henry to come inside at once. Fortunately, baby Alexander was napping in his bed.

She closed the doors and windows, even though it was stifling inside. Locusts were hopping on the floor and they quickly stomped on them or swept them outside. They watched through the windows as locusts hit the outside of the house and landed in her garden, devouring every part of the plants. She quickly grabbed a bushel basket and tied a shawl around her head.

"Henry, keep everyone inside!" she shouted to her oldest child, a mere seven years old. "I have to try to save the garden." She tied the shawl around her mouth and nose, ran outdoors, and tried frantically to pick vegetables before the locusts could eat them. She was sickened when they landed all over her but she wanted to keep as much food as she could for her family. They crawled up her legs under her long dress and tried to chew on her clothing. They were indiscriminately eating everything they could find. She gathered as much as she could before she was terrorized by the insects crawling on her, then ran for the house.

As soon as she got through the door, she stripped off her shawl and dress and threw them back outside as they were covered with locusts. She shook all the remaining insects from her underclothing and from the vegetables she had gathered and stomped them all. The children acted like it was a game until their mother collapsed on the floor sobbing. Her sweet little boys put their arms around her neck to comfort her, and the little girls climbed in her lap.

"It's just a bug, Mama. Don't cry," six-year-old Frankie told her.

She laughed, wiping her tears, and pulling them all into her embrace.

"You're right, it's just a bug. There are just so many of 'em." She put on a different dress.

As the locusts swarmed into the cornfield their gloom blocked the sun. Locusts pelted the roof like hail, and they watched out the east window where they could see Chris struggling to get the horse and oxen in the stable. The oxen didn't pay much attention to the insects, but the horse was shaking his head violently, trying to ward them off. After about twenty minutes, Chris appeared on the porch, batting the locusts off his clothing and shaking out Mary's dress and shawl before coming indoors.

"I can't believe how many locusts came. There must be a million right out in our field," he declared. "They are eating everything in their path—the corn crop, the wheat shocks, even the pasture grass."

"How do you get rid of them?" Mary asked.

"You can't. You wait until they have eaten everything, then they will move on. But they will have laid eggs in the soil, so you have to turn that up to try to destroy the next generation."

"But we can't let them eat all of the crops. We need that for food, to sell, for the livestock ..." her voice trailed off when she saw the hopeless look on his face.

"It's the dry weather what brought them here. If it started raining, it might chase them off. Some farmers are burning their fields to drive them out, but that is dangerous in these conditions." He dipped a cup of water out of the bucket by the sink and sat to drink it.

Mary just stared at him in disbelief. They had overcome many obstacles just getting to this place in the middle of nowhere. They had built houses, outbuildings, outhouses, and torn up the sod to plant crops and gardens and trees. They had raised cows and pigs and chickens and children, for God's sake. And now he was going to let locusts destroy it all? She could not fathom that.

The next morning Chris announced they needed to dig a trench around the house. Henry and Frankie were drafted to help, and the younger children were told to stay indoors. Mary wrapped herself up in the shawl, tied handkerchiefs around the boys' mouths, and put hats on their heads. The locusts were not as thick in the morning.

Maybe they will leave us alone, she hoped. They dug a trench about twenty feet away from the house. Fortunately, most of the sod in that area had already been removed when they built the sod house and the frame house, but Chris had to get the oxen team hitched to the plow to break up one area behind the house. Chris explained this was for prairie fire protection, but it might also keep the locusts farther away from the house. If they could keep an area around the house free from combustible material, such as grass or leaves, a fire should not advance toward the house.

It took them most of the day to dig the trench in the hot August sun. About the time they were finished, the swarm of locusts increased again and were lighting all over them. The next day, they planned to set a small fire they could control outside the perimeter to destroy some of the vegetation to increase the fireproofing.

They didn't get a chance. About four o'clock in the morning, Mary woke to cries from Alexander. She was nursing the one-year-old when she smelled smoke. From the south window, she could see smoke and distant flames on the horizon. She woke Chris, who ran outside to see what was happening. The horses and cows were making a racket, having smelled the smoke. He came back in and said it looked like it was at F.C.'s farm. He asked Mary to soak a blanket in water. He saddled his horse and rode toward the fire with the wet blanket.

Mary didn't see him again until late afternoon. She kept an

anxious eye on the windows, and even let the children out to play for an hour or two in the morning, but the smell and sight of smoke permeated the air. She had just made supper and fed the children when Chris returned. She met him on the porch. He appeared to be all right, just covered with dirt and soot.

"We got it put out," he said, sinking down on the porch rail. "Just leave the horse for now, I will tend to him after I eat something." He tied the horse's reins to the porch post.

"Tomorrow morning we should just get in the wagon and head to Lincoln, and catch the first train back to Chicago," Mary said putting her hands on her hips.

"Don't be silly, Woman. We're not going anywhere. The fire could start again at any time," he said wiping the sweat off his brow with his sleeve.

"You said it yourself," Mary cried, her voice rising, "the locusts are eating everything—everything we have been growing the last five years. And if they miss anything, the prairie fires will probably get that. There will be no food, not for us, not for the livestock. We will all starve. I am not going to stand by and watch it happen. It was bad enough the blizzards and market crashes nearly wiped us out. Enough is enough! We are leaving this *Höllenloch*!"

The look he gave her told her that he was bone-tired and out of patience.

"Now stop it, I mean it. You ain't going anywhere. That's nonsense. Now get me some dinner, I don't want to hear any more about leaving." He clomped into the house, but she didn't follow him. She knew he would find dinner on the table.

Instead, she turned and ran to the sod chicken house. There were locusts in there, of course, but she plopped down on one of the hay bales. She was almost too frustrated to cry, but the tears did come in spurts. The chickens, bless their little hearts, were trying to eat the locusts, but they couldn't keep up.

He can't expect to stay here after this. We might not make it through the winter with the food we have set back, and the locusts may get to that for all we know. We have already borrowed money to plant the corn crop, how are we going to pay that back? It was never like this in Indiana. We always had enough rain, and the crops were fine. Please God, I want to go back to that time in Fort Wayne when I only had to worry about my schoolwork. She cried for how much her life had changed, but she knew there was no going backward. She cried for her five children and the one in her belly. How would she feed them? What if the fire came again and burnt them all up in their sleep? Would the locusts start eating their house? How are we going to keep the locusts out of the well and our water? We have to escape this madness, she thought.

But she knew Chris would never leave. He would never let the children leave. She couldn't leave without him. Even if she wanted to, it was his wagon and his horse. Women didn't own anything. She had no money of her own to buy food or train tickets. Even her widowed mother, who was able to own her homestead, didn't have the patent for the land ownership yet, and she was out of money too. Everyone counted on the sale of the crops to the freighters who transported them to markets. She had to stay. She had to stay and have more babies who would probably starve too. Well, maybe not if she starved first.

Now I know I am getting delirious, she thought. That night was the first time she'd felt absolutely miserable since she'd been married.

She was good and mad and decided to stay mad, at least for the night. She watched the chickens settle into their nests. They made little clucking noises, as they went to sleep. She took off her boots and smashed as many locusts as she could with her heel. She had seen snakes in the henhouse before, so she got the revolver from its nail on the rafter, then curled up in the corner and fell asleep.

She woke once toward morning when she realized her breasts were full and she needed to nurse the baby. He's probably crying, she thought. I am going to let his father try to solve that problem, she decided, and went back to sleep for another hour.

A little before dawn, the chickens started raising the alarm. She woke with a start to find a red fox standing in front of her, ready to pounce on her favorite hen. She didn't hesitate. She grabbed the revolver and shot him. Then she calmly picked him up by his tail and walked back to the house, just as Chris came stumbling out the door. She dropped the dead fox at his feet.

"Let's eat him," she said as she walked into the house, past her confused husband.

"That woman is going to be the death of me," he muttered as he took out his knife and reached for the fox to skin it.

After that night, Mary didn't feel the same hope which had followed her all of her twenty-six years. A cloud hung over her, a cloud of locusts perhaps. In the next few weeks, she often dissolved into tears for no apparent reason. She felt like even God had abandoned her. Disappointment and discouragement clawed at her soul like a badger. Once she'd shut down her feelings, she could at least keep her anger and tears at bay. She went about her routine but wasn't much interested in eating, or playing or reading with the children, or working in her garden. She weaned baby Alexander so he didn't depend on her as much.

"Mary, what's wrong? You haven't been yourself lately. Are you still mad at me for some reason?" Chris asked her in bed a few weeks later. "The locusts were a nightmare, but they didn't wipe us out."

"I know, but I don't know what's next."

"What's next? You're having another child soon. You are not eating enough, it's no wonder you don't have any energy. You hardly even pay attention to the children. When I try to get close to you, you pull away. How can I fix this?"

"Tell me there's not another disaster coming. That there won't be insects, hail, prairie fires, lightning, or drought destroying our crops. How bad would it have to get for you to leave?"

"I'm not leaving. This is our home. We will make it, whatever comes. How could you stop believing that?"

She couldn't answer, but she let him hold her while silent tears ran down her cheeks. She didn't want him to understand how dark her world had become.

By the time Mary went into labor in late November, she lost a noticeable amount of weight, despite the late stage of her pregnancy. F.C.'s wife, Gesine, and Gussie came to help usher the infant, Gunther, into the world. At first, they thought he had died. He was blue and small for a full-term baby, but when they turned him and gave him a smack on his behind, he gasped and cried and the two helpers rejoiced. Mary, however, appeared listless and uninterested. She was so weak that Gesine offered to be a wet nurse, since she was still nursing her baby, Minnie.

"You have to eat. You're going to eat if I have to feed you myself. If you don't, tomorrow I am taking you to the doctor. You are starving yourself," Chris told her a week later after Gesine had left for the evening.

"I'm just not hungry anymore. I don't think it matters."

"Of course it matters. You have a husband and six children who need you, who love you. How does that not matter?"

She ate the food he put on her plate. She knew it was wrong to make Gesine and Gussie come over and help with the cooking and the children. She knew her husband was starting to resent her. She knew she had to try to feel better. She began to silently pray for help.

By now, Auguste had become concerned as well. Auguste wrote to Alexander for counsel. He had opened a practice in Chicago but promised he would come to Nebraska in a few months. In the meantime, he sent several potions he said had helped other young mothers.

"Frankie's leg is not getting better," Chris told his parents when they were over for a visit in January. "He says he wasn't kicked by one of the animals and he didn't fall, but he can't walk over to John Henry's for school. He is in too much pain. I have been taking the boys on horseback every day. I'm gonna have to take him to Lincoln to the doctor tomorrow."

"My brother will be here in a few weeks," Mary argued. "I think we should wait. He told me to always contact him if Frankie needed any medical attention since he was Alexander's first patient."

"I don't care what little agreement you had with your brother, this is our son we are talking about, and I don't want him to lose his leg because we waited too long," Chris said emphatically.

"If you want to take him to Lincoln, go ahead," she snapped, as she went back to making supper. "Doesn't matter what I want, does it?"

Mary could hear Chris talking to his parents in the other room, although he acted like she was out of earshot.

"Is Mary all right Darling?" she heard Elisabeth ask him.

"I don't know anymore. At least she had an opinion. That's more than I've gotten out of her lately," Chris said turning his back to Mary. "She has been taking an iron tonic and some other smelly potion her brother sent her. I think it might have opium in it. I am not sure if it is helping."

The next morning he was helping Frankie bundle up for the long ride into the big city when Mary started getting herself wrapped warmly as well.

"I asked Elisabeth last night if we could use their buggy. She is bringing it over and will watch the children while we're gone," Mary told him.

"You want to go along?" Chris asked. "You've hardly set foot out of the house in months."

"Why wouldn't I? He's my son too."

"It is necrosis of the tibia or the shin bone, I'm afraid," Dr. Strickland told them. "The bone is not getting enough blood to it, and he needs surgery to repair it. The best place to perform the surgery would be at the hospital where they have sterile facilities. The nearest hospital is St. Joseph's in Omaha. I'm sorry to say I have to go to New York soon, and I won't be able to schedule this until I return in about seven weeks. There isn't anyone else here who has performed this operation."

"My brother can do it," Mary spoke up. "He is a physician at Rush Medical in Chicago."

"I wouldn't suggest taking the boy so far, but if the doctor can come here, he can certainly use the hospital's facilities."

Before they left for home, she sent Alexander a telegram asking him to consult with Dr. Strickland.

"What makes you think your brother knows anything about this surgery?" Chris asked on the ride home.

"He will. I just know it."

In early March, Mary and Chris took Frankie to Omaha on the train and Dr. Alexander Von Mansfelde met them at the hospital. He assured them he could do Frankie's operation, as he had performed this many times in Chicago.

"Alexander, if one of your own children needed this surgery, would you do it yourself?" Chris asked him pointedly.

"It depends. If we were in Chicago and one of my colleagues could perform surgery on my child, it would be better. In such a case, I would assist. But I understand there is no one else here qualified to do Frankie's surgery."

Mary and Chris were nervously waiting in a salon at the hospital during the surgery.

"How many times did your brother say he had done this surgery?" Chris asked Mary. He massaged one palm with his other hand, where his tendons seemed to be swollen and tender.

"I don't know for sure. I think he said about thirty times. He said he has to operate on both Frankie's tibia and knee, and sometimes, it is just one or the other."

"You certainly looked happy to see Alexander."

"I am so happy to see him. I told you he would come. If this is the next disaster, at least he can fix it."

"You seem to have a lot more faith in your brother than you do in your husband," Chris said with more than a little bitterness.

My faith is in God, Mary started to say. But before she could respond, her brother came into the room and announced the operation went well, and they would be able to see Frankie shortly.

After spending the next few hours tending to their son, Chris seemed reassured and went home to the farm. They didn't want to leave the other children in someone else's care too long.

The hospital had sleeping quarters for parents of young patients where Mary stayed to be close to Frankie. Alexander spent most of his time with them.

"I am happy to see you aren't expecting again," Alex chided her, only half in jest. "I think your husband should leave you be. Isn't six children enough?"

"For some people. But maybe not for us. Of course, this is not your concern. Are you having more children with your wife?" she countered. Julia and Alex had three daughters: Julia, Johanna, and Belle. It did make her realize her husband had been "leaving her be," as Alex had put it when she was not feeling like herself these past several months. It was time to rectify that.

After ten days, Chris returned to Omaha to retrieve them and found Frankie sitting up with his color back and a splint covering one leg. Mary stood by his bed and greeted Chris with a radiant smile.

"Isn't it wonderful, Chris? He is doing so much better since the surgery."

"And how are we doing, Mary? You are in a cheerful mood," Chris smiled and planted a kiss on her lips.

She wrapped her arms around him and clung to him for a long time. When she didn't let go, he wrapped her in an embrace.

"I know I have been so sad lately. I haven't been very fair to you and I'm sorry," she said softly leaning on his shoulder, with tears in her eyes.

"Sometimes life is sad. You weather the storm."

"Alexander said he has seen other women with symptoms like mine. Something bad happens and it triggers an unshakeable feeling of melancholy. You don't have an appetite, and that just makes it worse. If you don't eat, you don't feel like doing anything. I feel like I have been drowning in sorrow for the past six months. Alexander thinks I am getting better, but I need your help."

Chris brushed a loose hair away from her cheek. "When I think of all the danger and hardships I have put you through, coming out here … what can I do to help?"

"This." Mary slipped her fingers in his hair and kissed him in a way that showed she had forgotten her son was in the room. He tightened his grip around her lifting her off her feet while keeping his mouth on hers.

"*Eeww*," protested Frankie, covering his eyes. "Stop with the icky stuff."

They stopped kissing and laughed.

"Son, someday you are going to want to kiss a girl when you grow up. We're just trying to show you how it's done." Chris teased him.

Mary knew this was a turning point. Her prayers had been answered. She was again able to see her husband and their special life on the homestead through the lens of love. Even though there were more tragedies, she was able to cope much better after she saw she could come through the darkness if she was patient.

Alexander stayed in Nebraska for a few more weeks. After he had a nice visit with his mother and Gussie, he stopped by to see Mary one afternoon.

"Sis, I think maybe you had the right idea. I think I like the frontier. I'm not going to farm, but I can be a pioneer in medicine right here in Lancaster and Douglas counties. The hospital in Omaha said they would love to have me, and I can do my own experiments like I used to with Colonel Reed. I'm sending for Julia and the girls. We'll find a place in Lincoln for now, but we will see each other more."

Mary and Chris weren't done having babies, not by a long shot. Mary Wilhelmina, named after her mother and aunt, was born in 1876. She was called "Bertha" to avoid confusion. In 1878, baby Paul was born but died from influenza a few months later. Little Gunther came down with it first, and he died at the age of four. Both boys were buried behind the new chicken house on the north side of the homestead. Mary's melancholy returned after that double blow, but she was able to bring herself out of it over time.

She went on to have Christian Christle in 1879, Herman Julius in 1881, John John in 1883, Arnold Fred in 1885, and Otto William in 1887. During her last pregnancy, Alexander told her she had developed a metabolic disease. He said her body was not processing sugar correctly and it could be dangerous for both her and the baby. Dr. Von Mansfelde advised her not to have any more children because her condition could prove fatal, but she did have one more child, Elizabeth in 1890. She gave birth to a stillborn child in 1894 at the age of 46.

"I'm done with this baby business," Mary said to Gussie, a few months after the stillbirth. "I told Chris I shouldn't have any more babies after Otto was born, but you know how he is. I guess I still can't resist his charm after all these years. But now I think he understands it could hurt my health. Besides, I think he is finally slowing down. He should be at his age."

It was a warm evening in May. They were sitting outside the porch watching their younger children playing in the yard.

"Have you ever thought about what our mother managed to accomplish in the last twenty years of her life?" Mary went on. "She came on the wagon train with us and claimed a homestead for herself. If she didn't work the plow or build a house herself, she watched my children so I could do the physical labor."

"And once the well was dug, we planted the trees and garden ourselves. But she had a little trick. She'd bake pies or put up preserves to try to entice one of her neighbor boys to come over, and she would put them to work. That's how I met my John, you know. He came over with August Lindekugel to help build the chicken house," Gussie laughed.

"I think you might have been the enticement that day, not the peach pie," Mary teased.

Gussie and John Heulff married in 1876 and moved to his place two miles south.

The year before Auguste died, she sold her homestead farm to August Lucke, Fred Lucke's brother, and she moved in with Alexander and Julia. They had a beautiful place east of Lincoln in Ashland, Nebraska. It was lush with ash and linden trees, and a lily pond filled with goldfish.

Mary was so proud of her brother, too. He had become a leading authority on many medical topics, had helped to create the state medical society, and taught at the medical school in Omaha. He served as Lincoln's first health officer and began reporting weather events for the weather service. He also brought a hospital to his new hometown of Ashland. She knew Chris thought Alexander was a little too full of himself, and he wasn't the only critic he had, but she loved him just the same.

Chris and his brother, F.C., both got involved in politics. The precinct held the local elections at Chris and Mary's farm. Chris had served terms as road supervisor, school treasurer, and delegate to the county convention. F.C. was elected to the state legislature in 1889. He was also a state assessor, a justice of the peace, and served on the school board. John C. Severin Sr. died in 1892, but he lived to see his sons and daughters accumulate a quantity of land he had only dreamed about back in Iowa; finally, they were prospering.

Mary thought about the Severin and the Siedschlag clan again a month later when a traveling photographer came by and asked if he could take a picture of the family. Mary wanted a photograph with all her children. This was her legacy. She had borne fifteen children and managed to keep twelve alive and healthy under trying circumstances and hostile living conditions. Of course, her husband had provided the lifestyle they enjoyed, but she was the one who held the family together.

She gathered all the family together on a warm June day, and they patiently posed for the portrait. She was pleased to see her children were all in their Sunday-best clothing, some of which she had made herself. Her older children looked like proper young ladies and gentlemen, and the younger brood of boys managed to keep their suits clean and free from tears, at least while the photographer was afoot.

Mary had days where she didn't feel well and her energy waned, giving her a sense of foreboding, so this photograph was particularly important to her and her family's history. Once the finished print was delivered, she thought it was a good likeness of everyone.

Mary could see something else in the portrait. She saw her son Frank standing tall and strong: his leg never bothered him again. She saw little Frankie and Henry bouncing along in the covered wagon. She remembered snatching up Augusta and Anna when the locusts came. She winced at all the mischief little John, Christel, and Herman got into when they were younger. She saw Bertha with her telltale disapproving pout. She saw her own hand behind Betty, holding the four-year-old in place. She saw her husband's deep-set steel-blue eyes reflected in each of their eight sons. And she saw a little of herself in each one: the lessons, loyalty, and love of land and family she had instilled in them. Chris and Mary had planted the seeds of the Siedschlag and Severin family here, as surely as they planted the corn and oats. It was up to the next generation to see how far they would grow.

SIEDSCHLAG/ SEVERIN FAMILY

AUGUSTE TAPP--HERMAN SIEDSCHLAG

        CHILDREN:
        ALEXANDER (AUGUST WILHELM) SIEDSCHLAG AKA
        VON MANSFELDE
        MARYA MARIA SIEDSCHLAG
        HERMANN SIEDSCHLAG
        AUGUSTA "GUSSIE" SIEDSCHLAG AKA MANSFELD

ELISABETH LINDEKUGEL----------------JOHAN CHRISTIAN SEVERIN SR.

        CHILDREN:
        JOHN CHRISTIAN SEVERIN JR.
        JOHN HENRY SEVERIN
        WILHELMINA SEVERIN
        FREDRICK CHARLES "F.C." SEVERIN
        JOHANNA "MARY" SEVERIN
        AUGUST F. SEVERIN
        AMELIA SEVERIN

MARY SIEDSCHLAG-----------------------------------**CHRISTIAN SEVERIN**

        CHILDREN:
        HENRY SEVERIN
        FRANK J. SEVERIN
        ANNA MARIE SEVERIN
        AUGUSTA JULIA SEVERIN
        ALEXANDER CARL SEVERIN
        UNIDENTIFIED SON WHO DIED AT AGE 4
        MARY WILHELMINA "BERTHA" SEVERIN
        PAUL SEVERIN
        CHRISTIAN CHRISTLE SEVERIN
        HERMAN JULIUS SEVERIN
        JOHN JOHN SEVERIN
        ARNOLD FRED SEVERIN
        OTTO WILLIAM SEVERIN
        ELIZABETH SEVERIN

Left: John Christian Severin Jr. and Marya Maria Siedschlag's wedding photo October 14, 1866

Below: Family portrait 1894
Back row: Alexander, Augusta, Frank, Bertha, Henry
Middle row: Anna, Mary, Elizabeth, Otto, Chris
Front row: Christel, Arnold, John, Herman

NELLIE

CHAPTER ONE

June 1916

"We are going to like it here," twenty-year-old Zella Zerpha Smith announced as she and her nineteen-year-old sister, Nellie Irene, were unpacking trunks and rearranging the second-floor bedroom in their grandmother's farmhouse in rural Sherman County.

Nellie scoffed, "You can't just decide for both of us. When Daddy told us he couldn't work at the sandpit any longer, I was surprised he wanted to move to western Kansas to farm with Mom's family."

She looked out the window and saw her grandmother, Henrietta Payson, and her mother, Ida Smith, feeding the chickens to the delight of their two little nieces, Lazetta, two and a half, and Beth, twenty months. Nellie went on, "I mean, what is there to do here?"

"At our age, we have to go out and make our own fun. Maybe we can take Grandma's buggy into Brewster tomorrow. I'll bet we meet some real cowboys."

"Silly girl, you are always thinking about men. Don't forget we have to find ourselves jobs."

"That is the perfect excuse to go to Brewster as soon as possible. There must be some way to advertise there are two trained house helpers available for hire to a good family," Zella said. "We can tell Mom at dinner."

The next day, Nellie and Zella did go to Brewster, but they were accompanied by Ida, little Lazetta, and Beth. After subscribing to the local newspaper and posting notices about their availability as domestic servants on the post office board, they headed for J.P. Horney's General Store. The first item on the list was to try to find some shoes for the little girls. Ida approached a lean young man with wavy red hair. He pointed her in the direction of the children's shoes, then he approached Zella and Nellie.

"Are you girls new in town? I don't believe I have seen you in here before and I never forget a purdy face." He grinned. "I am Ben Johnson, at your service."

"Pleased to meet you, Ben," Zella answered. "I am Zella Smith and this is my sister, Nellie. We just moved here from Nebraska, but you probably know my grandmother, Henrietta Payson."

Nellie nodded in greeting, then went to help her mother wrangle shoes onto four flailing feet.

"And the children? Are them yours?" Ben asked.

"Oh no, I'm not married. Those are my sister's children," Zella said, glancing over at the little girls who were now having their feet measured.

What Zella meant was Lazetta and Beth were the children of her older sister, Ruby, who had died six months earlier from pneumonia. After much discussion, her husband had agreed to let Ruby's parents and siblings take the younger two girls with them to Kansas while he kept the oldest daughter, Thelma, with him in Valley, Nebraska, where one of his sisters helped him.

"So, Zella," he began, "Do ya need someone to show you around town?"

"I think we saw all the businesses in town right here on this street. Do you have a movie theatre or an ice cream parlor hidden somewhere?"

"Well, no. It is a small town. We may have to go to Goodland to have fun. How about I pick you up on Saturday night and show you what I mean?"

"*Hmmm*. Maybe. Come out to Henrietta Payson's ranch around seven Saturday evening, and we will see if my parents and grandmother approve. You said your name was Ben Johnson, right? How old are you?" Zella asked.

"I am twenty-one; an' you?"

"Well, I will be twenty-one next month, how do you like that?" Zella smiled sweetly and flounced over to the benches where Ida was finalizing her selections for the toddlers' footwear.

At dinner, Zella announced she had a date with Ben Johnson, that cute red-haired fellow from the general store, and they would all get to question him on Saturday evening.

"What exactly do you know about him, Sweetheart?" Henrietta asked. "J.P. Horney hired him about six months ago when he came to Brewster, but no one seems to know why he came here. J.P says he grew up in north-central Kansas, but his family all moved to eastern Nebraska. He says he seems to go to Goodland every weekend. That's a good twenty-five miles away."

When Ben came to pick up Zella that Saturday night, he was forced to explain that he had not found many single friends in Brewster so far, but he had met some dandy young men in Goodland, so he went there on his time off from work. He was sure Zella would have a good time.

Unfortunately, Zella didn't have a good report when she got home around 1:00 a.m. Sunday morning. Her father, Arthur, let her in, the smell of smoke and whiskey in her wake. She told him the evening had not been her kind of fun. He gave her a disapproving look but said nothing.

Nellie was anxious to hear the details of Zella's big date when her sister got into their big bed.

"I don't think we hit it off," she yawned. "He took me to this private club where his friends went to drink and dance. It is illegal to buy booze here in Kansas, did you know that? The whole state is dry. Ben said that is why there are so many private clubs. We danced a little at first, and he is a good dancer. But later he was dancing with other girls and drinking with the boys. I barely saw him for an hour. He's a regular good-time Charley. The next I saw him, he was half-drunk and tried to get me to sit on his lap and give him a kiss. I'd just met him and I didn't want to kiss him. So he pulled another girl on top of him and put his hand on her thigh. Those girls in the club work there just to entertain the men. They look like hussies in short low-cut flouncy dresses. He was smoking most of the time. Not how I wanted the evening to go. I hope there other available men in this town."

Nellie was shocked. "Zella, you must be more careful. You were lucky to have escaped. We should just go on double dates if that is what these Wild West men are like."

Zella didn't go out in Brewster again for a while, as she took a position working as a domestic for a lady in Kanorado, Kansas, near the Colorado border. Nellie was hired by Mabel Horney, who was married to J.P. Horney's nephew, Glenn. Mabel had just had a baby and needed some help for a few months. Ben was invited to some of the Horney family dinners since he worked at their store. He attended one of those dinners a few weeks after Nellie started working for the Horneys.

"I ain't seen Zella in town," Ben said when he could speak to

Nellie in the Horney's parlor. "She avoiding me?"

"Oh, no. She went to Kanorado for a job. I think she is enjoying it."

"I see. I don't understand how you are taking care of Mrs. Horney's baby. Who is taking care of your little girls? Doesn't your husband farm?" he asked.

"My little girls? I don't have any…you mean my nieces? Those are Ruby's, my oldest sister. She died last year. Her husband and oldest daughter are still in Nebraska, but Mom is taking care of the little ones. We all help, of course. Even my brothers help. Harry is fifteen and Verner is thirteen."

"Oh, so you ain't married? Maybe some Saturday night—"

She interrupted and put her hand in front of his mouth before he could finish, "I'm not a party girl. No dancing, no booze, no cigarettes, no thank you." She walked away to help Mrs. Horney prepare the dessert tray.

Nellie thought he had gotten the message that she wasn't interested in him. Her next job was forty miles north of Brewster in Bird City, Kansas, working for Mr. and Mrs. Gray who had a big house to clean. Their twenty-nine-year-old son, Eustis, came by the house frequently. Like Brewster, there wasn't much to do in Bird City, but Eustis and Nellie would sit on the porch and talk in the evening, and sometimes take a picnic lunch out to his farmland on Sundays. He was dependable, as comfortable as a worn-in boot and Nellie enjoyed his company.

Nellie didn't see Ben again until she ran into him at the general store nearly a year after the Smiths had moved to Sherman County. Arthur and Ida Smith had bought their own farm and were busy working it along with their two teenage sons. Zella had been home to visit, but she was still working in Kanorado.

"Nellie, you're back!" Ben rushed up to her when he saw her come through the door of the store. He acted as though they had been friends the whole time she was gone.

"Hello, Ben. How have you been?"

"Tell me you missed me as much as I missed you. There are no girls as purdy as you in this town," he said in a low voice, moving in closer to her, evoking some suspicious looks from the other patrons in the store.

"Don't be silly, Benjamin. I don't know you well enough to miss you, and you've probably been cavorting with those dance hall gals in Goodland," she answered smugly.

"My name is not Benjamin, it is Benona. You're right. We should get to know each other better. I have been out to your dad's farm a few times, and I helped him put up a fence. I'll come out tonight and we can talk more." He went back to the cash register to ring up a sale for an older gentleman who had been waiting impatiently.

Nellie was both confused and flattered. Had she done something to encourage his attentions? It didn't matter. She had a real thing going with Eustis, and Ben probably was just looking for a handy girl to talk with. No harm in that. But he had some nerve paying her mind when he'd been out with her sister first.

She was standing on the fence of the horse ring that evening when he drove up in a horse and wagon with some seed in the back that Arthur had ordered. Harry and Verner were riding horses they had gotten the previous week. They both greeted Ben as though they knew him well.

He jumped out of the wagon carrying a bouquet of partially wilted wildflowers and presented them to her. That was the last thing she expected.

"You are full of surprises, Ben Johnson."

"I wanted to tell you the news. I signed up for the army. I have to take a physical examination, but I think I will be going this summer. They said I was one of the first ones to sign up from these parts. I'll be in uniform and everything. I may even go to Europe to fight those Krauts. Won't you be proud of me, Nellie?"

He did seem like he had matured if he had joined the army. Most of the farmers she spoke to in Bird City hoped to avoid being drafted, saying they were needed on the farm to supply food.

"Well, Ben, the army might be just what you need. I'm sure the whole town is proud of the young men who are going to fight in this war."

That was enough encouragement for him. He stood up on the fence railing next to her chatting about the horses. Her brothers soon convinced Ben to saddle up one of the other new geldings, and the three riders raced across the pasture, whooping and laughing when the lead changed.

Nellie watched them for a bit and then slipped into the kitchen to put the flowers in a vase.

"That man is sweet on you," her mother observed, watching Nellie arrange the bouquet. "He's stopped by here often and we see him at the store. He has asked about you a dozen times. I told him you were working in Bird City and I didn't know when you would be able to come home."

"Really Mom," Nellie said. "Zella went out with him and she didn't even have fun. Besides, he is going into the army and I am going back to Bird City. There is another lady who wants a housekeeper, Mrs. Overturf. I may start working there part of the time. And there is Eustis. I can't just forget about him."

She expected Ben to leave after the ride with her brothers, but her parents invited him to stay for dinner. Afterward, he asked her to come out to the barn to show her something. She was a little concerned about what he meant until he pulled out a tin of cigarettes he had rolled himself.

"It is time you learned how to smoke, Nell. All worldly women know how to smoke. It is considered chic," he told her, lighting a cigarette for himself and one for her.

She wasn't sure she was chic, but she decided this was her chance to try it. Predictably, she choked on the first few puffs. Ben showed her how he could blow smoke rings, and stood very close to her, trying to intermingle their smoke. He even put his hand casually around her waist as they both laughed at her attempts to master smoking.

"I don't know about this. But I did have fun trying to learn," she said.

"I have a lot to teach you, Nellie," he said pulling her close. His breath was hot on her neck when he nuzzled her ear.

"That's what I am afraid of." She pushed away and stomped out her cigarette. As they walked back to the house he took her hand and it felt romantic, something she didn't expect. She found him exciting in some odd way. He was nothing like Eustis. He had experience with women, with liquor, with smoking, and God knows what else. He was a little dangerous. She found it made her want to know more, despite her fears.

The next day Nellie went back to work for Mrs. Gray in Bird City. On her day off, she helped Mrs. Overturf clean house, so she didn't have time to come back home all summer. She continued seeing Eustis. She realized there seemed to be a spark missing in their relationship. Chemistry, she had heard the other girls call it. He was a perfect gentleman, and she began to wonder how perfect that was.

About a month after she last saw him, she got a short note from Ben saying he'd passed his physical exam and would be leaving in September for Camp Funston in northeastern Kansas. He planned to go back to Ashland, Nebraska, to see his family beforehand. America was gearing up to meet the threat to democracy and everyone in Bird City was talking more about the war now. Nellie tried to pretend she didn't care that Ben might be facing danger, but she couldn't put him out of her mind.

He showed up unexpectedly one afternoon in September. The Grays had gone out to see some friends and she had just cleaned up after working hard all day. She was sitting on their porch drinking coffee when a noisy Model A truck came lumbering down the dirt road and Ben jumped out of the passenger seat. Her heart leaped a little at the sight of him. He was smoking a cigarette and, as soon as he reached her, he offered her one.

"Do you think I remember how to do this? I haven't had one since." She put the cigarette in her mouth obligingly and let him light it. She marveled at how it seemed like she had just been with him in the barn back home when she hadn't seen him in months.

He pulled her up and leaned against her by the front door. "I had to see you, Nellie. I leave tomorrow. I want you to write to me. I know we are just gettin' to know each other, but we can do that writin' letters. See, here's the address they gave me. I got your address if you got my other letter. Just tell me if you move, okay?" He handed her a small piece of paper with his name, rank, and address printed on it. "If you don't want to do this for me, do it for the country. You women need to keep the soldiers' morale up. You gotta kiss me now, Nellie, for good luck. What if something happens to me, and you never have another chance?"

She took the paper but didn't answer him. The next thing she knew he was holding her head on both sides and kissing her mouth. Before she could object, he backed away, ran down the steps, and jumped back in the truck. His buddy, the driver, waved and smiled and they took off with a roar and a cloud of dust. Her heart was still pounding when she saw Eustis walking toward the house staring first after the truck and then at her.

She started working as a live-in domestic for Mrs. Overturf shortly after Ben left. She made more money, which was the primary reason she had changed jobs. But she knew it would be awkward to continue working for the Grays once their son told them what had happened.

"What the hell, Nellie? Who was he?" Eustis had demanded. He threw her cigarette down on the ground as she stuffed the paper with Ben's address on it into her blouse. "Since when do you smoke?"

"He's a friend from back home, and he's leaving for the army. He smokes."

"What I saw was hardly just a friendly buss on the cheek. I don't think proper young ladies go around kissing anyone like that."

"You know what I think? He knows how to kiss. *Properly*."

Eustis just stared at her. "I guess you are not the girl I thought you were."

"Funny," Nellie said. "You're exactly the guy I thought you were. You could take a few pointers from my friend there. He knows how to heat things up."

Eustis didn't seem to like that remark at all and he stormed off. She had surprised herself when she defended Ben and admitted the way he had caught her off guard had given her a thrill. Nellie thought it was a shame she had to make Eustis jealous before she ever saw him display any passion. If only he had tried to kiss her with that much intensity well, she wouldn't be working for Mrs. Overturf. In her own little rebellion, she started smoking more. The Overturfs didn't seem to mind, as Mr. Overturf smoked every day.

Ben's letters left her a little breathless too. Not at first. The first two letters were in sloppy penmanship, and full of grammatical errors. She didn't even know how far he had gone in school. But the third letter she received was noticeably better. It was written in a much more elegant style and hand. He told her he was with the Quartermaster Corps Remount Depot Automatic Replacement Draft. The Quartermasters were charged with most of the administrative duties at the camp, kind of a behind-the-scenes function, to assure the fighting men had whatever they needed— artillery, food, clothing, and even horses in some cases. His section was designed to step in when there were casualties closer to the front lines. So far, they had not been deployed, but they were always ready.

What surprised her most about his letters was they were becoming more romantic. Ben started talking about her eyes and her hair and how she moved and even started quoting poetry. He once wrote:

> "And fare thee well, my only love!
> And fare thee well awhile.
> And I will come again, my love,
> Though it were ten thousand mile."

She didn't identify this was from the Robert Burns poem, "A Red, Red Rose" but she knew it had a familiar ring. The idea he would even steal someone else's poetry impressed her. Maybe he was a diamond in the rough. What was even worse was she knew she was falling for it. Was this why he wanted to write letters, so he could tell her what was really in his heart? Could she trust it was true?

She had to respond in kind. To do otherwise would have been unkind. She didn't quote poetry, but she acknowledged she was thinking about him and worrying about his safety, although it sounded as though he was not about to go anywhere near a battlefield. The camp was one of the largest in the country for training soldiers, and it appeared his unit had their hands full attending to the men there.

In September, he was granted leave for five days after he had been in Camp Funston for a year. He asked for permission to come and visit her family in Sherman County; she took time off from her job and borrowed her father's car to meet him at the train in Brewster. As soon as he grabbed her and spun her around on the platform, she knew the whole town would have them pegged as a couple. Things had definitely changed between them. He looked healthier and stronger and his red hair was very short.

After they got into the car and had some privacy, she confided, "Those letters you wrote were beautiful. I think they made me fall in love with you."

He started laughing. "Them letters were written by Dewey. He writes letters for all of us guys. He's good, right? I can write letters to my mother, but when you want to impress a woman, well, Dewey's the guy."

"Wait, what? You didn't write any letters? Then I guess I am in love with Dewey instead."

"Oh, no, no, no. Dewey's married, for one thing. I paid him to write a little news about the corps, what I have been doing, and he adds some romantic junk. That's his special touch. He's got books of poetry, and he's kind of a wimp if ya know what I mean. We all protect him from the camp bullies because he writes a great love letter. I bet he writes for ten different guys in our squadron. Which is probably not hard, cuz we all do the same thing. He's kind of like our secretary."

It was pretty pathetic that he paid someone else to write such lovely words. But at least he owned up to it. I guess he could have gone on fooling me, she thought. And despite her disappointment about the letters, they did enjoy each other's company while he was there. Her parents and brothers were entertained by him. They all laughed at his jokes, and he even showed them how he'd learned to juggle. He had several funny stories about army life.

Ben convinced her to sneak back out to the car after it got dark.

"I've been dreaming about kissing you again for a whole year. It is a terribly long time to wait," he said, grasping her head in his hands as he had before. He took his time, nibbling gently on her upper lip and working his way down her neck, pulling her into his lap.

She thought her instincts were right before. He certainly did know how to kiss and didn't seem to get tired of it either.

When it was time for him to catch the train back to Camp Funston, he held her tightly and vowed he would miss her even more than before.

"You know I used to think you were a bad boy," she teased.

"Make no mistake about that: I am a bad boy. I will always be up for a good time, the wilder the better." He winked at her. "I just learned how to act like a good boy."

She would come to understand how true that was.

Nellie had a break after the Christmas holidays, so she went to see Ben at the army camp. There was a place nearby often used by visiting family members.

She was supposed to meet Ben Friday evening at the Oxford

Hotel in Junction City, a short walk from the train. He estimated he'd arrive around 6:00 p.m. and they would find a place to eat dinner. He would have to report back to the barracks by 5:00 p.m. the following day. She would spend Saturday night at the hotel and travel back home on Sunday. When he had not arrived by 7:00 p.m., she began to worry. The hotel was kind enough to let her call the camp, but they were not able to provide information regarding a specific soldier.

She went ahead and had some dinner and went to bed, but she didn't hear anything the next morning either. Finally, she spotted some other soldiers in the lobby of the hotel and asked if there was a way to find out what happened. Corporal Winston and Corporal Lee were happy to try to help her.

"Who are you looking for, Miss?" Corporal Lee asked.

"I was supposed to meet Corporal Ben Johnson last night, but he hasn't shown up and I haven't heard from him," Nellie said.

"Johnson…Winston, isn't that the guy they put in the infirmary last night? No, the night before last."

"Yeah, I think it might be. He was pretty beat up. I hope that is not your fiancé," Winston replied.

"What do you mean? He was hurt? Was it some accident?"

The men both roared with laughter. "Nah, nothing like that," Lee said. "He was at a speakeasy, I guess and didn't pay his bar tab. The bouncers don't take kindly to that sort of thing. You know they can't call the police, since speakeasies are illegal. So the bouncers, well, they take care of the deadbeats to set an example. I guess he drank more than he could pay for. You gotta be careful in those joints. Sometimes the girls there will steal your wallet."

"Don't ask me," Winston added, "I try to steer clear of those places, nothing but trouble. But when I got a glimpse of him, it wasn't pretty. I couldn't be sure it was him with all the blood, but I think he had red hair."

"But I don't understand why he would have been in town at all. I thought he was on duty until Friday night, and then he was supposed to be here," Nellie wondered aloud.

"Lady, if that was him, he probably didn't know what day it was. I'd say he is lucky someone dragged his ass back to camp," Corporal Lee said.

With the new information, she called the camp infirmary. They wouldn't let her talk to Ben, but they did confirm he was there and had a head wound, a concussion, a dislocated shoulder, and multiple sprains and lacerations.

Unfortunately, there wasn't another train back to Brewster before the one she was booked on, so she just waited in her room. She was grateful she had brought a book to read on the train. She decided she was not going to write to him, and just see what kind of explanation he came up with.

It was three weeks before she got a letter from him. I can just imagine what he got Dewey to write for him this time, she thought, as she tore open the envelope. She read the letter, then blinked. He hadn't explained anything. It was like he'd forgotten she was coming to see him. She wondered if he had forgotten because of the concussion. She pulled out the last letters she had gotten talking about her trip. Yes, he had said he'd meet her there on Friday evening at 6:00 p.m. In the absence of an apology or explanation, she decided she would not write back.

Although she was back at her parents' home, she didn't reveal to them what had happened on the trip. But after she got the letter, she decided to confide in Zella, who had finally come home.

"I just hope you weren't planning to marry this bum," Zella said frankly. "He is just not the kind of man you can trust. Whatever happened to that nice fella, Eustis?"

"Eustis is engaged to some girl he met after me. I think she's only twenty years old," Nellie said and wondered if she should swear off men entirely.

Ben wrote several more letters asking why she had not written, but she did not respond. She was back in Bird City and ran into Eustis at the library one evening in February. He offered to walk her home since it was getting dark so early. Although he talked about his new girlfriend, she couldn't help but notice he seemed interested when she said things had cooled with Ben. However, when they arrived at the Overturfs' house, they found Ben sitting on the porch steps smoking. He was dressed in olive green army fatigues and boots, and she thought he must be freezing without a coat. Before she could speak, Eustis leaped up the steps and pointed his finger in Ben's face. The men were immediately in verbal combat causing Mr. Overturf to rush out of the house to prevent blows.

"You!" Eustis began loudly, "Haven't you caused her enough trouble?"

"What do you mean? Who do you think you are? Nellie, what are you doing with this jackass?" Ben said, keeping his eyes firmly on Eustis's. "Don't tell me this is your ex-boyfriend!"

"There is no need for fighting," Mr. Overturf said. "You boys just come inside where it is warm and talk like gentlemen."

He introduced himself to the two younger men, and indirectly to each other. Nellie was glad Mr. Overturf was there as the voice of reason because her head was spinning. But as soon as she followed them inside and the two men sat on the couch, they both seemed to turn on her.

"Nellie, didn't you break up with him?" Ben and Eustis said, almost in unison.

Nellie looked at both of them and decided there was no need to answer.

"Ben, what are you doing here? Tell me you aren't away without leave."

Ben jumped to his feet and put his hands on her shoulders. "Of course not! I got an emergency leave just for tonight. I have to be back by 1700 hours tomorrow, and I borrowed my buddy's car. It's a long drive. Why haven't I heard from you, Nell? It ain't because of him, is it?" He glanced at Eustis in disdain.

She studied Ben: he was standing in good lighting for the first time. His bruises were faded but he had cuts on his face, including a sizable gash on his forehead which appeared to have been stitched.

She turned to Eustis. "Eustis, I appreciate you walking me home. Why don't I talk to you in a day or so? I need to straighten some things out with Ben. Mr. Overturf, I am so sorry we caused a commotion, I think everything is under control now."

Eustis looked at her with concern and gave Ben a warning glare, but quickly left the house, clattering down the porch steps. Mr. Overturf nodded and retreated to the bedroom in the back.

"Come out to the car with me," Ben ordered.

"It's cold outside, let's just talk right here."

"It's private in the car, c'mon." He pulled her by the elbow and guided her out to the car, which was parked on the street in front of the house. She grabbed a blanket laying on the couch on her way out the door. Arguing is not going to keep us warm, she thought.

"What do you think you are trying to do to me, giving me the silent treatment? Are you back with your old boyfriend?" he demanded.

"Tell me what happened the weekend you were supposed to meet me in Junction City," Nellie said evenly.

She could see that surprised him. "Whaddaya mean? I couldn't come. I got hurt, I was jumped by a couple of thugs."

"You stood me up. I came all the way on the train just to see you and paid for a hotel room, and you didn't come. You didn't even write to me to apologize or explain. You just ignored it. So what really happened?"

"Okay, I see you're pissed off about that. Truth is, I don't remember everything. Someone stole my money and beat the crap outta me."

"Try again."

He looked at her questioningly, then dropped his gaze to his feet, "I don't know who you've been talking to …" he began slowly. "I went to this here club in Junction City, it's a little shady, but I'd been there before. I went with a couple of other fellas to celebrate one of their birthdays the night before we were supposed to meet. I thought they left without me, while I was talking to one of the girls. I went to pay the tab, but I was short. I offered to give them an IOU, but they said they already had an IOU from me and they was gonna take it out of my hide. At first, I thought they was kidding. They wasn't. My friends musta found me on the street or I'd probably be dead. I know it sounds terrible, that's why I didn't want to tell you."

She let him stew for a minute or two, and he didn't look up. He reminded her of when her little brother had been caught eating half a pie that had been set up on the windowsill to cool.

"I still haven't heard an apology," she finally said, pushing the blanket toward him when he started shivering.

"Jeez, you sound like my mother. It wasn't my fault, you get that, right? I wanted to be there with you. I couldn't get out of the fucking bed. I don't even think I knew where I was for two days." He finally looked up at her, and she thought she saw tears in his eyes. "I survived though. I thought about you the whole time I was trying to get better. And you don't even send me a letter when I needed to hear from you most."

"You're impossible!" she said stunned that he was trying to blame her.

"Damn straight," he answered. "That's why I need you." He wrapped the blanket around his back and arms and pulled her to him, enveloping them both. "I would have never thought of a blanket."

She didn't know why she was allowing him to kiss her, or unbutton her coat to put his cold hands around her back. She had heard there was a fine line between love and hate, but she'd never understood the expression before that moment.

CHAPTER TWO

By the time summer started, things had changed for both of them. Nellie left Bird City and moved back in with her family. She had learned more domestic skills working for the Grays and Overturfs. She had learned to sew from her mother when she was just a child, but she had a chance to make dresses, boy's suits, shirts, quilts, and draperies while she was employed. Mr. Overturf had generously bought her a new sewing machine which he insisted she take along when she left. Once she was back home, Nellie started sewing some clothing for her growing nieces. She began to think she could go into business as a seamstress.

Ben had finally been discharged from the army in May, having endured a war in which he, and tens of thousands of other soldiers at Camp Funston, had never fought. After a quick trip back to see his parents in Ashland, he settled back into life in Brewster, working once again for J.P. Horney at his merchandise store, and living in an apartment above it. He got his old Buick out of the Horney's storage shed and tuned it up.

Zella was also living back in Brewster, working as the "Hello Girl," or telephone operator. Zella was not pleased to see Ben and Nellie were again becoming closer.

"I think you should go with him to one of those clubs, Nell. That is where he seems to run into problems when he has too much to drink. Go see for yourself if you have anything to worry about."

"You're right. I don't know why I shouldn't go. I know they are illegal, but I hear they are quite popular, and you don't hear of anyone being arrested just for going to a club," Nellie agreed.

Ben seemed surprised when she said she wanted to go to a speakeasy with him. "I don't know if that is going to be fun for you. Have you ever even tasted liquor?"

"If you think going to a club is fun, I think I should see why you like it."

She saw why he liked it pretty quickly. They went to his favorite spot in Goodland. She had never seen waitresses in such scanty outfits, with bare arms and even their knees showing. If I had to make a dress like this, it would be cheap and easy, she thought. Hardly any fabric or shape, like they are wearing pillowcases.

"I've never seen you in a suit before. Spiffy. Is that what they call pinstripes?" Nellie asked Ben once they were seated.

"It's all new. Worsted wool, pinstripes, white shirt with attached collar. I even sprang for new shoes." He stuck one shiny black shoe out for her inspection. "I got tired of wearing fatigues for so long."

"Well, I feel a little drab in a lace blouse and long skirt after looking at you."

"You should get a dress like the ones the hostesses wear here. Very modern."

Very brazen, she thought.

When the bartender put two shot glasses in front of them and poured whiskey into them, she gulped hers with one quick motion. It seared her tongue and throat and she started coughing. Ben burst out laughing. But after the first shot settled in her stomach and they had smoked a couple of cigarettes, she found it was easier to have the second and third.

Then they started dancing. She remembered Zella saying Ben was a good dancer. He did the first dance with one of the hostesses, who was an excellent partner. She wondered if he had danced with her often or how well he knew her. When he pulled Nellie onto the floor, she felt a little lost and embarrassed as she knew everyone would compare her dancing to the other girl's. She had only danced with her father at Ruby's wedding ages ago. But about that time, the whiskey kicked in and she no longer cared. She just tried to follow whatever Ben was doing. He was laughing, swinging her around, and doing some crazy moves. A few dances later, she felt her stomach churning and she barely made it out the back door. She pulled Ben along with her, as she still had ahold of his hand.

"What's wrong, did I step on you? Are you okay?" he asked.

She responded by upchucking all over his shiny black shoes and pinstriped cuffed pants.

"Dammit! I knew you should have taken it easy on that whiskey. You stay here until you're done …ya know. I have to clean this off."

He went back inside and she sat on a chair on the makeshift patio behind the club. She didn't know how long she sat there with her head in her hands, waiting to feel better, when she realized Ben had not returned. She tried standing up, and when she felt steady, she went back inside the smoke-filled club. She was happy she had not vomited on her own clothes or shoes.

She went back to where they had been sitting but Ben wasn't there. She looked around and finally spotted him at a table in a dark corner canoodling with his previous dancing partner. A half-empty bottle of gin sat on the table with two nearly empty glasses. Her first impulse was to just walk out the door, but she remembered she was in Goodland and had no other ride home. She acted on her second impulse. With tears rolling down her cheeks, she slowly walked up to the table where they sat. She stood there, apparently invisible as they were stuck in a lip lock. She surveyed the table, then picked up the bottle of gin and poured it into their laps. The hostess screamed. Nellie started for the door before Ben even got to his feet. Suddenly, she felt much better.

On the way back to Brewster, they got into a serious row. Looking back later, she figured this might have been the argument that set a pattern for them. A number of similar fights followed. Nellie wanted Ben to be more responsible and settle down. He wanted to go out drinking and have fun with his friends, including dancing or making out with other women. He didn't see any harm in that, as the hostesses were paid to entertain the men and entice them to revisit the club. She knew he often drank more than he should. She would hear from the Brewster gossips that Mr. Horney had to go upstairs and drag Ben out of bed on Friday or Saturday mornings.

The only good thing about these quarrels was making up afterward. Ben kept trying to get her to come up to his apartment at night so they would have more privacy, but Nellie became increasingly aware of what privacy might lead to.

"He's never going to marry you, you know that. He probably will never marry anyone, and die old and alone," Zella predicted one evening in October after the latest disagreement had come to her attention. Nellie didn't bother arguing with her sister. She knew how she felt.

Ben was planning to come to the farm for Christmas dinner. Five days before, Nellie had stopped by the store. She was trying to tell him about all the family and friends who would be attending, and how they were connected.

"My father's mother, Annie Robinson Smith, lives in Otoe County, Nebraska, but her brother, David Robinson, lives here. He married Carrie Reed, who was a sister to my mother's mother, Henrietta Reed Payson. They all got together when they lived in Nebraska. So my granduncle and grandaunt were married from two different sides of the family. Aunt Carrie died, but their son Harvey is coming to my parents' house for Christmas. Grandma Hen is coming, as well as her son, Clarence. You know them, of course.

Also, Camilla and George Weatherhogg, are coming in from Douglas, Nebraska—"

He cut her off. "I'm going back to Ashland for Christmas. My pa is not doing very well, according to my ma's letter. I am not sure how long I will be there. I told Mr. Horney today, and I will try to get a train ticket tomorrow."

"Oh, well, of course, you should go. I hope your father recovers. Will you let me know when you make plans?"

He agreed to contact her when he knew more, but he seemed distracted.

She didn't see him again before he left. The holidays came and went and the gift she made him remained under the Christmas tree until she finally put it back in her room.

She didn't hear from him the whole month of January, and she now understood how he felt when she stopped writing to him when he was at Camp Funston. She didn't know how to reach him in Nebraska, and even if she had, she wasn't sure what she would say if she wrote to him. She had to assume his father was still very ill or had died, and he was needed there. By mid-February, she asked Mr. Horney if he had gotten a letter from Ben, but he said he had not heard anything either. Mr. Horney had hired one of his nephews to take Ben's job for a few months, but Ben's replacement was leaving town in June. He had not rented out the apartment yet.

She tried to put Ben out of her mind. She decided it was best to move forward on her own. She accepted another job as a domestic, this time in Goodland, working for a Mrs. Arthur Vail. Her mother promised to forward any letters that came for her.

In late May, she went to one of the clubs where Ben had taken her the previous year. She went with Esther, a young lady who lived next door to the Vails'. When she ordered a drink, one of the owners of the club recognized her.

"Hey, Nellie. I haven't seen Ben for months. What's he up to?"

"Oh hi, Gabriel. This is my neighbor, Esther. I am not sure what is going on with Ben. He went back home last Christmas and I haven't heard from him." Nellie said.

"Wow, that surprises me. He told me he was crazy about you. Here, try one of our new drinks. It's the Goodland Gooze. Like Goose but with a 'z'. Vodka, orange juice, schnapps, and a secret ingredient."

Nellie and Esther both tried the drink, and soon Nellie was dancing with Gabriel and it felt like she was free for the first time in months. As with most of the clubs, the place was dark and smoky, even with the back door open. A bearded man wearing a black shirt and pants and a fedora was sitting in the back watching them. His stare made her a little uneasy. She asked Gabriel if he knew him. Gabriel glanced toward him and stopped dancing.

The man came forward lunging at Gabriel, fists flying. Gabriel backed away, pushing Nellie behind him. The bouncer was on the other man in a flash, knocking off his hat, and Nellie realized it was Ben.

Gabriel recovered quickly. "Hey, Ben. I didn't recognize you back there. Why don't you go out to the back room, and I'll get you a couple of free drinks. The usual?"

Ben didn't say a word, he just picked up his hat, glared at them, and retreated to the back room. Gabriel excused himself and went to get the drinks for Ben. Nellie sat back down with Esther, who seemed to think the whole thing was exciting.

"Are those men fighting over you? Golly geez," she said.

About five minutes went by before Nellie saw Gabriel return from the back and head for the bar where he helped other patrons. She went to the back room, not certain whether she was glad to see Ben or not. The windows were open and the warm May breeze was blowing in, making it more comfortable than the rest of the place. The smell of stale cigarettes in the overflowing ashtrays mingled with the perfume of the lilac bushes outside. Ben was sitting alone, at a table with two glasses in front of him. One was already empty.

He didn't speak when she sat down. He didn't even look up at first.

"When did you get back?" she asked. He looked so menacing with that beard, even though it was mostly red. She'd never thought about what he would look like with facial hair.

"Last night. Middle of the night, so morning. Like you care."

She waited for him to say more, but he didn't. He was just staring into his drink.

"I didn't know what happened when I didn't hear from you—"

"Don't start with me, Nell." He was now taking her in with flashing eyes, "Don't tell me I didn't write to you when my father died or to tell you when I would be back. My family ain't like yours with all your fucking relatives who were the founding fathers of the God damn county. Going back there was awful. Like reliving my crappy childhood. Everyone actin' like my father was a saint, when we all hated him. My brother and I were ready to kill each other, and I couldn't worry about what you were thinking. And my mother, she was always on my case, nagging me till I couldn't stand it… that's why I escaped from there when I was eighteen."

She started to say she was sorry about his father, but he interrupted her again.

"And you? What the fuck are you doing?" He made a sweeping gesture with his hand. His voice had been getting louder and more slurred as the outburst continued. "I went outta the farm to find where you went, and they told me you was working in Goodland. So I thought I'd just stop by my ol' watering hole here for a drink before I tried to find the Vails' place, and whaddayaknow. I've been dealing with all of this shit and here you are dancing and making googly eyes with my ol' pal Gabe. Son of a bitch. I guess you do like to have a good time after all. Well, I'm sorry I caught you. I'm sorry I came here to see you. I won't make that mistake again. You can go to hell!"

He got up, nearly pushing the table over in the process, and marched out the front door, slamming it loudly enough that everyone in the joint noticed.

Nellie felt her cheeks flushing as she sat there in stunned silence, fighting back tears. She waited for about ten minutes before she found Esther, and announced they were leaving. She felt every eye in the room on them. By the time they reached the street, Ben was nowhere to be seen.

Nellie was mortified after that night. She didn't ever want to go back to that club, and she was afraid to even go home. She didn't want to ask her mother or brothers if Ben was in Brewster because she didn't want to have to explain the whole ugly scene. About a month later, her mother did ask about him in a letter. Ida knew Ben had gone to Goodland because he'd come to the farm first, asking for Nellie. But the next time Ida saw him after he resumed working at Horney's Store, he was cool and businesslike. Great, she thought. Now I can never go back there either. How could he have been so nasty to her?

Mrs. Vail had plenty of work for her to do through the end of June, and she helped Nellie secure another job back in Bird City, working for Mrs. Vail's sister-in-law, Mrs. Danver. The Danvers went on a vacation at the end of July, so Nellie went back home to her parent's farm for the first time since March. She decided not to go into any detail about what had happened with Ben. She simply said she no longer wanted to talk about him. She thought it would be easier for her mother in particular, who continued to have some sort of contact with him if she didn't know what Ben had said.

Nellie had a nice visit with her family, although she felt like she was pretending to be happy. On the last day of her visit, her mother asked her to pick up a few grocery items in Brewster.

"You can't avoid the man forever you know," Ida commented when Nellie gave her a panicked look.

"Wanna bet?" she answered, as she herded seventeen-year-old Verner and six-year-old Lazetta into the car with her.

Ida had written out a grocery list. Nellie stood in the street outside the store and counted out what she hoped would be plenty of cash into Verner's hand, and told him where he could find the items inside the store. Verner didn't understand why she didn't just go in with him, but he cooperated. She watched Verner and Lazetta walk into the store, and saw Ben gazing at her through the open doorway. The beard was gone, and he looked like he used to back when they were together. She quickly walked a few doors down and sat on a bench near the post office, wringing her hands until the younger Smiths appeared.

Her life was busy back in Bird City. The Danvers had two rambunctious sons, who were about the same age as Nellie's nieces, and she ended up taking charge of them much of the time. For the first time, she thought she did want to have her own children, so maybe she ought to find a new boyfriend. Eustis had gotten married in July, while she was in Sherman County, so he was done with her for certain.

She had started attending church with the Danver family and

had met a couple of nice men there, but nothing had come of it so far. In late September, she received a letter from Ben, postmarked from Ashland, Nebraska. The letter explained that he had gone back home because his older brother, Charles Edward, known as Ed, had gotten into a serious automobile accident while driving to Omaha. He had been in the hospital for several weeks but was supposed to go home any day. Ben said he would have to help Ed into the bathroom and down the stairs because his whole leg was in a cast. He asked if he could come to see Nellie when he was able to come back to Sherman County and gave her his address in Ashland.

Nellie was touched he went back to help his family once again, especially since it seemed to be so hard for him last time. Most of her heartache and humiliation had gone away, and maybe she should see him at least one last time. She wrote him a newsy letter about what was going on in Bird City and said she would be willing to talk to him.

One Saturday afternoon in mid-November, she took the two Danver boys downtown to the ice cream parlor. They had just gotten their sundaes when Ben sat down in an empty chair at their little round table.

"Hot fudge, my favorite," he said, picking up her spoon and taking the first bite. The little boys laughed, wondering who he was. He gave her a sidelong look and raised his eyebrows, trying to gauge her reaction. Nellie just shook her head and smiled. When he turned on that boyish charm, she found him hard to resist.

They took it slowly; it was as if they hadn't dated before. Since the drive to Bird City was farther than it was from Brewster to Goodland, he often came to see her on Sundays, when they were both off work. She was able to go home for a week around Thanksgiving and Christmas, and he came to the family celebrations at the farm.

He no longer talked about going to the clubs and seemed to enjoy spending time with her little nieces, and the little Danvers. At the same time, he didn't talk about anything serious and didn't explain what had happened when he was back home.

Nellie continued working for the Danvers until March when Mr. Danver got a job in Kansas City and the family moved. The Overturfs were members of the same church as the Danvers. When they had heard about Nellie's job ending, they offered to have her come back and work for them. She agreed to start in April, after a two-week break so she could go home.

She thought Ben would be happy about her going back to work for the Overturfs. "I will probably have more time to work on my sewing since they don't have any children," Nellie said as she and Ben walked out to the barn to feed the pigs.

"I think it is time we got married," he said bluntly.

She looked at him with confusion. "Married? What? I thought you didn't want to get married, too much responsibility…too much boring—"

He cut her off with a wave of his hand, "I know, don't remind me. I said a lot of crap. I changed my mind. I dunno, maybe it was those kids. Seeing you with those cute little boys, just made me think. I mean what the hell are we waiting for? Do you want to get married?"

She made him wait a moment while she pretended to ponder the question. Then she shrugged. "Sure, why not?"

They decided to get married on the Fourth of July, which fell on a Monday. They could be married by a minister in Goodland in his parsonage.

The next few months flew by with a flurry of preparations.

Nellie knew brides were often getting married in big white dresses, but she didn't want that. She wanted to look modern. It was 1921, and she decided she should update her look. The first thing she did was to go to a hair salon in Bird City and ask them to cut her hair in one of those new bobs. She had worn her dark brown hair long and pulled back in a braid for many years, so they were reluctant to cut it all off, but she was sure it was time.

She went to the fabric store and found a pattern for one of the new "flapper" drop-waist chemises with a big collar. She even decided she should wear it just below her knees, which was the current style. She didn't want white because she wanted to wear the dress for other special occasions. She chose an antique rose pink and added fancy trims and lace to make it elegant.

She even got some perky little T-strap, two-inch heels to compliment her outfit. She knew she had spent more money on herself that day than she ever had in her life. It's lucky we are getting married in the heat of the summer and I won't need a coat, she thought.

In May, one of Verner's classmates, Floyd Fiechter, had a party for his eighteenth birthday. Ben, Nellie, and Harry were also invited. It was the first time anyone in Brewster had seen her new haircut, and they were all raving about it. She was a little worried to see Ben's reaction.

"You don't look like you," he said. When she frowned, he grinned and added, "You look like one of those movie starlets."

She gave him a quick peck on the cheek. They had fun at the party with everyone trying some of the new dance steps after Floyd's parents got out the gramophone.

Floyd's older brother, Frank, came in about 10:00 p.m. He had been visiting some friends in Kansas City and had picked up the latest slang words, or "flapper talk," as he called it. "I'm not going to tell you all of them with ladies present, but here are some of the common ones: bee's knees, which means it's swell; gams means a lady's legs; phonus balonus, or nonsense; you slay me means you are funny; zozzled means drunk; giggle means to water down the booze, and manacle means a wedding ring. Have you all heard these?"

"How would anyone know what you are talking about if you use those terms?" Nellie laughed.

"Says the lass with the lovely gams," Frank answered, as Nellie blushed. "See, you catch on once you use them. I'm Frank, by the way. Sorry if I was too fresh."

"I am Nellie, Verner's older sister. And this is Ben Johnson, my fiancé," she added quickly.

"Yes, she is about to get a manacle," Ben chimed in.

CHAPTER THREE

"When do expect your family to come for the wedding, Ben?" Ida asked when he was filling her grocery order. "We should probably have them out for dinner."

"No one is coming from my side of the family. It's a long way, and I wouldn't have much time to spend with them."

"I hope we can meet them eventually. At least that keeps the wedding luncheon smaller," Ida said cheerfully.

The wedding went off just as they planned. Zella, despite her reservations, stood up with Nellie as her attendant, and Harry stood up with Ben. Since it was a hot day, they were happy they were saying their vows at 11:00 a.m. They had a lovely cool luncheon in a private dining room at the Hotel Neu, which was a big stone mansion. By 2:00 p.m. they were bidding the last of the guests good-bye, and Nellie turned to hear her two brothers laughing uproariously at something Ben said.

"What were they laughing at?" Nellie asked as Ben led her up the stairs to find their modest bridal suite.

"I told them I was 'going to Dance the Married Man's Cotillion,'" Ben grinned. "It seemed to fit the occasion."

"We're going dancing?" she asked.

"No, that was one of the new slang phrases Frank told us men about out on the porch at that party. He had many more, but I've forgotten most of them. They were all about sex," he said locking the door behind them.

"Wait, are you saying you just told my two little brothers we're going to—"

He cut her off with a kiss. "We're on our honeymoon!"

Married life found them busier than she expected. She had been away from Sherman County for most of the last few years, and now they had a chance to spend time with family. Nellie had moved into Ben's apartment above the store. She went out to her parents' farm about once a week, and they also spent time with Harve Robinson and sometimes with his brother, Bertie. Harve took them to the county fair and even took them on a camping trip to Colorado. He usually paid for the big expenses, since he was an established farmer, and seemed to enjoy getting to know Ben, treating him more like a younger brother.

When Christmas rolled around, Ida invited Harve, Bertie Robinson, and Bertie's wife, Arcelia, to join them for dinner at the farm. Her relatives had started hinting Nellie might be in a family way, which made her a little uncomfortable. She was already wondering why she wasn't pregnant and didn't want everyone else thinking about that.

The previous year, things had gone well for Nellie and Ben, so she was caught off guard when she found a bottle of whiskey in one of the dresser drawers. There was some sort of label on it that appeared as if it had come from a drug store. She put it on the kitchen table, and when she asked Ben where it came from, he seemed defensive.

"When I was back home with my brother, he told me the doctor gave him one of those prescriptions for alcohol. Ed said it was an easy way to get liquor. Just take it to the drug store, and as long as the prescription is good, they sell you more, no questions asked. So I was feeling kinda sad, cuz it's been two years since that whole thing with my pa and all, so I asked Doc about it. He says, 'no problem', and gives me a prescription. He said most of the men in town are getting their hooch that way. It's perfectly legal."

"I had no idea you could do that," Nellie said. She opened the bottle, poured a little into a glass, and started to drink it.

He exploded, "What the hell, you can't have that. Are you nuts? Get your own damn bottle." He grabbed the glass and the bottle and stormed down the stairs and out into the freezing January night.

What the hell indeed, she thought. I haven't seen him act like that since…well, maybe he just told me. This goes back to when his father died. Still, he didn't come back for hours. She went to bed, and hoped he had his key.

If he had been feeling sad, he had hidden it well until that night. Afterward, she had to describe his mood as dark. She didn't touch his bottle of whiskey again, but she noticed the amount changed regularly. He must be consuming it daily. He started going out at night again driving his car. He didn't tell her where he was going, but she guessed he was going back to the clubs. She was asleep when he got home, but he would wake her up, smelling like whiskey and cigarettes, and expect her to perform her wifely duty. He was hungover after those nights, and she had to roust him out of bed to go downstairs to work.

If that wasn't bad enough, by February he began to blame her for not being pregnant. "There must be something wrong with you. I've been doing my part, you should be pregnant by now. Go see Doc and find out what the problem is."

She had heard sometimes the problem is with the husband, but she didn't want to argue. She also wanted to know why she wasn't pregnant, although, with the way he was acting lately, it might be for the best. She made an appointment to go see the local physician, Dr. Hays.

After the exam, she felt repulsed. She had not anticipated the doctor would make her undress and put his hands on her. She figured he would just ask her questions and tell her his diagnosis as he had when she had a stomach ailment.

"You're too anxious, my dear," Dr. Hays told her. "Everything looks normal down there, but I am writing you a prescription for a bottle of alcohol. Your choice, whiskey, vodka, or gin. Put an ounce or two in a glass and down it once or twice a day before your husband comes home. Relax, have fun. You're practically a newlywed. You might want to smoke more cigarettes. That will help your nerves and it will all be good for the baby when you get pregnant."

So she got a bottle of vodka from the druggist and several packs of cigarettes and got relaxed enough to pass out and forget about that humiliating experience. When Ben came upstairs shortly after 5:00 p.m. he found her lying on the bed, a cigarette burned down to ashes in the kitchen.

"Nellie, what are you doing? Where's dinner? You aren't making dinner? Are you sick?"

She got up and smoothed down her hair and dress. "*Hmmm*?"

"You're not sick," he continued, looking at the vodka and the ashtray on the table. "You're zozzled."

She sat down at the table and looked at him drunkenly, propping up her heavy head on her hand. "I went to old Dr. Hays. He said if I have to do the mattress jig with you, I'd better be zozzled."

She watched the insult sink in. Everything seemed to move in slow motion, and she could watch angry lines pop up on his forehead.

All at once, he laughed aloud. "He never said that! You made a joke, Nell. God, I almost forgot you had a sense of humor!" He dumped the ashtray into the garbage. "Well if you are going to drink, you have to remember the first rule: as soon as you start to feel your head spin, you've got to put out the cigarette. You could have burned this place down, and the general store below us with it. If that went up in flames, this whole block is gone. Would you want to be known as the woman who burned down Brewster?"

She shrugged. "I'd be dead, who cares?"

He chuckled. He had never had to deal with a drunken wife. He picked up the bottle of vodka. "Okay, so it says right on here no more than two ounces per dose. How much did you drink? Was this full?"

In response, she just laid her head on the table. She sure was relaxed. And he did seem awfully attractive as he scooped her up to put her back to bed. Maybe the doctor had a point.

The next morning she had a massive hangover and couldn't stop throwing up, so she knew she couldn't drink so much again.

After that, she limited the amount of vodka she drank in the evening, putting it in her coffee at supper. And surprisingly, Ben stopped going out at night and they began to have fun with each other again: dancing, playing, or just talking. He finally started opening up to her about the problems he'd had with his family, and why he was reluctant to take her back to Nebraska to meet them.

The vodka was no longer bothering her, but at the end of March, she felt nauseous every morning and told Ben she thought she should stop drinking. When it persisted, even without the drinking, she went back to Dr. Hays. At least this time, he kept his hands off her. He told her it was likely she was pregnant and they tested her urine. A week later, Dr. Hays' nurse, Sarah, called the Horney's store and gave the news to Ben, because they didn't have a telephone up in the apartment.

Nellie hadn't been out to the farm to see her parents since Christmas. Things had not been going well at the beginning of the year, then she started feeling poorly, so she'd put off a visit. Now that she knew she was expecting, she took the car out to the farm and hoped she would find them at home.

She saw her father out mending a fence. She parked in the middle of the road and got out to talk to him.

"Good morning Missy. What brings you out this way?"

"Oh Daddy, I just couldn't wait to share the news. I'm expecting a baby. You're going to be a grandfather."

"That's wonderful, Nellie. But I reckon I'm already a grandfather. You haven't forgotten about Thelma, Lazetta, and Beth, have you?" he said, picking up his hammer again. "Now you hold this board right here for me." She did as he asked and he pounded several nails in place.

"Of course, I know you already have three granddaughters, but this will be different. I will get to enjoy watching you be a grandfather. And it might be a boy. That would be different."

"*Hmmm,* doesn't seem so different to me. Of course, we sure do miss your sister, Ruby. She should have been able to see those babies growing up." He suddenly seemed more concerned. "You will have to take good care of yourself now. Be sure your husband is doing all the heavy lifting."

"Yes, Daddy. He's fussing over me already. Where's Mom?"

"She was hauling all of the rugs out to give them a good beating the last time I saw her. 'It's a good day for spring cleaning,' she said. Go on, I know you want to talk to her. I'm mighty pleased for you, Pumpkin; mighty pleased."

Ida was back in the kitchen when Nellie reached the house. "Mom, can you believe it? I am officially with child." She put her hands on her middle as if the pregnancy was visible. Ida gave her a hug, and they sat down and drank some tea.

"You've been pretty busy these past few months; we've hardly seen you," Ida said. "Is everything going all right with you and Ben?"

Nellie smiled. "Of course they are going well; I'm pregnant, aren't I? What could be better than that in a marriage?" Her mother was giving her one of those looks that told her she could read her like a book. "But sometimes, things are not as good as I would like, I guess."

Ida patted her hand. "My darling, marriage is work. Not just work like mending fences or beating the rugs. The relationship takes a lot of work. It's not all fun or romance. That's why you take vows when you get married. It's serious. Both people have to work together to keep things from falling apart."

"I don't know, Mom," she said staring at her teacup to hide the tears in her eyes. "Ben didn't want to get married for a long time because he wanted to have fun and not be so serious. I'm not sure the baby is going to be fun. I mean you have to take care of a baby all the time."

"Babies are also fun, you'll see. The first time your child smiles at you, or learns to crawl or walk, it's just magnificent. Just cheer up. If you are happy, Ben probably will be too."

The morning nausea finally went away by mid-April, but Nellie began getting dizzy when she tried to get out of bed or up from a chair. She assumed it was just part of being pregnant and didn't mention it to anyone. She felt a little better for a day or two. One afternoon she was taking a few groceries up the stairs from the store when she passed out on the fifth step and tumbled back down the stairs. There was a door separating the store from the staircase, but Ben heard the noise and ran to see what had happened. Dr. Hays' nurse, Sarah, was shopping at the time and ran in right behind Ben. Nellie regained consciousness after a few minutes.

"What happened, Nell? Did you trip on the stairs?" Ben asked.

"No, I don't think so," Nellie said, as Sarah dabbed her forehead with a wet towel. "Everything just went black and I remember sinking to the floor. I have been getting dizzy lately … quite a bit I guess."

"Anemia," Nurse Sarah said at once. "Or at least that's what it sounds like."

They took Nellie to the doctor's office. He suggested she stay in bed as much as possible until the dizziness subsided and said Nellie should be eating spinach, organ meats, chickpeas, peas, or just regular cuts of beef to increase her iron intake. The doctor also said he may need to take a blood sample every couple of months if she continued having symptoms.

When Ida heard what had happened, she insisted Nellie come stay with them at the farm at least for a few weeks, or until she wasn't dizzy. Ben agreed it was a sensible thing to do. The first few evenings she stayed with her parents, he came out for dinner and they all tried to force her to eat everything on the list of foods the doctor had given her.

"Enough! If I ate all of that I'd be so big I'd never make it up a flight of stairs!"

After the first few nights when he'd seemed concerned about her health, Ben was noticeably absent. Nellie knew that on one of the nights, he was planning to go to Goodland to meet with some other veterans who were trying to start a Legionnaire's Post. The previous November, Ben had taken Nellie with him to a convention in Kansas City of the new American Legion. She had enjoyed meeting some of his army pals, including the infamous Dewey. She assumed Ben was working late the other nights, doing stockroom work or ordering goods. But when she tried calling the store around 9:00 p.m. on several occasions, he didn't answer the phone. They had told their families if they were calling them on the store phone, to ask the operator to ring twenty times. That way they would know it was a personal call, and they would go downstairs to answer it.

When Ben came back after a week to check on her, she asked him where he had been in the evenings.

"I don't know. I might have been over at my friend Wayne's place. We may have gone to a club in Goodland. Maybe I was just passed out. Don't worry about me, I can take care of myself."

But she was starting to worry, not about his health, but the pattern emerging again.

"He may be taking advantage of my absence to get himself in trouble again," she thought.

After three weeks, she was able to return home, but she had to check in with Dr. Hays more regularly than before. Ben encouraged her to go to bed early and she had to admit she tired more easily than before. A few times she noticed he had gone out after she was asleep. Then he stopped bothering with any pretense and flat out told her she was the one who had to take it easy but that was no reason for him to stay home.

"Some of us guys from the Legion have been going to a new club in Goodland. I feel like I know everyone there. It's just harmless fun and most of the people hanging around there are married. So chances are I'll be spending my evenings there. I could take you, after ...ya know ...you're not pregnant." He was backing out the door as he spoke.

Nellie trailed after him, calling down the stairs, "After I am not pregnant, we will have a baby to take care of in the evenings, so no, I don't think I will be going to a speakeasy any time soon! And don't try to crawl all over me when you get back."

This is not fair at all, she thought. Why should he go play with his buddies and the dance hall girls while she stayed home to take care of her health? Maybe when the baby comes, I will let him stay home and take care of it while I go and play around. That would show him.

As her pregnancy progressed, Ben began going out more often and made several hurtful remarks implying she was getting fat.

"I wish you would just stay home," she said simply.

"I can't even dance with my wife anymore, let alone love it up. You should see yourself, it's like you swallowed a balloon," he said with contempt. "You can't blame me for wantin' to spend time with some real dolls."

"You do remember those wedding vows you took a little more than a year ago? You know the part about being faithful unto me and forsaking all others?"

"Hell, I didn't even know what 'forsaking' meant. I still don't know. Don't wanna know either. Besides, there is an exception for when you are having a baby. They don't talk about it when you're gettin' hitched, but everyone knows that when the wife is as big as a house, making whoopee just don't work. The husband has to find some other accommodation. That's the word Wayne used, 'accommodation.' I thought it was pretty funny. Such a big word that just means—"

"Cheating," she supplied.

"No, that's what I am saying. It can't be helped because of the situation. But, go ahead, be mad. You're always mad at me for something. I might as well make it worth it. I'm going to the juice joint."

Men! she thought. She was too disgusted to waste her tears. Are all men so self-centered?

She thought about her father. She couldn't imagine him ever talking to Ida that way. Ida would probably throw a pan at him if he did. Nellie hoped Ben was all talk and no action when he threatened to cheat on her, but she had no way of knowing. She still had never met anyone from his family. After the baby comes, she would make sure that happens. Maybe if she did, she would finally understand his behavior.

On Monday, November 13, Nellie woke up about 8:00 a.m. with alarming pains. Luckily for her, Ben was asleep beside her.

"I think this is it. You'd better fetch the doctor," she gasped.

"But it's too early. The office won't open until nine o'clock," he said, rubbing his eyes.

"Go call his house. I'm having the baby!"

Dr. Hays was on another call and by the time he arrived, he determined it was too late to try to head for the hospital in Goodland. Dr. Hays and Nurse Sarah sent Ben downstairs to go to work.

Mid-morning, Sarah came down to the store and found Ben. "You can come back upstairs now," Sarah said. "You have a handsome son."

He put the "closed" sign on the door as soon as the customers cleared out. He went up to find Nellie cradling the newborn, wrapped in a pink and blue blanket she had made herself.

"You are lucky you weren't up here for the labor. I gripped Sarah's arm so hard, I might have broken it. I think I used every swear word you ever taught me," she laughed ruefully.

"And then some," he agreed.

"What? You don't mean you could hear me?"

"Everyone could hear you. I had to convince old Mrs. Doolittle it was the wind howling. But most of the customers had better hearing than she does."

She laughed until she was crying. "Just tell me my mother didn't come in."

"Oh, no, no, no. If she'da come in, I would have sent her up for a front-row seat to your profanity."

They had talked about baby names the week before and had a short list for boys.

"I want him to have the same initials as me. We might not have another son. I like the name Burl. There was a guy in camp named Burl Ames, and he was a big strong fella. So you go ahead and pick the middle name, as long as it starts with an M, okay?"

"In that case, I am choosing Melvin because I like how that sounds with Burl. If you have a short first name, it is better to have a two-syllable middle name. It just seems to work. We could also use Monroe, your middle name."

"Nah, I think he should get his own name. Besides, my name confuses folks. They shoulda just named me Benjamin because everyone thinks my name is Benjamin. They ain't never heard of Benona. And when I was little, my ma called me Benny. I couldn't get rid of that once I got to school. And Monroe is a perfectly nice name, after a president. But somehow people even misspell that. I am just happy I got an easy last name, but it means you need an unusual first name."

"Well, Burl Melvin, what do you think?" she asked the sleeping infant. "I think he agrees."

The Smith clan enjoyed the new baby over the Thanksgiving

weekend when Ben, Nellie, and Burl stayed over at the farm. Zella came home and brought her latest boyfriend, Herbert Hess. Herb had been born in Arkansas, and done some work in Colorado, before starting a job on a farm nearby. Nellie thought this was what families were supposed to be like, everyone at different stages of life: her nieces, her brothers, her sister, her parents, and now her baby. She thought life would only get better.

They decided to finally visit Ashland for Christmas. Mr. Horney was able to find someone to cover for Ben for a week, and they took the train all the way. Nellie was nervous about meeting her in-laws for the first time.

"It will be fine. You've got the prize now," Ben assured her, glancing at the baby. "We both do."

On the long train ride, he attempted to fill her in on his brothers and sisters, most of whom she would be meeting soon.

"My oldest brother is Frank, it's Joseph Franklin, but he goes by Frank. He still lives in north-central Kansas where I grew up. When the rest of us moved back to Ashland, he was already grown, married, and had kids. Frank is thirteen years older'n me and thinks he's the boss, always. Some people would say he's a 'by the book' guy. To me, he is just a prick. I tried living with him after I left home but he threw me out. That's when I moved to Brewster. We got in a fistfight the last time I saw him after Pa died. I doubt if we will ever get along. Ma told me he wasn't coming for Christmas.

"My sister, Blanche, and I get along fine. She has rotten luck with men. Her first husband, Bill Stewart, was great. They had three children. But he died and she married George Vorse. What a loser he was. She already had three little kids and he wanted to dump his two on her besides. He abandoned her without warning and without money and high-tailed it to Denver. At least he took his kids with him. She's been trying to support her family on her own by dressmaking in Lincoln.

"Ed is the next in line. He was the one I came home to help after the accident. I dunno what it is about Ed, but he always seems to need help. Maybe it's Ma who says that. He's not married, still lives at home.

"We won't get to see William, he lives in Quincy, Illinois. I haven't seen or heard much about him since Pa died, but he's okay.

"Let's see, Claude Americus is next. How'd ja like to have that name? He married Marguerita. She's a real firecracker, much too exciting for Claude. I can't wait to see her again. You will think she is fun too. I think they have a little girl who looks like her mother.

"I had one more brother, Timothy. That is also my grandpa's name. He died at age two. They had me a year after, so I was the replacement kid. I bet they wished he'd survived instead.

"Beulah is younger'n me. She married Elmer Hall after I left home. They have three children, I think. One of them is Ben. They should be there."

Claude and Ed met them at the train station, and Nellie was taken aback at how much Claude looked like a bigger version of Ben. She decided it might be better not to mention that. When they got to Arminta's house, his mother embraced Ben like she hadn't seen him for decades.

"Benny! You too skinny, I can feel your ribs. Are you eating? I feed you here, don't worry. You stopped smoking and drinking, yeah? You are father now, you have to behave," Arminta admonished.

"The baby, Ma. Just look at the baby. Oh, and this is Nellie, my wife," Ben said.

Arminta cupped Nellie's face tightly in her hands. "You have the face of an angel. You must be an angel to marry my Benny. He has the devil in him. I guess ya know by now."

Before Nellie could object, Arminta had whisked the baby out of her arms and was showing little Burl to the rest of the company.

"What did I tell you? My mother," Ben said to Nellie in a low voice. Nellie just smiled, a little overwhelmed with all the relatives in the house.

She sat down in the nearest empty chair, and an adorable little girl of about three with dark ringlets of hair came up to greet her.

"Well, hello there. I'm Nellie. What's your name?" Nellie leaned down to look her in the eyes.

"Ruby." The little one said quite clearly.

Nellie wasn't sure exactly why her eyes filled with tears and she felt like she was going to faint again. Beulah, Ruby's mother, knelt next to Ruby and put her hand on Nellie's knee.

"Are you all right, Honey? What is it?" Beulah asked kindly.

Nellie was so embarrassed, she got up and rushed out of the room, even though she had no idea where she was going.

"Sorry, Beulah," Ben explained. "Ruby was Nellie's sister's name, and she died. Nellie will be fine in a minute." He followed Nellie into what turned out to be the kitchen.

"I'm sorry, Ben. I've already made a fool of myself in front of your family in the first five minutes!"

"No, don't worry. If you cause a little drama here, you fit right in." He put his arm around her and brought her back into the living room.

There were times when he was truly sweet, she thought. She just wished it happened more often.

She'd waited a long time to meet Ben's family. Over the next few days, she curled up in the corner in Arminta's antique rocking chair, holding Burl even if he was sleeping. If anyone else was sitting in the rocker, Arminta made them move so Nellie could sit there with the baby. It gave her a good vantage point to study the family, and how they all interacted. For the most part, she could see Ben's assessment of the others was correct.

His sisters seemed to both dote on him and ask him for advice. They were under the impression he owned the general store now. At one point, Blanche asked Nellie to convince Ben to move to Lincoln, because she relied on his counsel, and Burl could see his cousins, who were now teenagers. Beulah's three children were all little. In addition to Ruby, there was six-year-old Ben, and Colleen, who, at age one, was trying to walk.

Edward barely acknowledged Nellie, and she noticed he rarely got a chance to speak while his siblings dominated any conversation. She decided he was the shy one. Ben was right about Marguerita. She made a grand entrance when she arrived, demanding to hold the baby and smothering him with kisses. Nellie could only laugh and comply. Marguerita was trailed by her toddler Doris, another dark-haired beauty.

Nellie thought Claude had married a woman like his mother, Arminta. Both women were pushy, but Nellie enjoyed watching them trying to get everyone to do what they wanted. She did see why Ben got mad when she tried to reign him in. His mother had done that to him his whole life.

On Christmas Day, Ben seemed surprised when his brother, William Perry came to dinner. William said he'd moved to Lincoln about a year ago, but he was lucky the acting governor didn't extradite him to Illinois. He said he would tell them about the terrible week he'd had after dinner. When he pulled Ben out onto the porch, Nellie went along, not wanting to miss this story. William offered them both cigarettes.

"I don't know what got into Helen, my wife. I came back to Nebraska after Pa died two years ago and decided to stay. I thought it might be better to be closer to Ma. I worked for Burlington Railroad, but I was injured and then laid off. Helen came once but left again. There wasn't much of a place to stay; the workers were sleeping in boxcars. Even after I left the railroad work and started selling nursery stock, she refused to come back. I've tried everything to get her to move here for the last two years. So in February, I filed for divorce and she didn't respond."

He took a couple of drags on his cigarette and continued the story. "So here I'm thinking I just have to wait for the court case. On Wednesday, these Illinois deputy sheriffs show up at my workplace and tell me I am under arrest for wife abandonment! I was dumbstruck. I had to spend one night in jail until my lawyer got me out the next day. Two days later, I had to go before the acting governor so he wouldn't send me back to stand trial in Illinois. Acting Governor Pelham Barrows is a real horse's ass on top of everything else. Barrows was pushing around all the attorneys and his own staff just to show everyone he was in power. He got mad at my attorney at one point and was going to sign my extradition papers just to piss off my lawyer. But my lawyer apologized and Barrows backed down."

"Anyway, Helen is claiming I left her destitute, which was never what I intended. Apparently, she told her lawyer I should pay her thirty-five dollars every two weeks, which was twice what I was making. That made no sense at all. I'm sure there will be some chance to settle things up if they don't throw me in the hoosegow. I'll tell you, I don't know if I'd ever get married again after this."

He cast a wounded look at Nellie after that last remark.

"And the rest of the family doesn't know about this?" Nellie asked tilting her head toward the house.

"Hell yes. They all know. It was on the front page of the local newspaper. Twice."

Ben whistled. "I'm surprised you didn't go out and get rip-roaring drunk."

William said, "I wanted to. With my luck, I'd probably get arrested for that."

By their last evening in Ashland, everyone had gone home except Ed. They were sitting in the living room, and Nellie was admiring the family portrait hanging on the wall. Nellie wondered aloud about Ben's father, "Tell me about Marshall."

Arminta looked a little uncomfortable and Nellie assumed she was still grieving. She began apologizing, but Arminta stopped her.

"Marshall was fine man, good husband, good father. He was a Teamster, ya know. He protected his family and worked hard, but he was demanding. He didn't put up with backtalk from the children. No sass. No siree. His word was law. Frank is like Marshall. He had to follow the rules, but when we got down to little Benny, things were looser. Frank always said we were too easy on Benny and Claude."

"You always knew where you stood with Pa," Ed said. "But you'd better run when he got out the strap." Ed and Ben laughed, but Nellie wasn't sure how that could be funny.

"Remember that time he made me paint Grandpa's barn?" Ben asked his mother. "He didn't like the way I said somethin' or other, and I had to paint all day long. I could barely move the next day. I think I was about ten."

"That's nothing. He threw me in the river, and told me to learn to swim," Ed said.

"They are exaggerating, Honey," Arminta said when Nellie's eyes got big. "He loved his children, but he showed them the world was a tough place and they had to be ready."

By the next day, Ben and Nellie were both eager to board the train for home.

"So now do you see—?" Ben started to say after they were en route.

"I see," she interrupted and leaned against him, swaddling the baby once more.

It was just after quitting time one day in late January when Ben walked into the kitchen like he was in a trance and plopped down on a chair. "Nellie, guess what Mr. Horney told me? He's selling the damn store. I'll be out of a job and we'll probably have to find somewhere else to live."

"What are you talking about?" Nellie asked, trying to get her fidgeting infant to nurse. "I don't know why Burl is fussy today. He is usually hungry."

"Maybe he knows our whole fucking world is blowing up."

"Start from the beginning. What exactly did Mr. Horney say?" She put the baby on her shoulder to comfort him.

"He just told me he and the wife talked it over at Christmas and they are going to retire and move to Colorado. No one in his family wants the store. He asked me if I wanted to buy it, but he already has someone from another town who offered him a fair price. There's no way I could come up with that kind of dough. He didn't mention the apartment, but it's part of the building, so I guess we're out on our asses."

"But he didn't say you would be fired or that we couldn't keep living here?" she tried to clarify.

"No, but the new owner is probably planning to run the place and will need a place to stay here."

"I think you are jumping to conclusions. Let's wait until you know more. There may be ways you could raise the cash. What if my father or your brothers wanted to invest?" She stood up and walked back and forth with the baby on her shoulder, as he seemed to be drifting off.

"I suppose we could think about it, but I can't see me working in this place forever. I mean I would like to have my own business but without all them overhead expenses. There is a lot invested in inventory here," Ben said. "Maybe this is a sign we should move on."

"Move on? Like where?"

"Well, my sister is still begging me to move to Lincoln, Nebraska, to be near her. I dunno. Didn't your parents say there was a small farmhouse their neighbor wanted to rent? I don't see myself raising crops and all. You have to have so many acres for crops here. Maybe we could have some animals … pigs or milk cows … or ducks."

"That might be nice. It would be closer to my parents' place, and the nieces could come over and play with the baby."

He kept working as before and they didn't discuss it again for a few weeks, until one evening when Nellie said, "I think my mother talked to her neighbor about their farmhouse for rent."

"I have been working on another idea. Have you ever sewn a man's suit?" Ben asked. "I mean, I know you have made dresses, shirts, and clothes for your nieces, but a man's suit has to fit pretty well or it just looks cheap."

"I made suits for my brothers when they were about sixteen and eighteen. They turned out nicely, but they were still growing and grew out of them."

"Do they still have them? Maybe we could use them as samples."

"You've lost me, Ben."

"Well, this was Mr. Horney's idea. He feels kinda bad about me losing my job right after the baby. He sent me to Goodland to talk to this Mrs. Borne. She and her husband have a tailor shop and they want to expand to Brewster. They are in a partnership with a place called Strauss Brothers, and that's where they get all of their nice fabrics. They make suits for men and boys, and do hat cleaning, blocking, alterations, pressing, cleaning, and repairs. She said they updated some of their equipment last year, so they would let me use the old things, just to see how much business we could do here. But with you being a master seamstress, it seemed like it might make sense."

"But when would I have time with a baby?" she asked.

"You could manage. Blanche is working as a dressmaker and has three children and no husband."

Yes, but they are not babies, she thought. "You'd have to learn to do everything but the sewing part. Could you handle that? Could you operate those machines, and block and clean hats?"

"I'd have to learn, of course, but Mr. Borne would teach me. Ya know my brother, William, opened up a cleaners and pressing place in Lincoln, so how hard could it be? And here is the best thing: Mr. Horney said he would put up the money for the startup costs. He even said maybe I could start it in one of the back rooms of the store, as long as the new owner is okay with that. I think this could be what I have been looking for." She could see he was getting excited about this new venture.

"And where would we live? Can we stay here?" she asked, still not sure he had thought this through.

"Well, that part is not clear. I'd have to see what the new owner of the store wants to do. There may be other places we could put the business with apartments above them. The block across the way, where the newspaper is, might have some space." He was already planning it in his head.

Nellie thought he was charging ahead without much consideration for the risks. Within a few weeks, they were moving across the street and opening a storefront north of the newspaper office. Ben got the equipment from the Bornes and took out an advertisement for his tailoring and cleaning establishment before she even knew about it.

"Nellie! I need help down here!" Ben hollered up the staircase.

"Coming!" She was halfway down the stairs when Burl let out a wail: the noise woke him from his mid-morning nap. She crept softly down the stairs, hoping the baby would fall back asleep.

"Mr. Donovan here needs to be measured for his new suit. This fabric will be a perfect choice for spring weather," Ben said. Nellie took out her measuring tape and pencil and began recording the measurements she needed. Burl, meanwhile, kept up his insistent bawling, like an automobile engine throttling up. When she got down on her knees to take the inseam measurement, the client insisted she go check on her baby.

A few minutes later, she returned with a sniveling Burl, and handed him off to her husband, and resumed her measuring task.

"Nellie, the baby needs to be changed," Ben complained, wrinkling his nose.

"I will take care of that when I am done. Or why don't you go ahead and change him while I finish with Mr. Donovan?" Ben held the baby at arm's length and took him outdoors instead, and Burl resumed howling in the cool March wind. Mr. Donovan seemed to be in a hurry to get out of the room after that. After he left, Ben and Burl came back inside.

"Nellie, you can't bring the baby into the business. How do you think that looks? And smells, for God's sake. This is supposed to be a sophisticated shop."

"Mr. Donovan told me to go tend to the baby. It wouldn't kill you to change his diapers you know."

"It might." Ben handed Burl back to her and covered his mouth and nose with his hand.

That was just one of the kinks they had to work out in their system, she thought. Burl was not napping as long anymore, which gave her less time to work on the sewing. She thought about asking one of her nieces to come to help her after school, but one day she was busy, and the next day there was no new business.

Ben's response to the business getting off to a slow start was to add something else.

"Look at this deal I found! They were selling this shoe repair business in Goodland, and I was able to buy all of their tools and supplies for a song. This will be a great addition to the tailoring shop. I am going to start advertising that tomorrow." Ben started unloading the boxes he'd just bought. "Maybe we can even make Burl his first pair of shoes."

"Ben, I love your enthusiasm, but do you know the first thing about repairing shoes?"

"Not yet, but I will learn when I have a customer."

Ben didn't like having time on his hands, or at least that was the way it seemed to Nellie. As long as he had work to do, he kept busy. But she noticed he wasn't good at sitting around waiting for customers. After a month or so, once the weather improved, he started leaving in mid-afternoon. He'd lock up the shop, but customers sometimes pounded on the door, thinking he must be upstairs. Nellie would have to go down to see what their business was about. He never told her where he was going, but it was pretty clear when he came home drunk after she and the baby had gone to bed.

"Ben, a couple of gentlemen I didn't know came by to have their shoes shined yesterday. Are you doing shoe shining now? I didn't know what to tell them, and it made me uncomfortable being alone in the shop with two strange men. Where did you go?"

"It's important to go out and meet new people when you have your own business. I will have to go to Goodland more often for that. I put the sign out we were closed. They shouldn't bother you."

"But you don't even tell me you are leaving …" she began.

He raised his index finger. "Don't give me any crap, Nellie. I'm warning you. I got enough problems."

She dropped it after that. She started going to her parents' farm one afternoon a week so they could see the baby, catching a ride with Zella. It didn't take long before they ran out of money. They were two months behind on rent. The business was not breaking even, and they didn't have another income to supplement it. They sold off what they could and had to give up the apartment in town.

Ben was surly on the day they had to move in with her parents.

She thought he would have left town that day, except he had no cash for gas let alone liquor.

"This is your fault. People told me they came to the store on Thursday afternoons when I was out drumming up business, and you weren't there to help them. And how many of those suits have you made or repaired? That was supposed to be the money maker."

"I did all of the orders you gave me," she said. "Maybe Brewster was just too small a town for that kind of business."

"Ya know nothing about it." He stomped out and brooded on the back porch, cursing that he'd even run out of smokes.

It might have been more accurate to say she and Burl moved in with her parents. Ben was rarely there and didn't want to explain his whereabouts to any of them. She told her family he was working on the next project, but again, Ida saw right through her brave front. At least with her mother and nieces there to entertain little Burl, Nellie could start sewing again. She was able to get some clients by advertising in the local paper without much expense.

At the beginning of the year, Ben's mother sent him the train fare to go back to Nebraska for a month to help with a new crisis with his sister, Blanche. When he came back to Brewster, he was ready to start the next endeavor. He suddenly seemed to have some capital to invest but didn't tell Nellie where it had come from.

"One of the neighbors is willing to sell me five dairy cows," he explained one evening at the Smiths' dinner table. "I've been talking to the new store owner in Brewster. He said if I bring milk to the store every morning, he would sell it for me. I also think I could line up some customers who would want fresh milk delivered every day or every other day. Do you suppose I could keep the cows in your barn until we can afford a place again?"

Arthur looked dubiously at Ben, but then caught a glimpse of little Burl tottering across the room babbling to himself.

"On one condition. You and Nellie have to take complete responsibility for the cows. Cows need to be milked twice a day, they have to be fed or put out to pasture, and the stalls have to be cleaned out. Whatever they need, it is up to you two. If one of my sons has to do any cow chores, or if I have to step in because you went to Goodland and got yourself drunk, those cows will be mine. The very first time. And I want that in writing."

Nellie said, "Of course, Daddy." She looked at Ben, who was turning red.

"You ain't the one I'm worried about, Missy."

"Understood," Ben said, obviously uncomfortable. He seemed surprised that Arthur was being so inflexible.

Later that night, Ben asked his wife, "When exactly did your father become so goddamned hard-nosed?"

"Probably about the time we moved into his house. He has never approved of drinking." Nellie smiled to herself. "It will be okay, you'll see."

Nellie kept her sewing business going, but got up every morning to milk cows and feed them while Ben delivered milk in town. He did the evening milking and chores. He was so tired by the end of the day, he didn't mention going out, even when he started to accumulate some savings. Things were finally looking up again. Little Burl was into everything. He thrived on the farm and seemed to love all of the attention from the extended family.

Zella invited Herb Hess to Easter dinner and they announced they were getting married in August. Zella wanted Nellie to help her with her wedding dress and they immediately started making plans.

One Sunday afternoon in mid-May, Nellie was outside weeding

the garden. Bertie Robinson drove up in his truck. His sons Everett and Keith, who were about the same ages as Nellie's brothers, were with him, along with his friends, John Lister, John McDaniels, and Fred Sussex, in a separate car. Nellie stood up to greet them.

"Is Arthur inside?" Bertie asked briskly. He was not smiling, which wasn't like him.

"Sure, do you want me to get him, Bertie?"

"No, Nellie. You should stay out here. We have some business to discuss." All six men went into the house. Cousin Bertie had been there many times, so she wasn't surprised when he knocked quickly and all six men walked into the house. Suddenly, it occurred to her they may be bringing bad news. Maybe someone was hurt in town. She ran through a mental checklist and everyone in her family was nearby, even Zella was indoors talking to her mother. In a few minutes, her father called out to her.

"Nellie, go fetch Harry from the barn. We need to speak to him right away."

What would all these older men want with twenty-two-year-old Harry? She found Ben, Harry, and Verner in the barn trying to throw a rope over the rafters so they could swing from the hayloft to the ground floor.

"Harry, there's a bunch of men up at the house who need to speak to you. Bertie and Keith and Everett, and several others. Daddy said to come on," Nellie called out.

"Oh, God!" Harry wailed. "She must have told her parents."

Nellie, Ben, and Verner all looked at Harry in surprise.

"Who told her parents what?" Ben asked, putting a hand under Harry's arm when he looked like his knees were buckling.

"Lucina Mae?" Verner guessed. Ben and Nellie looked at him like he knew something more. Lucina was closer to Verner's age than Harry's, but still three years his junior.

"Lucina told me last night she thought she was…*um…* knocked up." Harry cleared his throat. "We decided we were going to check it out at the doctor next week, but it sounds like she must have told Bertie."

"What? How old's Lucina? Ain't she still in grammar school?" Ben said.

"*Uhmmm.* …she is seventeen. She just turned seventeen." His voice squeaked like it had when his voice changed.

Nellie opened her mouth but couldn't find any words. This was the last thing she expected from her kid brother who was playing pirates in the barn moments ago.

Harry looked like he might start crying. "What do you think they are going to do to me? They can't put me in jail, can they, Ben?"

"Nope, the age of consent in Kansas is sixteen. It's not illegal if she was willing. But you better get up there," Ben said, giving Harry a gentle push toward the house, "before they come after you …with shotguns." Harry turned around in panic.

"He's kidding, Harry. Go!" Nellie pointed at the house. Harry slowly gathered his courage, walked up, and disappeared into the house.

"I can't believe it. I didn't know they were seeing each other," Nellie exclaimed.

"I think they kept it secret," Verner said.

"But you knew," Nellie countered, turning on him.

"We share a room. I figured it out."

"Wait a minute, isn't Lucina Mae your cousin?" Ben asked.

"Sort of. Bertie and Mom are first cousins through Grandma Hen and Aunt Carrie being sisters, and Dad and Bertie are first cousins through Uncle David and Grandma Annie being brother and sister. So Harry and Lucina are second cousins. Like double second cousins. By the way, how do you know what the age of consent is?"

Ben shrugged, "Came up once when I was in the army. Just the kinda thing every man should know."

Verner looked up at the house. "I wouldn't want to be in his shoes right now. Dad's gonna skin him alive."

"If Bertie doesn't beat him to it," Ben added.

Harry and Lucina were married in Salina the following weekend without any violence involved. Bertie had some connections across the state in Abilene and arranged for Harry to get a job there before it became obvious Lucina was in a family way.

In June, Zella announced at dinner they had decided to have their wedding in Hays. It would be closer for Herb's relatives if they came from Arkansas. After the wedding, they would go on to Abilene for a few days for their honeymoon. That way, they could visit Harry and Lucina.

Both Ben and Arthur looked doubtful. "That's too far for us to go," Arthur said. "We are milking cows, and Ben here is selling milk every day. If you can't get married within an hour or so of here, we can't go. It's that simple."

Zella looked crushed. "You're making me choose between one family and the other," she cried. "Nellie, you have to come. I need you to be my attendant."

"We'll have to see, Zella. I have a child now, and I have been milking every day too."

Zella and Herb left abruptly. In the end, it was decided Arthur and Ben would stay home to tend to the milking, along with help from Verner. Ida and Nellie, along with Burl, would attend Zella's wedding. They had to change trains at Stockton, so the train ride took all day, which meant they had to stay overnight in Hays.

Ben wasn't happy with Nellie when they got back to the farm. "Don't ever do that again. You left a ten-year-old to cook for us, and we had to do all your work and your mother's besides. What was your stupid sister thinking getting married halfway across the state? I bet she expects your folks to throw her some kind of reception here because no one showed up at her wedding. Arthur was steamed about it too."

She was expecting her father to take the same attitude when she served him breakfast at dawn the next morning, but he only smiled and said he was glad they were back safely.

A year later in October, thirty-year-old Zella had a baby boy, Verner Arthur. Nellie couldn't have been more excited when she took three-year-old Burl to the Hess farm to visit the baby Art.

"Look at us, Zella. How perfect is this? We both got little boys and they can grow up together just like we did," Nellie said. Harry and Lucina Mae's child was a son too, Adelbert, but he was still in Abilene. "Oh, I sure hope Herb has given up that idea about moving back to Arkansas."

Despite encouraging Zella to stay near home, Nellie was beginning to wonder how much longer she could expect Ben to be happy on the farm. They had finally moved to their own place, but that just meant they didn't have family members to help out with the child care or chores. Taking a day off was out of the question. Ben had bought five horses and five pigs, in addition to the cows, so there were many animals with just the two of them to care for. She no longer had time to sew, and missed that. For one thing, it was cleaner. Nowadays she felt like she was always up to her knees in mud and manure. And trying to keep a little boy out of the muck was impossible.

She could tell Ben was wearing down from all the farm work too. He was drinking more now that her parents were not watching over them, and he'd even found someone nearby to supply him with moonshine. Nellie tasted it and found it horrible. But she got her prescription refilled and started drinking vodka again in the evening. More than once, she forgot to put little Burl down for the night. Fortunately, Lazetta, now eleven, had come to stay with them to help with Burl, and she quickly became skilled at getting him to sleep and putting out forgotten cigarettes.

"Nell, if I said I wanted us to move to Lincoln, Nebraska, what would you do? I know your family ties are here in Kansas. I just want to be sure you wouldn't pull a stunt like William's wife did and refuse to follow me." They had been up most of the night with a sow having piglets, and were trying to wake up, sipping pre-dawn coffee in front of the stove in the kitchen.

"Of course I'd go with you. I don't know what happened between William and his wife, but that's not normal. It sounded like revenge to me," she said, yawning.

"Okay, good. I got a letter from William, and he said I could come to stay with him for a week or a month while I look for a job. He said Lincoln is growing quickly and there are jobs available. The railroad is hiring, and the phone company and they need men to work on the streets. William runs a dry cleaning place. It's not very big, but he said he can always use a good seamstress to repair clothes. You could work for him. If he don't have enough work for you, he knows all of them cleaners in town. I think he said he bowls with them. I don't know when he took up bowling, for Christ's sake, but I guess he is pretty good at it." Ben said.

"You've been planning this a while."

"Before I leave, we'll sell all of the livestock and anything else we don't want to take. Once I get a job, I'll send for you and Burl. But it might be easier if I have some money coming in first. That way, we could get our own place when you come."

"When are you planning on doing this? Burl will be four in November, and it would probably be best if he started school there," Nellie said.

Ben looked at her curiously, "You don't mind moving? Here I expected you to have a problem with this."

"You know what?" she groaned slightly, resting her head on her hands. "I don't think either one of us was cut out to be farmers."

Ben laughed. "That may be the truest thing you ever said."

She agreed with her husband that moving to a larger city was best for all of them. In particular, she thought her child would get a better education and wouldn't have to leave school to help with the farming as her brothers had done.

Ben didn't waste much time putting the plan in motion. By September, everything was sold, and he left on the train for Lincoln. Nellie, Lazetta, and Burl moved back to her parents' farm.

"I will miss seeing little Art grow up. And I will miss Lazetta and Beth too, they are just becoming young ladies," Nellie told Zella, who was helping her pack some things. "Can you believe we have been here for ten years? I can still see those two little girls chasing around after Grandma Hen's chickens."

"Just tell me you will be back for nice long visits," Zella said.

She decided it was time to start calling her son Mel, short for Melvin, his middle name. If he was going to start school soon, he would have to tell all the new children his name and they might think Burl was too unfamiliar. Children can be cruel, she thought, even if they don't mean to be. She worked with him for a week or two, until he would always say his name was Mel when she prompted him. I should have done this before he learned to talk, she chided herself.

By mid-October, Nellie got the train tickets from Ben. He had gotten a job with the Chicago, Burlington & Quincy Railroad Company, commonly called Burlington. One of the best things about working for a railroad, he said, was they got standby railway tickets for next to nothing, so she could travel back to see her folks, or they could come to visit her. He said he was a machinist helper, and it was hard work but he was excited about learning the job. She said a tearful good-bye to her parents, sister Zella, brother Verner, her nieces, and nephew, and set out with little Mel for the big city.

CHAPTER FOUR

On the long train ride to Lincoln, Nellie sat next to an older man who said he was writing a book about the history of the American railroads.

"If your husband is working for a railroad, he is likely to be injured, and almost guaranteed to be laid off every year. That's the reality of the rail industry today," he said soberly. "Yes, ma'am, the railroads were once the lifeline to the American West, but the railroad industry has suffered greatly in the last twenty-five years, and the federal government took control over it during the Great War. The Chicago, Burlington & Quincy is one of many railroads competing for hauling goods to market. You know the farmers complained to the government about rate gouging for hauling their crops, so the government responded by lowering rates. The railroads tried to save on expenses by cutting wages, idling their rolling stock, and eliminating the less profitable routes. And there are several unions involved in representing railroad workers, and they use labor strikes to improve conditions. It's not like it used to be."

"Farming is not like it used to be either," Nellie answered. "We are hoping this move will be better for our son." She stroked Mel's back as he leaned against her sleeping.

Ben worked in the maintenance shop. Because he was unskilled and had very little seniority, he was one of the first to be laid off three months later. He was told he should be ready to come back any time if he wanted to continue to work for the railroad, although he was free to work elsewhere while he was furloughed.

So he was not working the first winter they spent in Lincoln, but he expected the layoff to be short-lived. Nellie was working part-time for his brother, William, at his cleaning and pressing store. William would drop off piece work to their apartment and she would estimate when she could complete it so he could return for it. Once they had a little money put aside, they decided they needed a telephone. This made it possible for Burlington to reach Ben, and Nellie could communicate with William. It was also nice to know family members could contact them more quickly if something urgent came up, even though long-distance was an expensive option.

Little Mel was doing a good job adapting to life in the city, although Nellie missed letting him run outside and play on the farm. There were other children in their building and on the block. Nellie was happy to have time to watch her child grow, and marveled at everything he learned.

Ben wasn't called back to work for five months the first time. He made a little money delivering cleaning for William and found a few other odd jobs, but it was getting hard to make ends meet. He had made a few friends during his short time at the railroad, and they knew where to go to get a drink in their town, even though Prohibition was still the law of the nation.

Early in August, Nellie got a letter from Zella, saying she thought she was pregnant. Nellie had to admit her first reaction was she was a little envious. She hoped for another child herself.

"Ben, can you get me one of those family vouchers for train fare back to Brewster?" she asked after studying the letter. "I am worried about Zella."

"Why, what is wrong with your sister? Are you homesick?"

"I dunno. It's like a premonition. Zella said she thinks she's pregnant and she keeps vomiting. The doctor thinks it is more than morning sickness. I believe there is something wrong with her, and I should go there. The last time I felt like this, Ruby was sick and she died."

He gave her a look like he thought she was a little crazy. "Well, I guess you could use a break. I will check on the tickets tomorrow.

You're taking Mel too?"

By the evening of August 24th, Nellie and Mel were on the train back to Kansas.

Verner met them the next morning at the train station and told her Zella was in the Goodland hospital. Her parents, Lazetta, Beth, little Art, and Herb were all there. Nellie didn't want to take Mel to the hospital, but it seemed like everyone who could watch him was there.

When she got to the hospital, her mother hugged her tightly and dissolved into tears. Nellie realized she had hardly ever seen Ida cry except for at Ruby's funeral, so that made her even more concerned. Everyone in the family was happy to see her and Mel, but they were all very worried about Zella. Herb had brought his wife in when she complained of abdominal pain and kept vomiting. Dr. Runnes told them he thought it might be an ectopic pregnancy, where an embryo implants in the fallopian tube rather than the uterus. The symptoms were also common to gallstones or an ulcer. They planned to do surgery the next day.

Arthur and Verner decided to take the children back to the farm. There wasn't anything for them to do in the hospital waiting area, and they would not be allowed to see Zella. When Nellie had a turn to visit with Zella, she couldn't believe how pale she looked.

"Nellie, thank goodness you came," Zella said in a frail voice. "I need you to help Herbert. He will be lost if something happens to me. I don't know if he can take care of little Art."

"Don't talk like that," Nellie said. "You're going to be here to take care of your son." She took Zella's hand but was surprised her grip seemed so lifeless.

"No, listen to me. I can hear Ruby. She is calling me. I know that sounds crazy, but I feel like I know what she felt like before she died. I know you came because you can feel it too. It is some kind of sister connection. You came to say good-bye. I am so glad you did," Zella murmured. "I need you to help Mom and Dad get through this too. You've always been the strong one. Look how you whipped that no-good husband of yours into shape."

Nellie laughed, but she was crying now. "You've never given Ben much of a chance. He's doing all right now. You'll get past this, and you can all come to Lincoln to see us."

The nurse came in to take Zella's temperature and told Nellie to leave and to send in Zella's husband.

Nellie did her best to comfort Ida, but Zella was right. The nagging panic she had was back. The next day, Arthur came back and waited with them during the surgery. Afterward, Dr. Runnes told them Zella might not come around for a while and they should go home. No one left, but only Herb was allowed in to see her. Zella regained consciousness, only to start vomiting again. The doctor was summoned. An hour later, the doctor reappeared to tell them Zella had died.

The next few days were a haze. Nellie saw her family alternate between operating by rote and falling apart. Herb didn't know what he should do, but Arthur helped him purchase a cemetery plot in Brewster for Zella, then he decided he should get two more: for himself and his little son, so someday they would be there together. The funeral was a small family affair. Nellie decided that she and Mel should stay a few more days to support her parents and Herb.

Young Art seemed to enjoy having Mel there to play with, and she thought how nice it was to be as oblivious as the children were. As Nellie sat and watched Mel entertaining his little cousin by trying to catch a baby pig, she had another tearful premonition. Somehow she knew that Herb would take the boy back to Arkansas to rejoin the Hess family. She would never see either of them again.

They say there is a calm before the storm. Nellie would think of the aftermath of Zella's death as the calm between storms. Ben had been afraid to take off work to come to Zella's funeral, with the job situation being so tenuous, but she was grateful he seemed to sense she needed his support when she and Mel returned home.

"Ya know, your sister never liked me," Ben said out of the blue one evening when Nellie seemed to be feeling depressed. "She didn't want you to marry me."

"I think she changed her mind. You must have liked her though," Nellie smiled slightly. "You did ask her out first."

"Because she told me you were married and had them two little girls. If I'd understood what she meant, I would have asked you out instead. You were the purdy one."

Nellie wiped away a tear. "Zella told me I was the strong one."

He put his arms around her and whispered, "You can be both."

He worked hard during the day but was home with his family at night when he wasn't working overtime, and they managed to put some savings away. He even started turning over most of his weekly pay to her when he discovered their nest egg was growing if he didn't spend anything. They had managed to do without a car since they'd moved to the city, and it was one of the things they were saving for now.

"William, I think Ben and I should open a bank account. How do you go about that?" Nellie asked her brother-in-law when she was working with him.

"I don't think you should do that right now, Nellie. I told Ben as much. From what I have seen in the newspapers, the economic climate is too risky. People have been spending money like it is burning a hole in their pocketbooks. Something is going to give. I am putting my extra money in real estate. I bought a big house, which should grow in value. I can take in tenants if I need to. If I were you, I would hang onto your savings."

She assumed William knew something she didn't and continued hiding her money in various locations in the apartment.

Mel had started school the previous year, in January of 1928. He attended the new Prescott School, which was about eleven blocks from their apartment. Now that he was in school, Nellie could work more hours. William didn't have enough work for her, so she worked at Modern Cleaners and Lincoln Cleaning & Dye Works. They had been able to purchase a used car so she could take Ben to work if he didn't catch the bus, take Mel to school, and drive to work.

Nellie decided the time was right to have another child. She missed having a little one at home and thought that at thirty-three, she might be getting a little old to have a child. Besides, things seemed to be going well for them financially and she thought she could go back to doing piece work at home if there was a baby.

But she had read enough in the ladies' magazines they kept at the cleaners to know she couldn't rely on the haphazard schedule of marital relations that they had fallen into. Most of the time, they hadn't even bothered with birth control. Between both of them working and a young child afoot, they weren't connecting very often anymore. According to the article she'd read, it was up to the wife if she wanted to encourage more attention from her husband.

Once she dropped a few hints about having a drink and going to bed early, it didn't take her husband long to join her. Sometimes, he'd even put their son to bed himself. All that was left to do was track her cycles on her calendar and hope for the desired result.

"Congratulations, Mrs. Johnson, you are indeed having a baby,"

Dr. Gerhardt told her at her appointment in June. "A little dividend should arrive by the end of the year."

"Gee, it worked just like it said in the magazine," Nellie told him pulling a small calendar out of her bag. "See, I have been writing down when I have been having my periods on this calendar every month. Two weeks later, the dates I circled, are when I was most likely to get pregnant."

"Interesting. I read something in a medical journal about that sort of thing. But the medical experts say that what you have marked there is the 'safe period' for couples who are trying to avoid having a baby. I guess you were just lucky," Her doctor smiled condescendingly.

Ben acted surprised this could even happen. "You're sure you want to go through that again? I mean not just having the baby, but the whole business of raising the kid? It just got easier now Mel is in school most of the day. You want to start over?"

"It looks like we're going to. I guess I have been thinking more about it since I lost Zella. I would like to have a daughter. But even if it turns out to be a boy, I don't think I will want any more than this."

Ben's attitude seemed to be that the baby was her problem, not his. He had been working pretty steadily over the past year and had taken on a new position as a locomotive packer. This meant he was often gone overnight as he traveled with the train. When he came home, he was covered in coal dust. They found a bigger place and moved in there in October when she was about seven months into her pregnancy.

Just a few days after they moved, Ben was laid off. That had happened several times already so he wasn't alarmed, except it seemed a lot more men were being furloughed with him on the same day. The rumor going around the union ranks was that Burlington was suffering from losses in the last few quarters and was making major cuts.

When the news about the bank failures broke, Nellie heard her neighbors and co-workers talking about storming their banks and being told they couldn't give them their own money, and she was very thankful she had held onto her cash. Now her only concern was someone would break into their house and steal her stash.

CHAPTER FIVE

"Good morning, Mrs. Johnson, I am here for the rent," her landlord said, standing at her front door.

"Of course, Mr. Hansen, come on in while I go get it. It's cold today."

She came back with an envelope filled with dollar bills. She stopped short and frowned as she counted them. "I don't understand. I had the rent money right here, but now twenty dollars is missing."

He took the envelope from her and counted it himself. "When will you have the rest? Before next month?"

"Yes, of course. You must believe me. It was all there two days ago."

"Don't look so frightened, Dear. Hard times have hit us all. I had to evict three families who were two or three months behind in their rent. They had their money in the bank and now they can't get it. As long as you are caught up by next month, I will understand."

"That's why I have kept my money in a safe spot at home. Only me and my husband know …" Of course, Ben, she realized. He had taken the money to go out drinking with his friends. She found a new hiding place for her stash and tried to work extra hours in the next month, but that was hard to do so close to her due date.

"Nellie, where is the money?" Ben bellowed, as soon as she walked in the door a week later. "I've looked everywhere. Don't tell me it was stolen."

She had put some in the hole in the closet wall just that morning, so she was pretty sure it was still there. "I moved it. We need it for rent and food and gas. Everything is tight right now with you off work."

He grabbed her arm roughly. "That's my money. You can't hide it from me. I can't go out without my money."

She shook her arm away and looked at him coldly. She could smell he'd probably already consumed whatever liquor they had in the house. "Fine. How much do you need tonight? I got paid today." He accepted a ten-dollar bill and stormed out of the house. She didn't see him again for two days.

They hadn't planned to do much for Christmas. The whole country was in the middle of a financial crisis. The three previous years they had gone to Arminta's in Ashland, but they both wanted to stay home this time. That turned out to be lucky for them, as Nellie went into labor just after midnight on Christmas. They called Ben's sister, Blanche, to come and watch Mel, and drove in lightly falling snow to the hospital. Little Donald Dean was one of three babies born in the Lincoln hospital on Christmas Day.

Blanche came over to visit a few weeks later. "One of the ladies I sew for, her husband said this is the worst economic depression our country has ever seen. He says the federal government doesn't even know how to solve the problems," she said, lighting her cigarette.

"Yeah, I picked a great time to add another mouth to feed, didn't I?" Nellie agreed. "The newspaper said in Omaha people are living on the street and standing in line at soup kitchens. Ben has had no luck finding another job. I can't work much with a newborn."

"I heard William had to close his cleaning business and take a job selling cars. At least cars are still in demand. His new wife, Esther, took a job as a beautician, and they took on four lodgers in their house. Can you believe it?"

Ben's loyalty to the railroad was rewarded to some extent when they brought him back as a locomotive packer after he was furloughed for a few months each year in 1929, 1930, and 1931. It was still hard, dirty, physical labor, and required him to be gone overnights, but with the overtime, he was making pretty good wages compared to most of the community. He had stopped turning over all of his pay to Nellie because he didn't want to ask her for spending cash, so she never really knew how much he was bringing home. She just made do with what he gave her.

After they'd left Kansas, she no longer had to worry about hiding Ben's drinking from her parents. However, when her father, Arthur Smith, died suddenly in 1933, her mother started making plans to move to Lincoln to be near Nellie and the boys. She knew she should invite her mother to live with them, but thought that would be disastrous. Ida moved in with another widow who needed some live-in help instead.

She'd come to accept Ben had two versions of himself. When he was working, he was on the job every day. He was scheduled to work for two or three days straight as a packer then had a few days off. He usually took those days to recuperate. But when he was furloughed, he went back to drinking heavily and she wouldn't know where he was half of the time.

If she objected to him going out with his friends they ended up arguing and he'd storm off anyway. After a while, she understood the arguments were pointless and she didn't like the children hearing them. Mel, at ten, was beginning to pay more attention to what was going on between his parents and would try to defend her.

One evening when Ben was furloughed and he had too much to drink, he got into an argument with Nellie and she told him to leave. He started to shove her, but Mel stepped in the middle and all three of them ended up sprawled on the floor.

"Stop it!" Don screamed, running into the kitchen in his pajamas before his mother grabbed him.

"You think these here boys are going to be on your side, don't cha?" Ben shouted at Nellie, standing up unsteadily. "Don't forget who the boss is in this family!"

By the end of 1933, Congress had passed the twenty-first amendment, and enough states had ratified it to close the book on Prohibition. Even after the repeal of Prohibition, there were state regulations that had to be set up before any store could sell liquor, or any establishment could legally serve it, and that took another year or more.

Ben stopped going out with friends to drink, but then they had to deal with his increasing tirades when he drank at home. He no longer limited his drinking to times when he was not working, and Nellie began to worry he might lose his job. He was still at Burlington, but now he was back working as a machinist, or sometimes a machinist's helper, which was the first job he'd gotten there. She'd tried to ask him why he was back at his original job.

"They are the fucking railroad. They can do whatever they want. I'm still getting paid, so just shut your face."

They had moved again, to a house she loved near Thirty-fourth and South Street. It was newer and had a big yard and room for all of them. After renting for a couple of years, the owner offered to sell it to them. They got a mortgage for the first time in 1936 from the American Savings and Loan.

On Burl Melvin Johnson's fifteenth birthday, his mother asked him to come home right after school so she could make his favorite dinner: chicken-fried steak and mashed potatoes. They had ice cream sundaes for dessert. Seven-year-old Donnie couldn't wait to tell his older brother that he had helped make the birthday cake that afternoon. Ben was even home and mellow for the occasion. Of course, he was still on his first bottle of beer.

"It's probably good you are all here," Mel said somewhat apprehensively. "I joined the National Guard Army Reserve this afternoon. They said I could join on my birthday, so I did."

"You joined the army? Did you tell them it was your fucking fifteenth birthday, or do they think you are eighteen now?" Ben asked derisively.

"Well, they didn't ask, I didn't tell," Mel said. "As long as I get paid to go to drills, I don't know what difference it makes."

"Because the army doesn't cotton to liars. That's what difference it makes!" Ben sniped.

Nellie glared at him, then turned a beaming gaze on her older son. "Don't mind him. I am proud of you, Darling. As long as they don't try to send you off to fight somewhere. At least not until you finish high school."

"Well, I did mention I was still in school and it didn't seem to bother them."

Ben stood, scraping his chair loudly across the floor.

"Can't wait until you find out what an adventure the army is," he said sarcastically. "I'm going down to the Bender. You all go ahead and have your party." The Bender Buffet was one of twenty or so retail beer establishments that had cropped up around the downtown and north Lincoln areas.

Nellie was relieved when he left them like this. He was putting a damper on things, which she could no longer hide from her boys. "So tell me more about this National Guard," she said, clearing off the dinner dishes and bringing out the cake.

During most of the 1930s, Ben and Nellie only had one car and sometimes it wasn't running. So even though they were near most of Ben's family in Ashland, years often went by without visiting them. Blanche had moved back in with her mother in Ashland shortly after Ben and Nellie moved to Lincoln. Claude lived nearby in Louisville, and William now lived in Seward. Beulah still lived in Ashland. Nellie had tried to get the boys together to go see Arminta when they were younger, but it became more difficult as time went on. Ben was not interested in visiting, as he said he didn't like seeing his mother getting old.

When Arminta died in June of 1938, they did go to Ashland for the funeral and spent the day with Ben's brothers and sisters. She finally met his oldest brother, Joseph Franklin, who still lived in Lebanon, Kansas. She found him to be very pleasant and she liked his wife, Edith, too. Ben barely spoke to either of them. Mel and Don were surprised to find out they even had an Uncle Frank. He seemed more like a grandfather to them, at age fifty-six. He took them out in the backyard to toss a ball around.

Edith pulled Nellie aside in the hallway. "Is Ben still drinking too much?" she asked bluntly.

Nellie was taken aback, wondering how this nice woman who was a stranger a few minutes ago, could possibly know about Ben's drinking. She wasn't sure how to answer if she should be loyal or honest.

"Never mind, the answer is written all over your face. Just promise me you will call us if things get out of hand." She handed Nellie a piece a paper with her phone number and address in Kansas written on it.

That is a funny thing about family, she thought, as tears filled her eyes. They are backing you up even when you don't know it.

Nellie saw less and less of her oldest son, as he was playing football and running on the track team. He had various other school activities and was doing National Guard drills once a month. But after a while, she began to suspect there was another reason he was so absent.

"Do you have a girlfriend, Mel?" she asked one Saturday morning, hoping to catch him off guard.

"Who told you?" he said, startled.

"Tell me about her."

"Well, I don't know if she's my girlfriend. I've been over to her place a few times. She lives on Fortieth Street. Her family has been real nice to me. Her father has a road equipment company, and her mother is involved in some society stuff. Eastern Star, I think that's what she called it. She has a sister and a couple of brothers. Her brother, Bob, is just a year below me in school."

"Her father owns his own company? What's her name?"

He hesitated, as though he was debating what to tell her. "Maryellen. Maryellen McCracken."

"Are they rich?" Nellie asked, still trying to figure this out.

"No, I wouldn't say that. I don't know, maybe. Her dad has a nice new Cadillac. She always seems to be getting new clothes. Don't worry about it. I like to hang out there. They have fun."

Nellie thought they were doing okay. She and Ben may have had their differences, but they were doing better than most folks had been during this long economic depression. They both had jobs. They could still eat, even if it was never anything fancy. They had a roof over their heads and even owned the roof now.

Nellie paid most of the bills herself, but Ben had offered to pay the mortgage bill every month because the American Savings and Loan office was near the Burlington yard where he worked. Sometimes, she paid it when he was not working. If he didn't have enough cash, he would ask her for part of it from her household fund. When he didn't ask for any, she assumed he'd paid it all himself.

That's what she thought until she opened a letter in January saying they had defaulted on their house loan, and American Savings and Loan was taking them to court. Ben made himself scarce that night, so she went down to the Savings and Loan office the next morning before work. She was shocked to discover the mortgage had not been paid in six months. To rectify things with the lender, they would have to pay all of that plus interest and a penalty. If they could not pay, their house would be sold once the case went through the court. If she wanted to avoid immediate eviction, she could pay rent, which was the same amount as the mortgage payment plus five percent each month, until the house was sold.

Nellie was both shocked and furious. Ben had deceived her about this, and she had been foolish enough to not check up on it sooner. He did come home that evening, and she asked Mel to take his brother to the library so they would be out of the house. She spread the letter out on the kitchen table, along with the list of payments and missed payments the savings company gave her.

"You told me you were paying the mortgage, but you didn't." She slammed her hand on the letter on the table. "Now they are going to sue us and sell our house."

"I never said I was paying the God damn mortgage." She felt his hot breath on her neck as he stood right behind her. "Those people are crooks. They don't deserve any of my hard-earned dough, or yours either. Hell, they are just as crooked as the banks," he said, opening up a bottle of beer. Nellie thought she needed the beer more than he did.

"We signed an agreement with them saying we would pay the mortgage amount once a month. You can't just welsh on a contract. Why didn't you just give me the money? I would have paid it. This is crazy! We are going to lose our house because you squandered the money away!" Nellie didn't care if she was nagging him, she had a right to be infuriated.

"See, this is what you don't understand, what you have never understood. I don't break my back every day so that I can spend my moolah on something as dreary as a house. What's fun about owning a house? Nothing. It just ties you down, the roof leaks, the heat goes out, you're paying for that. You have grass to mow and siding to paint, it goes on and on. I don't want to live like that. Life is supposed to be fun. We finally got rid of Prohibition. Let's live it up a little before we are too old to enjoy it. Once we had kids, you thought you had to be responsible. I don't want to be responsible. It is dull. God damn dull."

She thought his tirade was over, but it just got darker. And louder.

"Your problem is that you wanted to turn me into your father. I ain't your father. He didn't do so well either, did he? He's dead and your mother is working as a housekeeper just to survive. She ain't some rich farm widow now, is she? And what about your brothers? Verner, he ran off to Washington, and Harry took the farm. Where is your share of that? Harry with his child bride and three children. Children! That's all you women think is important. They just cost more money and they run off when they get old enough to help you. Where is that golden son of yours? He could be working instead of going out with his friends. Oh no, he has to play football like some big hero."

He'd set his bottle on the table. Nellie stood and grabbed it and took a swig.

"You can't drink my beer! What the hell?"

"Why not? I probably paid for it."

Without taking his eyes off hers, he grabbed the beer out of her hand and threw it against the wall, shattering the glass bottle. She didn't even look his way when he slammed the kitchen door behind him. At least he left the beer, she thought, as she opened another bottle with shaking hands.

In the spring of his junior year of high school, Mel got a job working part-time at Fairmont Ice Cream, a soda fountain near his high school. It was easy for him to go there right after school ended. Nellie wondered if he was really working so many hours, or if he was just avoiding coming home. She was surprised a few weeks later when he handed her a fistful of cash and said it was his first payday. He asked her to keep it in a safe place where his father wouldn't find it and blow it on booze.

"I will keep it for you, in a separate envelope. But when you get more, you may want to put it in the bank. I am thinking of opening an account in a bank now myself."

Mel had been reading about the Glass-Steagall Banking Reform Act in school, the law to protect consumer deposits in any bank. He agreed they should both open bank accounts. "But the money I handed you is to help with the household expenses, you know, like the mortgage payment and food."

She gave him a motherly embrace. "You're mighty sweet, Darling, but we're doing okay for now, as long as your daddy and I can keep working."

"I think you should ask him to leave. He is just mean to you, to all of us. I think I can make enough money we won't need him," he said seriously, suddenly sounding older than his sixteen years. "I know I won't be living here forever, but I can send you some cash."

"Oh, baby. You don't know everything about it yet. Husbands and wives. You just don't throw that away because of a few fights.

And you need to save for your future. So tomorrow, we will go down to the bank, *hmmm*?"

"Do what you want, Mom. But I think it is getting worse. Tell me when you need dough." He squinted at her, not quite believing the brave front she was putting up. "Or when you need help."

CHAPTER SIX

December 1949

Nellie found a seat in the back of the big courtroom in Wahoo, the county seat of Saunders County. She'd never been in a courtroom before and found it ominous. I should have never put our money in a bank account, she mused. How many times has Ben tried to spend money we don't have or write checks that he doesn't tell me about? He doesn't know how to manage money. Of course, they had lost their house when they defaulted on their loan, but you would have thought he would have learned from that.

The railroad moved them to Edgemont, South Dakota, for a few years while Don was in high school. When they left, they had to sneak out of town in the middle of the night because they owed back taxes and rent. That meant she couldn't keep in touch with any of her friends there.

They had moved to Ashland after Ben's job at the railroad ended, and moved her mother to a house nearby. He had been helping a local man hauling garbage, which meant getting up at about 3:00 a.m. He couldn't manage that when he was hungover. Sometimes he was still drunk at 3:00 a.m. She knew it was hard on him to be fired from a job that he didn't want to do in the first place. She finally had to get a job herself in Lincoln, and drive about twenty miles every day one way, just to cover the bills.

They had overdrawn their bank account in Ashland before. Mrs. Peabody at the bank always called her to let her know, and Nellie had kept a secret fund to cover those minor issues. But what had happened last week was more serious. She knew it, even if Ben didn't.

Mr. Landon, the county attorney showed up at her door. "Mrs. Johnson, there is a difference between writing a check against funds which are not yet posted to your bank account, and writing a check on an account that has no funds, or for an amount that exceeds what will be posted into your account. One is careless, the other is basically stealing."

"But I closed the account that the check was written on because my husband kept overdrawing it. I took the money out of that account and put it in a new one."

"Yes, but Mrs. Peabody said she told you she could not close the account completely without Ben's signature since it was a joint account. He wrote a thirteen dollar check at the liquor store on an account that only had two dollars in it. There is a warrant out for his arrest."

"Why are you so nervous, Nellie?" Ben asked her when he got home that day and found her wringing her hands and pacing the living room.

"I told you not to use that old checking account last week. Why did you write a check for thirteen dollars at Jim's Liquor?"

"I must have bought some booze. I was probably loaded. What's the problem?"

"There's no money in that account. I think they are going to arrest you."

"They won't arrest me over thirteen lousy bucks. Just give me the cash, I will take it to Jim tonight."

"I don't have the money, and I think it is too late."

When the doorbell rang, she opened the door. The deputy stepped inside and took Ben by the arm. She didn't think she'd ever seen him look so shocked.

She looked up with a start and realized they were calling Ben's case before the judge.

"You have been charged with uttering an insufficient fund check, Mr. Johnson. How do you plead?" she heard Justice Reader say.

She could barely hear him say "guilty" as she stared at him from the back of the room. He looked shorter somehow, as though the weight of the world had landed on top of him in the few days since his arrest.

The judge sentenced him to thirty days in the county jail and ordered him to pay the court costs. She watched them escort Ben back out of the room. He probably didn't even know I was here. Thirty days, she thought. I have thirty days to decide what to do. I could leave. I could be long gone in thirty days. But I can't leave Mom. She needs me, and she took care of me for more years than I care to remember. And now that my son and his family are in Lincoln, why should I leave them? No, I have to stay in this town now. But maybe I will change the locks.

The next day her mother came to see her. She didn't have to tell Ida what had happened. It was in the newspaper.

"I'm sure you're upset about this, Mom. So am I. But I don't know what to do anymore. He needs to get a job and then he would have some spending money at least. But he has to be sober for that. I know he drinks too much, but I can't stop him."

"Lord knows men are stubborn, and he is no exception. You can't control him, but you can control yourself. You can just say no. You can just say to him, 'if you want to live here with me, no more drinking.' This is a perfect time for him to stop because they won't let him drink in jail. He'll be sober for thirty days when he comes home," Ida said, settling on the couch.

Nellie sighed, "Oh, he'll stop at the liquor store or a bar on his way home, I'm sure."

"You're right. You can't wait. You have to tell him before he's released."

"Mom, I am not sure why you are talking to me about this now. He's been drinking as long as I have known him."

"Yes, I should have talked to you sooner, or someone should have. It's been a problem as long as you've known him. You just turned a blind eye. I guess we all did. But maybe, now that he's in jail, he's hit rock bottom. Sometimes you have to lose everything to see your mistakes. To change your ways," Ida said.

"But he did change his ways. He's always been a free spirit, but he tried to change because he wanted to be with me. Maybe I tried to make him into something he wasn't." Her knee began twitching up and down and she put her hands on it to make it stop.

"Don't blame yourself for one minute, Nellie. You are the best thing that ever happened to Ben Johnson, and he knows it. And that gives you some power. You can give him an ultimatum."

"You think I should make him choose between drinking and me?" Nellie asked spreading an afghan up over her legs as if she were cold.

"Are you strong enough to do that, Nellie?" her mother asked.

"I've always been the strong one," she sighed ruefully. "Haven't you heard?" After her mother left, she sat for a long time wondering what to do, fingering the afghan.

Months ago, one of the neighbors was going into a nursing home. He gave Ben his large green Amazon parrot, which Nellie found to be annoying, messy, and loud. Half of the time they had to keep him in the garage because he swore like a sailor. Ben had renamed him Dewey, in an unusual bit of irony, and got a kick out of trying to teach him new vulgar phrases.

When evening came, even though she didn't like the parrot, she moved Dewey's cage into the living room near the front door since she was alone. She hoped he at least would squawk if anyone tried to break in.

"Hells Bells. Damned if you do and damned if you don't," Dewey squawked and whistled.

"You know sometimes I would swear you are talking to me." She tried to look him in the eye but he kept bobbing his head.

"Screw you, Dewey, don't swear. Bad boy," he said.

She laughed at him and the absurdity her life had become.

"Good-night, Dewey." She started out of the room. She couldn't believe she was talking to a bird.

"Benny loves Nellie," Dewey squawked and clucked.

"What did you say?" She turned and came back, squinting at the parrot. The previous owner wouldn't have taught him that.

"Benny loves Nellie. Benny loves Nellie. Pretty boy."

"*Hmmm,*" she answered. "We'll see about that." She turned out the light and went up to bed. "We'll just see."

SMITH/ JOHNSON FAMILY

IDA MAY PAYSON---------------------------------ARTHUR EVERETTE SMITH

       CHILDREN:
       RUBY MARIE SMITH
       ZELLA ZERPHA SMITH
       NELLIE IRENE SMITH
       HARRY HARRISON SMITH
       VERNER THOMAS SMITH

ARMINTA JANE MCGUIRE-------------------MARSHALL PERRY JOHNSON

       CHILDREN:
       JOSEPH FRANKLIN JOHNSON
       BLANCHE MAY JOHNSON
       CHARLES EDWARD JOHNSON
       WILLIAM PERRY JOHNSON
       CLAUDE AMERICUS JOHNSON
       TIMOTHY GUY JOHNSON
       BENONA MONROE JOHNSON
       BEULAH MARIE JOHNSON

NELLIE SMITH--BEN JOHNSON

       CHILDREN:
       BURL MELVIN JOHNSON
       DONALD DEAN JOHNSON

Left: Nellie Irene Smith about 1914

Below: Marshall P. and Arminta Johnson family about 1910
Back row: Charles, Claude, William, Frank, Ben
Front row: Arminta, Beulah, Marshall, Blanche

KATIE
CHAPTER ONE

"Momma always said I was a daddy's girl. I didn't understand what she meant when I was younger. I mean, I loved my daddy dearly. Even though I was the youngest of seven children, my daddy was only twenty-six years older than I was. You see, Momma was married before to a man named Folkert Cross when she was twenty-seven years old and Folkert was thirty-one. They had two sons and four daughters, but he up and died on her. It's not like Momma wanted to get married again. She had her hands full with those children. Her oldest was only fifteen, and the baby was a year old.

"But the way Momma tells it, along came my daddy, a-courtin' her like she was a young girl again. By then, she was forty-three and my daddy was twenty-five. He told her she was the prettiest thing in Golden Township, even if she did have six children already. I guess it was lucky for me he had a hankering for older women. Of course, I asked him about it too. He said older ladies know what they are doing. They know about cooking and housekeeping and having babies. And he wanted a baby. Momma wasn't sure she could have any more at her age. But when she found out she was having me, she said Daddy was tickled pink. That sealed the deal, and they got married before I came along.

"I guess that's why I am a daddy's girl. He married an older woman with six children just to get little old me.

"Everyone calls me Katie. My given name is actually Frauke Jurgens Freese. *Frauke* means 'Little Lady' in German. You might expect there was a Catherine or Katrina thrown in there since they called me Katie, but no such luck. I'm happy with Katie.

"My Momma's name is Almt Janssen Meints, but she is called

Alma. Her last name was Cross for the twenty-four years or so she was married to her first husband, and now her last name is Freese. My daddy is Jürgen Hansen Freese. I was born March 23, 1870, in Golden Township in Adams County, Illinois. But when I was about a year and a half, my parents brought me and all those half brothers and sisters to Logan Township, Gage County, Nebraska. And I have pretty much stayed put."

"Do you tell that story to everyone you meet?" Hicke Baumfalk asked. We were outside the general store in Pickrell, Nebraska. It was a warm summer day in July of 1888, and I had found him sitting on a bench drinking lemonade. I sat down beside him.

"No," I laughed. "At least not like that. I thought it was important that you catch up."

"All right. I guess I am caught up." He tipped his hat in my direction. "My name is Hicke Welts Baumfalk. I live up there yonder." He gestured toward the Baumfalk farm north of Pickrell, in Holt Township. "I am waiting on my father, Dirk, who goes by Dick here. He is haggling about something with the store owner."

"Oh, I know all about you. Which is why I wanted you to catch up."

"You do?" He looked at me quizzically.

"You're one of those Baumfalk boys," I replied. "They said there are six of you, no … seven boys and four girls. Did I remember that right? I've met two of your sisters, Lena and Dena. They sound like twins, but I know they aren't. Anyway, they filled me in. I like to keep track of newcomers to this area, especially the younger ones. And I met your daddy once. You look like him, except younger of course."

Hicke had a strange look on his face like he didn't know what to make of me.

"You were in my brother Herman's grade, weren't you? I remember him talking about a girl named Katie."

"I liked Herman," I said. "I only saw him at school a few times, but we had a connection. He could have been my brother. And not like my half-brothers: they treat me like a kid sister. We could have been good friends if he hadn't gotten sick."

"Yes, we all miss Herman," Hicke said.

I needed to get our conversation back on a positive note. "But instead we can be friends."

"You think we should be friends? You think a twenty-three-year-old man should be friends with an eighteen-year-old girl?" A smile played at the corners of his mouth.

"Do you have a better offer?" I laughed at him, and sprang up and ran to jump into my father's arms so he could boost me into his wagon. I waved when the wagon pulled away. Hicke shook his head in amusement.

It's important to make a good first impression, Momma always said. I know I made an impression on Hicke the first day. Why it wasn't more than a week later, he showed up at our farm along with his brother, Wilt. They said they were there to talk to Daddy about trading some horses, but I knew it was more. Momma invited them to dinner and you should have seen the way they wolfed down Momma's fried chicken and mashed potatoes. They even had two helpings of apple pie, which I made myself. After dinner, Daddy and I took Wilt and Hicke back out to the stables.

I jumped on my horse, Rolf, in spite of my long black dress billowing out around me, and my short stature. Of course, I rode nearly every day.

"Come for a ride with me, Hicke," I requested. "He can ride Old

Master, can't he, Daddy? He's still saddled."

"Now, Sugar, we've got to get these horses on the wagon switched. That's what they came for," Daddy began. We both knew it was no use, he could rarely say no to me.

"But Hicke is my friend, and it is better to go riding with a friend. Besides, I can show him some of the farm."

Hicke mounted Old Master. "You can handle the horse swapping, can't you Brother?" His brother Wilt stared at him in amazement. When he turned the horse around to follow me, I was already galloping down the path behind the barn. "Giddy up, Old Boy."

I knew when I heard the horse's hoofbeats behind me, he was more than impressed. He was interested now. I have to be candid here. At eighteen, I wasn't the prettiest girl you ever saw. I had kind of a round face and a very high forehead. I wasn't particularly tall and I didn't have a nineteen-inch waist, no matter how tight I cinched my corset. But I knew how to use the advantages eighteen-year-old girls have when it comes to young men, short of endangering my virtue. I had four older sisters after all, and they were all married.

"Where are you going and what's the big rush?" Hicke called out.

I barely heard him, I was so far ahead of him in the trees. Rolf knew where I was going and slowed to a stop to let me slide off easily. I had my boots and corset off and my dress unbuttoned before Hicke seemed to understand what I was doing.

"It's pretty hot to run the horses so hard," he said, as he stopped his horse next to Rolf.

He dismounted and acted surprised to find me pulling my long black dress over my head, and running toward the creek in my white cotton combination undergarment. He'd probably never seen any women in his family wearing anything that short.

When I jumped into the creek, he seemed alarmed and rushed to the bank. I was up to my neck in the water and I'd let my long dark hair cascade onto my shoulders. I leaned my head back to soak my hair and smiled at him.

"Come on in. The water feels wonderful," I suggested.

"Are you sure? How deep is it?" he said, sitting on the muddy bank to remove his leather boots and Stetson hat.

"It's not too deep here. You can walk on the creek bed for about ten feet or so. I suppose it is about six feet deep where I am, but I'm treading water. I come here a lot in the summer. It's what I wanted to show you."

He motioned with his hand for me to turn around. I guess he didn't want me to see him in his union suit. It probably had some holes in it. I complied, and he slid off his pants and shirt and socks, then waded into the muddy creek.

"I don't know how you got me to do this, I'm not a good swimmer," Hicke said. I turned toward him again and moved closer, grabbing his hand and pulling him into the deeper channel. When his head went halfway under the water as the creek bed gave way, I let go.

"Hey, are you trying to drown me?" He gulped in some dirty water.

"You're fine, keep moving your legs back and forth like a pair of scissors. You kind of bounce in the water. Just move your arms around in a figure-eight motion," I laughed, while he tried to get the hang of treading water.

"Easy for you to say, girls are more naturally buoyant. Men are dead weight."

I could see him staring at my bare shoulders as the white fabric floated when I moved up and down in the water. He spotted a large branch protruding in the water and grabbed onto it.

"Okay, this is better." He seemed to assess the creek itself, once his fear of drowning subsided. "This is a pretty good creek, isn't it? How far does it run in your daddy's place?" He glanced over at the horses who had found themselves a shallow spot to wade and drink downstream from where we were.

"It goes quite a ways, I guess. It runs northwest from here into the Walkens' farm." I swam a little closer to where he had tethered himself on the branch. Suddenly something pulled me straight down beneath the surface, and I came up sputtering. He reached out and grabbed my hand.

"You okay? What happened?"

"I dunno, some kind of undercurrent I guess. There are holes all over under there, you have to be careful." I held onto his hand, although I knew the danger was over. He was about ten inches away from me now.

His slicked-back dark hair started to get wavy as it dried. I studied the line on his forehead from his hat. He had similar lines where his sleeves ended. He spends a lot of time outdoors, but clearly not in a creek. His chin and jawline were prominent and it appeared he hadn't had a shave for three, no maybe four days. He had kind eyes. They seemed to dance when he smiled like he was perpetually teasing. They looked sort of gray-green, but maybe it was only the reflection of the water. They were focused on me now, and I couldn't ask for more than that.

The sunlight that streamed through the trees was glistening on the water and I could feel its warmth. I closed my eyes and pushed my hair from my face.

"I must look a fright, soaking in this dirty water," I mused, twisting a strand of hair.

"Not at all. I was thinking about how winsome and natural you look. You're not very shy. I mean most girls wouldn't like getting all wet and muddy in the creek."

I was pleased by the way he was ogling me, but I knew it was time to go back. His brother was probably ready to start for home. I already knew Wilt had a girlfriend named Sarah, so he ought to have figured something was going on. Getting out of the water was going to be a little awkward though. This cotton undergarment was nice and cool under my dress, but since it was wet now, it was likely to cling to my skin.

"Turn around now. I'm going to get out," I requested. "When you want to get out, you should be able to walk right on the creek bed from here."

I started for the bank as he turned away, but when I was about knee-deep in the water, I glanced back to catch him peeking. He chuckled when I raced out of the water and back into the protection of the brush. I attempted to wring the water out of my clothing, shimmy back into my corset, and put on my voluminous dress. By the time I had braided my wet hair, and put on my boots, he was already dressed and ready for the ride back. He didn't say anything more that day, but I figured he didn't need to.

I told Momma later we'd be seeing more of Hicke Baumfalk. And sure enough, he showed up at our place again two evenings later.

I was sitting on the porch steps tossing an old ball to our dog, Twinkle, and my parents were sitting on the porch swing. Daddy was reading Momma a story out of the Beatrice newspaper when Hicke rode up on his horse, dismounted, and came up to the porch.

"Good evening, Mr. and Mrs. Freese," he said, tipping his hat in a formal fashion. "I'm here to pay a call on Miss Frauke if it is all right with you."

I had to stifle a giggle. He sounded like someone straight out of a book. Daddy seemed to take the hint though. With a nod to Hicke, he said, "Come along, Mother, let's go on inside now. It's getting late."

Hicke sat on the step next to me. I squinted at him in mock confusion.

"I told you to call me Katie. And what is this business about paying a call on me? I thought we were just friends."

"I called you Frauke because the other day, seeing you in the water, I decided you look like a Frauke. You reminded me of a wonderful teacher I had back in the Old Country. I had a schoolboy crush on her. You have typical German features."

I grimaced.

"No, I think German women are very healthy-looking." Hicke said, "Sturdy ...robust ... solid."

The scowl I gave him said none of those words were the least bit flattering.

He resorted to German, "*Prächtig*." That caught me by surprise and I felt the blush quickly rising to my cheeks. The last time I'd heard anyone use that word was when my older brothers were reminiscing about their favorite dancer at the burlesque show they'd seen in St. Louis. Of course, they didn't know I had been eavesdropping.

He looked embarrassed too and changed the subject quickly. "I was younger than you when I had to leave Germany. My older brother Gustav had been conscripted into the German army. My parents were afraid I was next, so at sixteen years old they got me on a ship to England where I worked as a cook's helper. Once I got to England, I found passage to America in the same way, helping the cooks. So I was the first one in my family to arrive in Illinois. I stayed with my uncle Tonjes and his family. My parents got everyone else out of Germany pretty quickly, but the whole first year I was afraid no one else would make it."

I thought I heard a catch in his voice at the memory. He quickly tried to cover his emotion by pulling me to my feet.

"Let's walk," Hicke said, and we started walking toward the stables. I slipped my arm in his and smiled.

"So, you are telling me you can cook?"

"I can peel potatoes. I do that quite well," he laughed.

When we got to Rolf's pen, I climbed on the first board of the stall door and stroked my horse's dark mane.

"You remember Hicke, don't you, Rolf?" I asked the gelding. Rolf snorted and seemed to nod, and we both laughed. Hicke came from behind me and wrapped his arms around my waist. When I turned back toward him, he kissed me gently while I held onto the stall door to keep from falling.

"You ruined our budding friendship," I whispered.

"I've got enough friends." He plucked me off the stall door, turning me to face him, and kissed me again. I wrapped my arms around his neck and kissed him back.

A few days later, on a Saturday afternoon, Hicke stopped by while Daddy was getting the wagon ready to make a run into Pickrell to pick up some feed. Hicke offered to get it for him.

"Katie complained I haven't taken her anywhere, so we could go do your errands in Pickrell if you like," Hicke said, with a mischievous grin. I gave him an admonishing look, but went and got my bonnet and parasol.

The ride into town was quiet. He held my hand with one hand and the reins with the other. When we got to the general store in Pickrell, he placed the feed order and we helped ourselves to the lemonade on the counter. Then we went around the corner to sit on the same bench where we had met. Several young women I knew walked by, but they didn't seem to see me. They were only staring at Hicke. Another girl waved at him from a buggy as she rode by.

After the feed was loaded into the wagon and we'd picked up a few food items for Momma, we started back to my family farm. For a short while, there was just the sound of the horses' plodding hooves pulling the wagon, a creaking wagon wheel, and the buzzing of flies around us.

"You seem to know a lot of girls in town," I prodded him.

He shrugged.

"How many other girls have you been seeing here?"

He heaved an exaggerated sigh. "I'm afraid I left a string of broken hearts back in Tazewell County, in Illinois, and Germany when I was in school. But alas, not lately. I guess no one here caught my eye. That is, of course, until you stormed into my life."

Two can play at this game, I thought.

"Honestly, I am not sure if I like you," I said, tossing my braid away from my shoulder.

He gave me a sidelong look. "Are you sure? You could have

fooled me."

"The thing is, I really love the way you kiss." I sighed, anticipating the effect my words would have.

"Whoa," Hicke said.

I wondered if he was reining in the horses or himself. The horses stopped.

"Well, now I am going to have to kiss you again."

"If you insist." I put the parasol up so we could hide from the view of others who might be passing on the road.

Our romance moved like a prairie fire after that. I had fun flirting with Hicke, but once he started getting serious, the flames kept nipping at the hem of my skirt. He often didn't come by until it was almost dark and Daddy and Momma had gone to bed. One night we argued because I wanted to sit on the porch and talk and he wanted to go to the barn where we could have privacy.

We had been sitting on the porch swing holding hands when he tried to pull me to my feet to walk to the barn.

"I don't understand you, Katie. You like to tease and toy with me, but when things start getting interesting, you're as skittish as a turkey at Thanksgiving," Hicke said.

"Maybe I find this interesting. What's wrong with sitting close and talking about the stars?" I tried to pull him back to the seat next to me, but he stood his ground.

"Maybe I want more. I think I am falling in love with you."

I did stand slowly and took his other hand. "We don't need to rush anything. We've only known each other for a few months. We're just having fun."

"So let's go to the barn and have some more fun."

I pulled back when he tried to guide me off the porch.

"Or maybe you don't feel the same way. Do you just like tormenting me?"

I could see he was getting annoyed now. It was true we had already spent several evenings frolicking in the hayloft.

"You must know I am crazy about you too," I said very softly, pulling him back to face me and wrapping my arms around his back. "You can kiss me right here and I won't get straw in my hair and dress." He did kiss me slowly, then glanced toward the open window to my parents' bedroom. He broke it off and backed down the porch steps.

"You need to decide if you want to move this forward. You can't lead me on like this. I have never been good at waiting." Hicke got on his horse and rode off.

I was a little stunned. I could tell by his expression he wasn't teasing this time. I let him kiss me. I even invited him to kiss me. So why is he mad? Things were going so well. Why is he trying to ruin it?

I should have known Momma would be awake and listening to the whole thing. The next day she hatched a plan to send me back east on an adventure.

"You're going on a trip, Darling," Daddy told me the next evening at dinner. Your momma has it all arranged. Your cousin Brune Meints is going back to Adams County, Illinois, to take care of some business for your Uncle Christian, and you're going with him. You'll probably spend most of the time in Quincy, according to what Christian said. It will be fun for you to see where you were born."

"But Momma," I protested. "What about Hicke? We're just starting to get close."

Alma interrupted, "That's what I'm afraid of, Katie girl. You have the rest of your life to tie yourself to one man and have babies. You're only eighteen. Go have a little fun, meet some new young people. Quincy is a booming town right on the Mississippi River. Hicke will be here when you get back. Christian is taking you both to the train station tomorrow."

Momma was right, as usual. I did have fun in Quincy with Brune. We stayed in "Calf Town," which is where many of the German immigrants first settled in Quincy. They called it that because most families had a cow tied up in their yard. We called on some of the Meints families who were still in the area, and it was fun to meet additional cousins. The meetings he arranged were with a group of attorneys who were trying to establish some property conglomerates in different states.

We spent most of the time meeting with Gerd Zimmerman, a young man who was a few years older than Brune, and three years older than me. He took us out to the beer garden overlooking the river and we drank beer and learned how to polka. I enjoyed dancing with him. Gerd had been born in Adams County on the west side of Illinois, like Brune and me, and his parents had also come over from Germany.

After about three weeks when it was time to return to Nebraska, Gerd came along with us. He was planning to start working on a conglomerate in Gage County and Brune invited him to stay at the Meints farm until he could get settled. I'm still not sure how it happened, but Gerd got the impression we were a couple. I suppose it may have been after he kissed me at the beer garden. Well, maybe he kissed me two or three times. He wasn't a bad kisser either.

The next time I saw Hicke was around the end of October. He

came riding up to the farmhouse, to the sound of Twinkle barking but found me sitting on the porch swing with Gerd. Brune and his brother John Meints were leaning on the porch rail, talking to my parents. I squirmed a little when I saw Gerd had his arm draped on the back of the swing. Hicke looked irritated when he walked up to the porch and was introduced to Gerd, but he shook hands with the men all around. Then he caught my eye and made a subtle motion for me to come down to the front yard and talk to him.

He pulled me a few yards away to get out of earshot. "Didn't you miss me?" he whispered, pulling me closer.

I kept my voice equally low. "Yes, I missed you, but we have company now." I glanced back at the porch to see who was watching us. Gerd was standing, watching me intently, but the others were at least pretending to give us some privacy.

"Show me."

I didn't understand until he grasped my head in his hands and kissed me firmly. I was surprised and broke away embarrassed. I could feel my face flushing, but I had missed the way he made my heart race.

"Hicke …" I tried to tell him he couldn't kiss me in front of my parents, but I couldn't manage to finish the sentence.

"Do you want me to come back some other time?" he asked.

"No, you should talk to Brune and Gerd. Hear about what they have planned. It might be something the Baumfalks want to get in on."

He sat on the porch rail with the others. My parents soon went to bed, and Hicke and I took their chairs. Brune and Gerd gave him an explanation about how the farmers could pool their resources and buy most of the land coming for sale in Logan, Holt, and Hanover

Townships. Gerd planned to handle the legal work involved and set up an office in Pickrell. I noticed Hicke was beginning to look uncomfortable. He waited until the other three men left before he launched into me.

"What in the Sam Hill is going on between you and that Gerd fella?" Hicke asked when we were alone.

"Nothing. We're just friends," I said. "It's getting late and —"

"Yeah, I know all about what you do to your friends, remember? But you gotta watch out for this fella. He's not only after you, he's after your inheritance."

"I don't know what you are talking about. Maybe you're jealous."

"What if I am? I am worried about what he's up to. Is he aware you are your father's only child and he owns 240 acres of prime farmland here?" Hicke asked.

"Well, yes, I think we discussed it early on. This is all Brune and Gerd's business, not mine. I went along because they brought me with them. It's not about me or Daddy's farm either." I had to look away because I was getting upset.

"You don't think he'd marry you to get the farm? That man has dollar signs in his eyes, not love."

"Why, what a terrible thing to say! You're the one who kissed me like you were marking your territory. It's time for you to leave." I turned and stormed into the house. But I was glad to know he clearly still cared.

I'd forgotten I'd agreed to go to the Opera House in Beatrice with Gerd the following Saturday evening to see a production of "Dr. Jekyll and Mr. Hyde." He borrowed Uncle Christian's carriage. It was a bit chilly, and I was glad I had bought a long wool cape in

Quincy. Before the play, we dined at Tivoli's Restaurant.

"I gather Beatrice is a much larger town than Pickrell. It might make more sense for us to live here. The county courthouse would be close by, which I would need for real estate transactions," Gerd said over dinner.

"Gerd, I am not sure what you mean. I can see why you would want to live here. I will be on the farm," I said.

"You must see I would be a much better husband than that farmer. What was his name, Hickey? We could live in style and dine out or go to the theatre like this whenever we wanted to."

"I hope you aren't proposing marriage because I didn't hear a question." I tried to laugh it off, but when he started to respond, I cut him off by putting my hand up. "Besides, you need a wife who is sophisticated and cultured. You might find one in this city."

He dropped the subject, at least for the evening. When the play was over, a frigid wind had moved in and snowflakes were beginning to swirl around us.

"It's going to be a cold ride home," I warned.

"I expected it to be, so I told your parents I made arrangements to spend the night, especially if the weather was bad. We can hole up overnight at the Davis House hotel. They claim to have those modern heaters in every room." When he saw the alarm on my face, he added, "Don't worry, my dear, I'm sure I can sleep on a chair or chaise and you can have the bed."

Gerd was true to his word, but he was probably warmer than a fresh-baked biscuit sitting right next to the heat, while I was barely warm enough in the bed wearing my clothes, cloak, and the two blankets they provided.

The next morning, the sun was shining on about an inch of snow. We would have been fine traveling the eight miles home the night before. After a nice hot breakfast, we arrived home to find Daddy and Momma had gone to church. I stood on the porch and watched Gerd leaving with the buggy.

Hicke passed him on the path from the road, and I could see him turn the horse around and look twice. I knew this wasn't going to be a pleasant conversation. I almost rushed inside and locked the door. But I didn't. I waited until he hit the porch and followed me inside. Before he even said a word, I could see he was furious. I expected him to yell and stomp around and accuse me of something I hadn't done. He did pace around a while and opened his mouth more than once before he spoke.

"I came by last night and you weren't here. I am obliged to put you out of your misery. Tell that Shyster Zimmerman you won't be keeping company with him anymore." He practically hissed out the words.

I gave him an exasperated look. "And why should I?"

"Because you are going to marry me," Hicke said a little more calmly but with more determination than affection.

Yes, that's right. Two proposals in less than twenty-four hours and neither one of them properly executed. What was I supposed to say? I sighed and rolled my eyes.

"Katie, you either agree to marry me today and we'll ask your parents when they get home or you'll get pregnant and you will have to marry me," he challenged.

"I won't get pregnant because I am not doing that bit with anyone, so don't even talk about it. Not until after I am married." I retorted.

He started unbuttoning the top buttons of his pants to make a point. "I should warn you, I come from a long line of very prolific German stock. They don't call it the Fatherland for nothing."

"Stop!" I cried in mock horror. I figured he was teasing me. I shook my head as he started to button his fly again.

"Okay, here's the deal. That was not a good proposal of marriage. I expect you to do better. You come back with flowers, or sweets, or maybe jewelry. Jewelry would be especially nice. Something romantic at least. Then I will give your offer serious consideration. Oh, and if you see 'Shyster Zimmerman', as you called him, tell him the same thing. Whoever has the better offer wins." I smiled. "Now go home. I need some rest. I didn't get much sleep last night."

It was his turn to roll his eyes.

I was napping at about 3:30 that afternoon when Momma spoke.

"I don't know what is going on, but you'd better come see this."

I rubbed my eyes and gazed out the front window. The yard was filled with people. I put my boots back on and went out onto the front porch. Most of Hicke's family was standing there, some of whom I hadn't even met. His parents, Dick and Folka, were sitting in a wagon filled with corn. His brother, Wilt had a bleating kid goat in his arms. Lena and Dena were there with a basket of eggs and three hens clucking around their feet. Fourteen-year-old Martin was there holding a pie. Frederick, who was ten, cradled a German's chocolate cake, and eight-year-old Diedrich was carrying a bundle of mums.

They were all watching me expectantly. Hicke was in the middle, and when he saw me he approached the porch. I covered my mouth with my hands and started to cry. He stopped in front of me and got down on one knee, which only made me cry harder.

"Jewelry was a little hard to find. I did find an antique locket my mother brought over from Germany," he said, holding it up. "The rest of this is…" He gestured to his family and the goods they brought.

"I know what it is," I said, starting to laugh with tears still streaming down my cheeks.

"Frauke Katie Jurgens Freese, would you do me the honor of being my wife?"

Because I couldn't speak any longer, I flung my arms around his neck. He stood up and swung me around, to the cheers of the Baumfalks and my parents alike.

"I've heard of a 'bride price' but I've never seen one," Momma said in wonder. "Sort of like a dowry in reverse."

"Sorry, but the livestock and the corn were for show. That's going back to my parents' farm," Hicke laughed.

Diedrich came up to the porch on cue, handed me the bouquet and I hugged him. The rest of the assembled Baumfalk family filed up to the porch and introduced themselves, and we all had pie, cake, and coffee, inside the crowded house.

It was the best proposal I could have imagined. I didn't think I would ever be so madly in love. Over the next few months, Hicke took me over to his parents' house a few times. His mother showed me some of her favorite recipes. It was nice spending time with his parents and his brothers and sisters.

But even before the wedding, I decided it was only fair to tell Gerd what was going on. A few weeks after Hicke and I were engaged, I rode Rolf over to the Meints place one morning. I was lucky Gerd was still there. He had been preparing to move to Beatrice. I met Brune at the door and he directed me to the back of the house, where I found Gerd packing his bag.

He looked up and smiled when he saw me standing in the doorway, nervously twisting a lock of hair. Since it was cold weather, I wore my hair loose and full around my face under my knit cap.

"Well, aren't you a sight for sore eyes? I'm sorry I haven't called on you, Katie. I wasn't sure where things stood anymore."

I felt remorseful then like I'd hurt my best friend. I walked up and put my arms around his neck, and hugged him. "You have been so special to me, Gerd. I don't know what I would have done in Quincy if you hadn't been there to make me laugh and to teach me how to polka. I was probably the only German girl there who couldn't polka."

He took my hands in his and backed me away from him to search my eyes. "I'm not the one, though, am I? I heard you plan to marry Mr. Baumfalk."

"Yes," I admitted. "That doesn't mean I don't care about you. I want you to find a girl who makes all of your dreams come true."

He thought that was me, I understood sadly, as I turned and walked away.

CHAPTER TWO

Hicke and I married in February at the Hanover Church, which was two miles north and two miles east of my daddy's place. Hicke's brother Wilt and sister Lena were our witnesses. Reverend Pooverlin was the Minister of the Gospel. Hicke wore the brown three-piece suit he said was his standard for weddings and funerals. I wore a blue velveteen and taffeta two-piece dress with a white lace collar and cuffs Momma and I found in Beatrice. It fit like a dream when I got it in late December, but at about the same time I bought the dress, I must have gotten pregnant. You see, it was too cold to go sneaking off to the barn at night, so I'd invited Hicke into my bed, and he started living with my family like we were already married. By the time we posed for the wedding photograph, I was nauseated, and my corset felt too tight.

Momma always said, "Just because you can have twelve children in twenty-four years, doesn't mean you should."

But I did. How was I supposed to avoid it? It would have been nice to have a magic potion you could take so you could enjoy married life without so many offspring, but I never saw one. And the first bunch of babies were mostly a joy. It got harder as we all got older.

Jurgen Hansen Baumfalk, Daddy's namesake, was born on a bright October morning. Hicke and Daddy were both busy harvesting the corn when the labor pains started. Luckily for me, we were still living with my parents so Momma was right there. I didn't want to do this on my own. I thought it would have been nice to have a midwife, but Momma convinced me she knew what to do. Her plan included a lot of walking though. She said this would speed up the birthing process, so we went walking out in the yard until I screamed at her to let me go back inside. I didn't want to drop the baby on its head.

She was probably right. Once we got back inside, it was only about an hour before the baby was born. Folka and Lena stopped by to check on me around noon, so they were the baby's first visitors.

When I held my baby for the first time, it hit me that I knew nothing about raising a child. After all, I was the baby in my family, so I'd never had to help out with younger siblings. Even Hicke had taken care of his younger brothers and sisters to some extent. When Hicke and Daddy got home and cleaned up, they were both excited and eager to hold baby Jurgen. It amazed me how much life had changed in a year.

Momma was a big help with the baby. With the crops harvested for the season, the men started working on building a house for Hicke and me. Daddy agreed to sell him some of the farm, so when Daddy started slowing down Hicke would take over more of the work. What would Daddy have done if I hadn't married a farmer?

By the time our second son, Grandpa Baumfalk's namesake Dick Hick came along, the house was finished, and we felt like we were on our own. I'd convinced them to add on more rooms than we needed in the beginning, and it was a good thing. We had five children by the time we were married ten years. Our first daughter was named Almt Ella Margaretha, after Momma and my half-sister. The next son we named Herman Friedrick, for the brother Hicke lost. The fifth child was Rekka Friedericka. I liked her name, it sounded very dramatic. She was the first one to be born in the Beatrice Hospital.

It was rare to gather the whole family for an outing, but in June 1897, we packed up the four children we had then and went with Dick, Folka, and my parents to Beatrice for the Chautauqua festival. Representative William Jennings Bryan, a Nebraskan politician, was the featured speaker. The previous year he had been the Democratic Party's nominee for President of the United States, and although he lost to William McKinley, he was the most famous person any of us had ever seen. He had also moved from Illinois to Nebraska, which made us all identify with him. The children were impatient when he started talking about the gold standard and why he favored the expanded minting of silver coins, but I found it inspiring that someone from Nebraska could be such an amazing speaker and command such large crowds. It made me wonder if I might be raising someone who could rise to such heights.

"Listen to this man," Hicke urged Jurgen and Dick since they were the oldest. "They call him the silver-tongued orator."

"Is his tongue made of silver?" six-year-old Dick wanted to know.

"No, Silly, but he keeps talking about silver. He probably eats it so it sticks to his tongue, like when you eat a cherry lollipop," little Jurgen told his brother.

We all had a laugh. I was pleased the children would be able to say they saw someone who had made history, even if they were too young to understand what it all meant.

Wilt remained close to Hicke and they often worked together, so it was natural I would become friends with Wilt's wife, Sarah. Wilt was one and a half years younger than Hicke, and Sarah was three years younger than me. They were married three years after we were and their oldest child, Robert, was the same age as Ella. Thomas was the same age as Herman. By 1899, we had seven children between us and tried to get together when we could so the cousins could play. I needed to hear another woman's voice sometimes, and Sarah was a blessing in that respect. I could always talk to Momma, but there are some things you'd rather discuss with someone in your own age group.

I was having a bad day, and I knew it before Sarah and her two little boys showed up at my house. It was hotter than a blacksmith's forge and my patience was wearing thin. Ten-year-old Jurgen, whom we had started calling George, and eight-year-old Dick were particularly driving me nuts, running in and out of the house, yelling and taunting each other and their younger sister. Things did calm down a little bit when Sarah got there, but that was mostly because I banned the older children from the house.

"I swear sometimes those boys will kill each other," I said. "And maybe I won't try to stop them! Goodness, why did no one tell me being a mother was so hard?"

Sarah smiled sympathetically. "Mine aren't old enough to kill each other, but sometimes I think about how I would kill them. Have you thought about that?"

I laughed at her exaggeration until I noticed Sarah wasn't smiling anymore. "*Uhmm* ...like what do you mean?" I asked.

"Well, they are small enough, I could still smother them or hold their heads underwater."

When I looked at her in horror, Sarah burst out laughing. "Don't tell me that hasn't crossed your mind many times with this brood. If I had five children, I'd be thinking of killing myself. What would your self-centered husband do then?"

This felt very awkward. I wondered how often she talked like this. But I knew Sarah liked to shock people even more than I did, so I chalked it up to her odd sense of humor.

"He's more patient than I am with the children," I shrugged, "He'd probably find some younger woman and it would be her problem."

After an outdoor lunch where the older boys launched a food fight, I could no longer tolerate them and sent Dick and George to the barn to clean out the stalls. Sarah had managed to get the younger children settled on the rag rugs for naps, and I sat and mopped the sweat off my face.

"You know what I really need?" I told Sarah. "I need to ride my horse. It has been ages since I rode. I miss the way my muscles work in tandem with Old Rolf's—the wind in my hair. I loved to ride when I was a girl."

"Go ahead, Honey. I've got everything under control here. You can go for an hour or two. You'll be back before your husband comes home."

I couldn't believe my ears. "Are you sure?"

When Sarah nodded, I jumped to my feet. "Oh my Gosh, I'm going! I can ride Rolf to the creek. Hicke and I did it once before we were married, and it was so …" I smiled at the memory. "Thank you so much!"

In the barn, I found the boys throwing horse dung at each other, and scolded them but good. I told them they'd better have the stalls in perfect shape by the time I got back or they would be in big trouble. I saddled Rolf and took off at a gallop. He seemed to miss it too, and I pulled the pins out of my hair and let it fly. I added a few extra miles to the ride for the sheer joy of it. I felt like I was eighteen again.

The horse ride was almost as good as peeling off my outer clothes and wading into the creek. I no longer had my combination underwear, I had taken to wearing a knee-length cotton slip under my corset. It was more forgiving when I was expecting. I was floating mindlessly, the slip billowing around me when I heard someone coming. Pretty soon I saw Hicke lumbering out of the brush. He sat on his haunches at the edge of the water.

"Come on in, you can join me," I said. "We haven't done this in years."

"It is tempting. You look like a water nymph or something out of Greek mythology. But I was getting worried. Sarah said you've been gone three hours. I'm not sure we should leave the kids any longer," Hicke said.

"Three hours! That can't be right. Is it time for supper? I was gone for about an hour or an hour and a half."

"She said you left before lunch."

"Then she's crazy."

"Well, that is another thing. Wilt tells me Sarah has said some pretty crazy things lately. I'm not fond of the idea she's alone with our whole family. Maybe your mother could watch them if you want to go riding again."

I started out of the water. "I'm not sure my mother would understand me wanting a break." I expected him to get up and move back when I came dripping out of the creek in my slip. "Are you going to move?"

"No ma'am. Right now I'm watching."

He probably saw his mistake when I walked right into him, knocking him over backward and laying my wet body on top of him. I thought it was going to be intimate but we both dissolved in laughter. The intimacy came afterward.

When we got back home, Sarah met us in the yard and she was frantic. That was not at all what I was prepared for.

"Katie, for heaven's sake," Sarah wailed. "I didn't know where you went. I saw the horse was gone, but you left the boys in the stable. They had pitchforks. And the babies were crying. I didn't know what to do. I think Hicke was here. He didn't know where you were either. I have to go. Where are my boys? They didn't go to the barn, did they? There are pitchforks there."

Hicke and I looked at each other. Finally, I walked up, hugged Sarah, and thanked her for watching the children. Hicke got Thomas and Robert out of the house and loaded in her wagon, and they left.

"Oh no," Hicke and I said to each other.

Afterward, I felt guilty for indulging myself. But I wondered if motherhood was pushing Sarah beyond her mental or emotional limits. I knew I didn't want to end up like her. Partly because of Hicke's concerns, I didn't see Sarah for several months. Then I started feeling guilty about avoiding her, so one morning after the older boys went to school, I took Ella, Herman, and baby Rekka over to Sarah and Wilt's farm. When I got there around noon I found Folka, Hicke and Wilt's mother, caring for Sarah's two little boys.

Folka wasn't expecting me, but she was always happy to see any of her grandchildren. "Goodness, they growed since I saw them. Look little Rekka, she running all over now," Folka said. Ella, Herman, and Rekka began playing with Robert and Thomas, and the toys they had strewn about.

I gave my mother-in-law a hug and sat down to chat. "I came to check on Sarah. The last time she was at my place, she seemed to be upset."

"She not here. Gone about a week. Poor Wilt, he fit to be tied. *Außer sich.*"

"I don't understand. Where is she?" I sometimes had a little trouble understanding Folka's mix of German and English, complete with various hand gestures.

"Strange man found her walking road to Pickrell. *Die kinder* here alone. She no tell him who was she. He gave her a ride to Pickrell and Reverend Gates came. He recognized her, had doctor examine her. They took her to hospital Beatrice, but she in the *Wahnsinnsstation,* how you say, madness ward. Wilt not able to see her. Thank goodness Reverend knew who was she. Why, anything could have happened to her," Folka said, fighting back tears.

I felt the tears filling my eyes too. "Oh, my goodness. Maybe something did happen to her. I mean, she's here all alone with the children all day. Wilt is usually out in the field. Maybe someone broke in or …" I didn't want to think about the consequences or how vulnerable we all might be.

"No, not *das*. She has rifle, and she knows how to shoot it if anyone comes she not trust," Folka explained.

I didn't like to imagine my unstable sister-in-law having a rifle handy. "When is she coming home? Can I help in any way?"

"Coming today with the children, *das ist gut*. Just knowing *das* family is here for her."

Hicke wasn't nearly so understanding that night when I explained what I had found out from his mother when we went to bed.

"You should stay out of it, Katie. If she has gotten so bad, she might be dangerous. You shouldn't take the children over there. I'll talk to Wilt. I'm sure there is a way he can handle this."

"But Hicke, you don't understand. Maybe she needs someone to talk to, someone who understands how hard it can be to be isolated with just little children day in and day out. I remember what it was like with two little boys running circles around me at that age."

"Don't be ridiculous. Taking care of children is your job, her job. It's what mothers do. It may get on your nerves at times, but most women don't go crazy. You haven't gone crazy, and you have five children."

I stared at the ceiling, a feeling of hopelessness washing over me. I feel like I might go crazy sometimes like I am trapped in my own mental ward run by children. He didn't get it.

It was a year and a half before I saw Sarah again, at a family gathering at Dick and Folka's house. I almost didn't recognize her. Her beautiful blonde hair had been cut short. When I recognized it was her, I went over and embraced her, but I could see Hicke giving me a disapproving look. She barely hugged me back, and I thought maybe she'd forgotten me. I was noticeably pregnant with Margaret, and she put her hand on my belly and smiled, but didn't speak. Her son, Thomas came up and asked her something I couldn't hear, and she turned and followed him outside. I stood there baffled, not knowing what to make of her. I don't know why I didn't follow her outside to speak to her privately. I always had the nagging feeling I should be saving her in order to save my own sanity.

The first few years of our marriage were blissful as wildflowers filling a meadow. We hardly ever had a cross word between us. When the children began getting older and more disobedient, I could see the differences in how Hicke and I dealt with them. They rarely challenged him, for fear of a swift and harsh discipline. He rarely had to impose the discipline because he was taller and had a booming voice. But when he was out of sight, I felt outnumbered and lost my temper with the children too often.

With a family the size of mine, some knew how to appease me, and others seemed to antagonize me. If George could make me furious, his brother Dick would calm me down or vice versa. It sometimes seemed like a little game they played, a game Ella and Herman learned all too quickly.

I no longer had any time to myself. I was used to that as the youngest child in my family growing up. If my husband wanted to be alone, he went to work in the field. I was grateful when he started taking our sons with him to do the farm labor.

Hicke was running into other problems. He had grown up farming with his father and brothers, in Germany, then in Illinois, and finally in Nebraska. It had been profitable, even when they were renting land until they could buy a farm. He was such a believer in hard work reaping its own reward. But when you have eight children and counting, you require a certain level of income too.

Hicke, his brothers, and my cousins all complained about falling farm prices and gouging by the railroads for hauling grain. Then there were weather issues too: it was either too dry or it wouldn't stop raining when it was time to harvest or plant. I suppose he was feeling a little trapped in his life too. He had too much invested in farming to pull up stakes and move to the city.

The country itself went into a depression starting in 1893. That affected farm prices and, according to the newspapers, one in six American men in cities lost their jobs. Banks and railroads were failing by the hundreds across the nation.

With all these pressures, Hicke and I started fighting with each other.

Our house was plenty large when we first moved into it with one child and one on the way. By the time we had eight children, they were sharing bedrooms. The younger girls had three in a room.

"We have to add on to the house," I told my husband, over dinner one night in September of 1906. "This baby I'm carrying will make eleven of us under one roof."

"You always act like that is so unusual. My parents had eleven children," Hicke said dismissively. "Where do you think I would find the time or money to add rooms to this house? It's fine. It's bigger than most of the houses around."

"Fine. I'll just talk to Daddy about it." I knew it was the wrong thing to say as the words were coming out of my mouth.

He slammed his mug on the table. "This ain't none of your daddy's business. You may have been a spoiled child when I met you, but times have changed. I don't want to talk about this anymore."

"You can talk to your children like that, but not to your wife!" I declared, a little louder than I intended. I marched out the front door, banging it behind me. I knew by now if we were arguing, leaving him to deal with the children was always a good strategy. I also knew he hated that.

I was surprised at how quickly he followed me outside. I glanced back at the house figuring chaos must be raining down with both of us out of earshot.

"Where are you going?" Hicke demanded.

I turned on my heel and waved my arms at him. "Maybe I needed to get out of the house because it is so crowded I can't breathe! Maybe I should go back to my parents and let them pamper me again. It's nice to find out after all of this time you thought I was a spoiled brat when you married me."

He took a breath. "Okay, I probably shouldn't have said that. You get so hysterical when you are expecting. Every little thing upsets you," he said, trying to reach out to me.

"What? You think I get hysterical when I'm expecting?" I shrieked at him. "Then I must have been hysterical throughout our whole marriage because I am always expecting!" I started to cry, which made me angrier because it seemed to prove his point. He put his arms around me, and I tried to push him back but he pulled harder until I caved into him. When I could speak again I added, "I'm not done talking about the house, you know."

He sighed, "Oh, I know."

When he tried to kiss me, I turned my face away and said, "Don't kiss me anymore."

"What do you mean? You said you love the way I kiss you."

"I do. I love it a lot. But that's what leads to the …" I put my hands on my protruding belly, "hysteria."

He wrapped his arms around me from behind, and put his hands over mine, and started nuzzling the back of my neck. His full beard tickled me.

I closed my eyes and relaxed my shoulders, enjoying the sensation spreading across my back. When I opened my eyes, I murmured, "We have an audience." He looked up then to see the children watching through the door and window.

"Well, then you'd better kiss me. We have to show them that married people disagree, they may even holler a little, but they still love each other," Hicke said.

I let him pull me back into a frontal embrace, then he kissed me like he did when we were still courting, the kind of kiss that made my knees weak and my heart melt. And we found we had a cheering section once more.

It turned out it wasn't only the children or my husband who made me angry: it was losing people I loved. I guess I had been protected my whole life. I had never lost a brother or sister, never even lost a child when I was pregnant. You realize the older people in your life are going to die and you will outlive them. But you still hope it doesn't happen.

Momma had been feeling poorly for about four months. I tried to visit often. She got to the point where she couldn't handle the noise and activity of all my children, so I tried to go there when the older ones were in school. I had four-year-old Martha and three-year-old Hicke Johannes to bring along. And I'd had another baby earlier in the year, Emma Clara. I did worry the baby's crying might bother Momma, but my daddy helped by taking her outside when I wanted to talk to Momma. He didn't want to hear what we were saying anyway because he knew it would be her time to leave us soon, and he couldn't bear it.

"Your daddy is going to need you, Darling, to help him get through this. I understand you have your plate full, overflowing really, with those children. My grandchildren and they are all delightful. But check in on him. I hope he will marry again, I honestly do. He knew I would probably go first when we got together, but it is different when the time comes," Momma told me.

"Don't worry about Daddy, Momma. I will be there for him," I said through my tears.

All of my half-brothers and sisters came to Momma's funeral. Johann was nearby, Antje, Mareka, and Margaretha were all living in Franklin County, Nebraska, and Klass and Trintje were in Gothenburg, Nebraska. Their families filled half of the church. Momma's brothers, the Meintses, and their families attended too. I sat in the front holding Daddy's hand as I had promised. Hicke and our brood were on my other side, surprisingly subdued.

I asked my father to come to stay with us for a few days, so I could try to help him. I hoped the activity of a busy household might take his mind off her death. But he sat off by himself most of the time, and I felt like I was failing him even while I was taking care of my own family.

I asked Hicke what I should do to help Daddy.

"Do what you do best, Katie. Talk to him. Make him talk to you, about Alma, about anything."

I tried that the next evening when my father had retreated to the porch after supper.

"Tell me about the day you and Momma got married. I love to hear that story."

"Don't ask me to talk about her, Katie. I can't do that. Not now. It will only make me cry," Daddy answered.

"Then cry. I'll cry too. Come in the house and we can all cry together."

We got through it somehow. Daddy was never the same though. That made me angry. He had always been my hero. He taught me how to ride, to swim, to shoot, to bale hay, nearly anything I could do on the farm. And now he was a shell as though the happiness had been knocked clear out of him.

After our next baby, Tena Lena was born in February 1911, we had to deal with the next blow. Dick Hikken Baumfalk contracted pneumonia in November and died after two weeks. I wasn't so close to my father-in-law, but it was worse to watch Hicke go through the same thing after I lost my mother. Not only were Hicke and his brothers and sisters enduring the emotional toll of losing their father, Hicke and his brother Wilt lived the closest to their parents so they were named the executors. Hicke, being the elder of the two, took on most of the responsibility. Wilt, unfortunately, was still dealing with Sarah's instability. Gustav was the oldest son, but he was farther away, farming near Harbine.

I didn't know much about wills or estates. When Momma died, everything she owned was in Daddy's name. She'd let me pick out a few trinkets she had saved, and my sisters also took things like ivory-handled hairbrushes or special plates.

But Dick owned real estate, had rental property, plus money at home and in the bank. Some people even owed him money, I guess, although we didn't. Hicke said this was all supposed to go to Folka. When she died it would be divided among her children, and one granddaughter, nineteen-year-old Bena DeVries. The last one surprised me. None of the other grandchildren were named in Dick's will. Bena had been living with Dick and Folka for most of her childhood and had helped care for him. Hicke explained the will was written to include Folka because Dick didn't always have Folka's name on the properties he owned. Married women had not been allowed to own property until about fifteen years ago.

Hicke and I had recently purchased some of Daddy's land and it was in both of our names, so it wouldn't be an issue regardless of which one of us died first. Hicke said we should make sure everything was in both of our names. It was an education, doing the probate, but it reminded us how fleeting our time on earth was.

I only saw Sarah one more time. She and Wilt came over to meet with Hicke about their father's estate, bringing the youngest two boys, six-year-old Wilhelm, and three-year-old Adolph. They were the same ages as Emma and Hickey, but they had not been around each other. In no time at all, the children were sharing toys and books and getting along fine. Hicke and Wilt sat at the table to work on some papers, so I took Sarah out to the barn to get out of the March wind.

"Tell me what has been going on with you, Sarah. I wanted to come to visit but it's been so hectic lately," I said somewhat cautiously.

"Well, I am better now. I was in the hospital for a long time. It wasn't like going into the hospital to have a baby. I know what that is like. After Little Adolph was born, everything got so dark. I came home with him, but he seemed like he didn't even belong to me. I wanted to nurse him and care for him, but he seemed like a foreign creature, not my baby. It was so confusing. It was scary. Even Wilhelm, he was only three and such a dear boy, but he suddenly seemed like he didn't belong there. They told me this happens to new mothers sometimes it's like a dark fog surrounds them. It has something to do with a chemical in your brain, I forget what they called it."

"I think I read something about it in the paper. So how did they cure you?"

"That wasn't fun. Wilt took me to a doctor and they committed me at once. I thought they would help me, but I don't know if anything they do in that place works. They like to give you ice cold baths as if freezing you to death will drive out your demons. I hated it because your hair gets wet and they don't let you dry off before you are shuttled off to bed, so your sheets get wet. I didn't think I would ever get warm again. Most of the time, they had you sit on a bench with other patients with nothing to do. But you learn pretty quickly you don't give those nurses any trouble or they will chain your leg to the bed."

Up to this point, I believed Sarah was completely lucid and talking like anyone else would, but now I wondered if she had imagined some of this. "They put you in cold baths and chained you up? How would that help? Did you tell your husband about this?" I cried in disbelief.

"Naturally he was busy taking care of the baby and Wilhelm, so he didn't come to see me for several weeks, maybe longer. It was hard to keep track when every day is the same. I did tell him when he finally came. He talked to the doctor, and I guess the doctor thought I was better so I came home. Honestly, probably all I needed was time, and the demons went away on their own. I never want to go back there again. I'd rather die."

"Don't say that, Sarah," I warned. "Please don't say you would rather die. Someone is likely to think you are crazy, and you might have to go back. It seems so unfair. Once they have decided you are on the edge, anything you say might be misinterpreted. Your children need you. You have to stay strong for them."

Sarah hugged me as she used to before any of this happened.

"You've been good to me, Katie. I hope you will watch out for my little ones if anything happens. I wish they had a mother like you." Sarah turned and walked back to the house, leaving me tearful and confused about her mental state.

Talking to Hicke about Sarah that night in bed was frustrating. He took Wilt's side and said it was a husband's duty to have his wife committed if he thought she posed a threat to their children. He dismissed the conditions she described to me as part of her delusion.

"I thought you were a little crazy when we first met," Hicke chuckled at the memory. "Right up front, you told me all of this stuff about your mother and how your daddy was so much younger than her. And when we went horseback riding, you undressed and jumped in the creek. That seemed pretty peculiar at the time. Then I realized it was just your way of getting my attention."

"You call it crazy. I call it effective," I snuggled up next to him. "And don't ever think about sending me away."

"I wouldn't dream of it."

About a year later when I was pregnant with baby number twelve, I again tried to convince Hicke to expand the house, and he finally agreed to build the addition after the harvest was done. He planned to frame in some extra rooms before winter set in, then finish the inside afterward. It was September, and Hicke, George, Dick, and Herman were all helping with the threshing. My little boys had grown into young men, but they were still firmly camped in my house and probably would be until they took wives of their own.

Only Ella had married and moved out, but her husband, Lubbe Rademacker, was out of town for a few days. She was staying over with us to help feed the threshers.

Hicke and I were sitting outdoors in adjoining wooden armchairs in the waning hours of the daylight. We watched the children try their hands at a game of croquet, a gift from a neighbor whose children had grown and moved away.

"I've decided this baby is the last one. I figured I should tell you. Once this baby is born, I am closed for business," I said firmly, trying to keep a straight face.

"I'm sorry to hear it," he said also using a serious tone. "And how many times do you reckon you have told me that?" He ran the side of his forefinger casually down my arm watching me try to hide my goosebumps. I turned my palm upward in anticipation.

My eyes flickered to his finger, still stroking my arm. "I don't remember. Maybe five or six. But this time, I mean it." I couldn't conceal the smile then.

"Whatever you say, my love. I'm going to bed. For some reason, I am tuckered out tonight. Maybe I am getting too old for threshing." He slid his hand into mine and squeezed it as he rose. "Can you round up this gang of ruffians yourself?"

Once I got everyone else to bed, I was pretty tired myself. I was always ready for sleep by the time I was five months along. Being pregnant meant I couldn't make it through the night without getting up to visit the outhouse. I was getting back into bed about 3:00 a.m. when I noticed Hicke was not breathing normally. He usually snored a little, but this was different. It was more of a gasping sound. I shook him awake, but he didn't even open his eyes. That's when I started screaming. If that didn't wake him up, nothing would. My oldest boys, George and Dick were the first to charge through our bedroom door, followed closely by Ella and Rekka.

I raced for the phone on the kitchen wall and frantically told the operator to get Dr. Boggs from Filley, my husband might be having a heart attack. I put Rekka on the line to hold for the doctor, and I went back to try to help Hicke. The boys and I tried to lift him to a sitting position, thinking it would be easier to breathe, but his breathing got fainter and he slumped in our hands.

"No!" I screamed at him, "You are not doing this to me! You are not leaving me with eleven children on my own! Breathe, dammit, breathe!" I tried shaking his shoulders.

"Momma, stop!" George told me and drew me away from Hicke. He was crying now. "It's too late, Momma. He's passed."

I surveyed the room, gasping for breath myself. Dick and Ella were crying too. Rekka was still in the kitchen holding the phone, but she was leaning on the wall weeping. Herman had come in carrying Tena. Margaret and Frauka were gathered next to Ella, and she drew them close to her. Martha, Hickey, and Emma tried to cling to me but I brushed them aside. I knelt next to the bed and took Hicke's hand which was slowly losing warmth.

"Don't leave me, my darling, I love you," was all I could say before the sobs overtook me and I buried my face on his chest. I heard George asking the older girls to take the little ones out of the room.

But Ella protested, "No. When the doctor comes, he will take him away. We need to say good-bye while we can."

I was vaguely aware of each of the children coming up and stroking my hair then and patting Hicke's shoulder or arm. I thought the older girls kissed his forehead. By then I wasn't sure of anything except that I wanted to wake up from this nightmare. When Dr. Boggs finally arrived nearly an hour later, George and Dick pulled me to my feet and helped me onto a kitchen chair. The older girls made sure everyone got dressed including me.

It probably goes without saying it was the worst night of my life. I kept replaying it all, wondering how it could have happened. I didn't notice anything when I left the house. Was I too sleepy to see he was fighting for his life? Would it have done any good if I had tried to wake him then? That rasping sound he was making when I came back will haunt me. I have heard people talk about a death rattle, maybe that is what it was. But he was fine. He had been teasing me, just hours before. How can someone be normal one minute and gone the next?

After they had taken Hicke's body away and the children had settled down, Ella and Rekka started breakfast. That's when my anger finally set in. And it set in but good.

I got up and went to the barn. Dick tried to stop me or join me, but I pushed him away. I thought I might saddle up Hicke's horse, Commander. My gelding, Rolf, had died years ago, and we had not gotten around to finding me another horse. I didn't trust myself to ride that morning. I went to the far side of the barn and screamed. I mean I screamed as loudly as I could. I picked up a shovel I found by one of the stalls and started beating it against the wall of the barn. I kept beating until my arms ached and I was losing my grip. I collapsed on the dirty floor and cursed. I was never one to use swear words, and Hicke rarely had but I cursed him, and God, and anyone else I could blame at the moment.

Finally, I cried. I was racked by gasping, uncontrollable sobs that shook me to the core. I held onto my belly when it seemed my abdomen was contorting in spasms. Twelve children. I had said, "don't leave me with eleven children" but there was one more. One more who hadn't even been born. This one would never even know his or her father. That led to another round of cursing and hysterical sobbing.

I don't recall how long I was in the barn. I remember being thankful I had children old enough to take care of the younger ones since their mother was having a nervous breakdown. Their father was, well …dead. I guess I had to face that sometime. The tears were spent for now, but the anger was still seething below the surface.

When I got back to the house, Ella had already called Daddy and Folka. Rekka sat me down and washed dirt and blood off my face. I guess I had gotten a little too close to the shovel. Afterward, a steady stream of relatives and friends arrived. I felt like a spectator watching someone else's life like I was hovering above the scene. I don't even remember much about the funeral except there were many people there. He was forty-nine years old. We'd been married twenty-four years. I thought my life was over too.

Daddy was the first one who was able to get through the wall I tried to build around my heart. We'd always had a special connection, and Lord knows he knew what I was going through. He acknowledged it was a whole lot different losing the love of your life at forty-nine than losing Momma at age eighty-three. But he also knew I had a lot of life left in me and my children were not getting enough attention from me in my current stupor.

He had offered to move in with us again, but there was not enough room. He suggested we go ahead with the addition I had wanted for years. He said he and the boys would get the lumber and other supplies and tools, most of which we had already. We could tear down the existing wall and add three additional rooms on the north side of the house, like the plans Hicke had drawn up months earlier. With pressure from some of the children, I agreed to go ahead with it.

The men had already done some of the framing when the day came to break down the wall on the north side of the house in November. The children had gathered to watch or help, in addition to Daddy and my son George's girlfriend, Annie Schmidt. George and Annie were planning to get married around Thanksgiving.

"Why don't you take the first swing at it, Momma?" Dick said. "After all, you're the one who has wanted this for so long." He handed me the heavy sledgehammer and I wondered if I could hold it up considering my small stature and advanced pregnancy.

I walked over to the wall. The siding had already been removed, so I was swinging at studs and the inside plasterboard. The first swing was somewhat wild, but I made a hole in the plaster wall. Everyone cheered. I guess they expected me to pass the hammer to someone else, but I kept swinging over and over again, grunting loudly, not so much to demolish the wall but to exorcise some of my pain.

George finally crept up behind me, grabbed my arm, and laid the sledgehammer on the ground. I almost hit him by accident, but he ducked.

"Enough, Momma. You've done enough. You're still carrying a child. Let Herman have a swing at it now." Annie came up next to George and gently led me back to where the rest of the family had been standing.

George reminded me so much of his father then, I could hardly stand to look at him. Dick resembled Hicke more, or how he looked in his twenties. They were more the same size, where George was taller. Often George would say something or move like his father, and I couldn't bear it. I appreciated how Annie simply stood with me and didn't try to make me talk. If I had to open my mouth, I was afraid of what would come out.

Even though those two older boys were rascals when they were little, they were a godsend in the months after Hicke died. They took over the farming, helped my daddy, and even went over to check on Folka. Margaret and Rekka kept the household running while I slowly began to join the living. With everyone's help, we finished the addition by Christmas and solved the overcrowding problem. I wasn't sure if I would be able to celebrate George's wedding, but Annie's mother was a great comfort and even gave me a glass of wine from their vineyard near Cortland.

As we got into January and the baby was expected, it got harder for me again. The children all seemed to sense this and gathered around more than usual. Even the little ones, like Emma and Tena, wanted to be held and to feel the baby kicking every chance they got. The older children decided Dick and Rekka would go with me to the hospital while George and Annie took over our house in my absence. They obviously were trying so hard to make me forget that one very important participant in the baby-making process was missing. Still, I got through it. I probably didn't cry any more than I had delivering every other child. I felt a little guilty when I remembered I had predicted Anna Hilka would be the last of twelve.

When you have had so many babies, the newborn care comes back to you even if it had been years. Holding and feeding Anna was probably the best medicine for me. Despite my pain, I appreciated that she was a gift from beyond the grave, which few mothers ever receive. Still, I knew the anger was still inside of me somewhere, waiting to erupt when I didn't expect it.

One day in April, we were cleaning out a cabinet because we were moving some furniture around. I found a set of ten china plates and a few cups one of my mother's aunts had left to her. She didn't need them at the time, so she had given them to me. I never liked them and had only used them a few times when we had a lot of company to feed. Some of them were even chipped.

The older kids were in school, and Tena and Emma were playing in the living room. Anna was napping in her bassinet in the bedroom. Ella was visiting, but she had gone to the barn for something. I dropped one of the plates on the floor, and it shattered into about eight pieces. I didn't drop it by accident, I did it deliberately. Tena and Emma, who were three and five, were startled.

"Come on girls, we're going to play a game. Let's take these dishes outside," I said.

As I hauled the box of dishes outside, I thought about how to do this with the least amount of mess to clean up. We went out to the shed, which had a nice stone wall without windows. I hurled a plate discus-style directly into the wall and it shattered. The little girls laughed, and I smiled.

"Now me!" Emma cried, and she threw a cup at the wall. It took a few tries before her cup hit hard enough to break. Tena stood right next to the wall in her attempt to throw a cup, but there wasn't enough force to do more than chip it.

I made them come back and stand behind me. I threw the rest of the plates one by one as hard as I could. We all cheered like it was an athletic event. I was starting on the cups when Ella suddenly burst upon us.

"My God, Mother, are you crazy? They're going to lock you up like Aunt Sarah."

I turned on Ella, and for a second I wanted to throw the cup at her. "Don't ever talk about Sarah like that again!" I screamed. "You have no idea what the poor woman went through. She died in that awful place." I threw the cup in my hand at the stone wall. After it shattered, I took both little girls in hand and marched back to the house. I left the mess of broken plates and cups and a couple of unbroken cups where they lay.

Sure, it seemed crazy at the time, but it felt so good. I had to endure all four of my oldest children chiding me for possibly putting the girls in danger from flying china pieces or at least setting a bad example. When your children become adults they forget you're the mother sometimes. Only Annie held back and listened.

"You're still angry," Annie said quietly when the others had left us alone. "I saw my Grandma go through this after Grandpa died. She never hurt a fly until he died suddenly, then gadzooks! She had a lot of temper tantrums."

"How did she get past it?" I asked her.

Annie shrugged, "She didn't. She died too."

By then, I knew I wasn't going to give up and die. I needed to take care of the younger children, and my father's health was beginning to fail. I started going over to his place a few times a week. I asked him to move in with me, but he said he felt closer to my mother at their place. How could I deprive him of that? My daddy, Jürgen Hansen Freese, died on December 19, 1915. They said his heart failed. I knew it had been broken. I was officially an orphan and a widow at forty-five.

CHAPTER THREE

While my daddy was ill, something else was happening to me. Wilhelm Heinrich Dissmeyer saved me from myself. I wish I could say I fell head over heels in love with him as I had with Hicke, but I wasn't capable of it in the shape I was in. But he truly was the friend I needed most at that time. He knew exactly what I was going through after Hicke died because he'd been on the same journey.

Hicke and I had known the Dissmeyer family for many years. Hicke's sister, Fulkelena, or Lena, had married Henry Dissmeyer in 1896. Henry's parents had lived in Illinois, then Kansas, finally settling on a farm southwest of Firth, Nebraska, which Henry and Lena took over by 1900. Henry's brother, August, married Hicke's sister, Dena, in 1897 and they lived on farms in Nemaha and Highland Townships in Gage County. So we had been to many family get-togethers that involved Dissmeyers. Wilhelm, or William, an older brother, and his wife, Mary, were often in attendance. They had stayed in Lincolnville, Kansas when the rest of the family moved to Nebraska. William and Mary had ten children.

They were kind enough to continue to include me on invitations to Baumfalk family events, even after Hicke's death. I don't recall exactly who told me William's wife had passed away, but at some point, I had heard about it.

In the middle of the harvest in 1915, I ran into William for the first time in several years. We were at Henry's farm, and the men were combining forces to do the harvesting and threshing, and the women were preparing massive amounts of food for the crews. Everyone ate outdoors on large plank tables, and there was general milling about and catching up during the breaks.

"Katie," William called out to me, "I haven't seen you at one of these in a coon's age. How are you?"

I struggled to answer that question in recent years. Was I expected to be "fine" or was I forever supposed to be a grieving widow?

"Better. It has been a tough few years, but today is a beautiful day."

I had the feeling he wanted to talk. "Come take a walk with me," William suggested.

When we started toward the trail by the pasture, he went on, "I was so sorry to hear about Hicke. He was a fine man and was admired by a good many folks."

I'd learned to steel myself for such a remark. "Thank you. I was sorry to hear about Mary too. When did she pass?" We were coming to the fence line now, and I traced my hand gently across the top of the fence as we walked.

"Just over two years now. September of 1913. Doesn't seem that long ago."

I stopped short and looked at him like he'd punched me in the stomach. "Really? September two years ago? What date?" I knew he would know the exact date his wife died.

"September 26th. She was forty years old. Why do you ask? What's the matter?" he said when he saw my expression.

I breathed out a sigh. "It feels a little eerie. I'm not sure why it should. Hicke died on September 13, 1913. He was forty-nine. And you're right, sometimes it seems like yesterday. And you know," I hesitated, "I'm still pretty angry at him."

"For dying?" William asked.

"Yes. It sounds silly, it's not his—"

He interrupted, "It sounds perfectly normal to me."

"Yeah?" I squinted at him dubiously. I caught myself pulling a lock of hair out of my braid, and twisting it in my fingers, something I hadn't done in years.

"I feel the same way. What gave Mary the right to go and die on me after everything we'd been through together?"

"Sakes alive, where have you been all of my life?" It sounded much too flirtatious after I said it. "I'm sorry, I only meant you seem to understand. If I tell my children I am angry at their father for leaving me or throw something in anger, they tell me to get over it like there is a deadline on grieving and I am long past it."

William laughed. "They must be talking to my children." Then he looked at me intently. "Give me your telephone number and address. I'm still living in Kansas right now, but I have been thinking about moving up here to see more of my brothers and their families. But I can at least write to you and call you when I am in this area. Maybe we could be mad at them together."

I laughed and agreed. No one had made me feel like myself in the past two years until that moment. Maybe Little Lady Katie hadn't died on the vine.

Even though I didn't want to think about William in that way, the truth is, for a man of his age, he was very handsome. It is completely unfair men can get better looking with age, while women seem to go the other way. I suppose it has more to do with having babies than anything else. I wasn't any raving beauty at eighteen, but at least I had a nice figure, which seemed to disappear with every additional pregnancy. I didn't mind having curves, but now it seemed like my curves had their own curves. What would a man like William ever see in me? Maybe it didn't matter since we were just going to be friends.

I received some nice letters from him. At first, he talked about his late wife often, but after a few letters back and forth, it seemed like we got the grief out of our systems and we wrote about our current lives and what was going on with our families. Sometimes he helped me figure out what was going on with the young men in my household, and I helped him decipher the behavior of his young ladies, although I was dealing with more girls and he was dealing with more boys at the time.

I saw William again when his children had a break around Christmas and they all came north by train to visit his brothers. He surprised me one day, riding up alone on one of Henry's horses.

"William? I'm surprised you had a chance to come all the way out here," I called, from the porch when I saw the horse trotting up the drive.

"I hope it is okay to come to see you. I took a chance," he said.

"Of course, come in. Some of the children are over at a friend's house. A bit of a holiday party. But the younger ones are here." I introduced William to Frauka, Martha, Hick, Emma, Tena, and Anna.

William sat by the warm stove and accepted a cookie Frauka had taken out of the oven. "This is nice," he said. "Your house is a good size for a big family."

I cast my eyes heavenward, "You hear that, Hicke? It's finally big enough for a dozen children!" I laughed at my own joke. "I had a little trouble convincing my husband to add onto the house." I gave him a tour of the place, and then we sat at the kitchen table.

"It's good to see you, Katie. You are looking well," he said. He appeared to be gathering his courage. "You know, I haven't done this for a very long time."

"Haven't done what? Visited a friend?"

"I reckon you can tell from our letters we are getting to be more than friends. That's why I came today. We need to figure out if we want to take this further. I live quite a ways from here. We spent all day traveling, making train connections in Junction City. We are miles from Junction City in Lincolnville, and Henry is a long way from Beatrice where we got off the train. I would really like to be with you, but we need to see if it is practical. We are long past the age where we are swept off our feet with caprice."

I couldn't quite believe this was happening. Again. In the past few weeks, the letters had been full of harmless flirting, or at least that was what I thought. Maybe I didn't dare think it would ever be more. Did I want it to be more? Why did I feel like I had to be alone to be true to Hicke's memory?

"I'm not completely sure I understand what kind of relationship you want," I said.

He glanced around at the children, who seemed to be completely lost in their activities. "Well, come into the bedroom, and I will show you."

That made me laugh. He couldn't mean …

"No, I'm sorry, that came out wrong." He was blushing now, something he probably expected he would never do again. "I just want to kiss you."

I was still astonished, but I let him take me by the hand to the bedroom. He pinned me against the closed door and kissed me several times.

"You thought I meant …" He glanced toward the bed, and I raised my eyebrows. "Well, not today anyway."

"So how exactly do you see this playing out, Mr. Dissmeyer?" I wiped my mouth, trying to get my head to catch up with my pounding heart. "I mean, what are you thinking? Surely you know I have nine children still living with me, and you have…what…six?"

"Seven, I'm afraid. I need to be sure we both want the same thing. If you are not interested in getting more involved, tell me."

I stared at him for a moment. "I don't reckon I can tell you that," I said, pulling him back into my arms.

William and I spent the rest of the day together, and he came back two days later and stayed the night. We decided we were going to try to make this thing work. We bundled up my children and took them over to Henry's farm so they could meet William's clan. When he got back to Kansas, he started preparing to sell his farm. I wasn't sure how George, Dick, and Ella would feel about adding a whole new family to our house and our farm, but the younger children who were still living here seemed to like his children.

I can't say I didn't have second thoughts about adding seven more children to my household. I mean, twelve children is a lot, but sixteen seemed unmanageable. I wondered what kind of trouble my kids would give him, and his kids would give me. But in the end, it should be about what works for William and me. Who knew how little time we had left to carve out some happiness for ourselves?

Luckily, William had a plan. He was a good planner. He sold his farm in Lincolnville in March but made arrangements for the family to continue to live in the house until school was over. While he waited, he began shipping any equipment he wanted to keep to his brothers in Nebraska, and they began hauling things to my place. By the end of May, they had shipped the belongings they had not sold, and William and his seven children arrived in Nebraska. William remodeled the house again, tacking on a new addition. He planned to create sleeping rooms for the older children, putting the boys together, then putting the girls together in separate quarters. The young ones were still sharing rooms like they were used to and were closer to us. It was chaos for a while, but it seemed to work. He also brought some apple, maple, and peach trees from their orchard in Kansas, and a few hens so his children would feel like they had ties to the place where they had been born.

Young George was still running the farm and William didn't interfere. His second son, August, also came by to help on the farm and with all of the other work going on. We'd planned to get married shortly after they arrived, but we postponed the wedding because we didn't have time and everyone that might come was busy with farm work in the summer. It didn't matter much to William and me when we tied the knot.

George was sitting at the dining table with me after dinner one evening in July while William was outdoors. He said he wanted to talk to me alone.

"Momma, you're not planning to marry William, are you?" he asked cautiously.

"Well, that's the idea, but we may not get around to it for a little bit."

"But how is that going to affect the farm? You and Father owned this farm together and you inherited some of it from Grandpa. If something happened to you, it would go to William and then to his children."

"We've got it all figured out, don't worry," I assured George. "We have a meeting set up with an attorney in Beatrice. Someone I have known for years, Gerd Zimmerman. He used to work on farm real estate transactions but now he does estates. We are going to separate the inheritance so that his children will inherit his money and mine will inherit whatever I have, including the farm."

"But how do you know he isn't interested in you for the farm?"

"Oh my God, you sound exactly like your father. He asked me the same thing once." George looked puzzled. I got up and searched through our kitchen drawer until I found what I wanted. I handed him the advertisement for William's farm sale in March.

"Read this. This is what he had in Kansas and sold to move up here. A farm with ninety-five acres of prairie grass, a creek running through it, fifty acres of bottom ground, thirty acres of wheat, and seven in alfalfa. Lots of running water and good timber. An orchard with apple and peach trees, 100 grapevines, two good wells, a house with seven rooms, a barn that holds thirty tons of hay, 500 bushels of oats, and sixteen horses. Does this seem like a man who is after my farm?"

"Well, I see what you mean. But what about his kids living here? If something happens to him, you will have even more young'uns to raise." He got a horrified look on his face and gasped, "You're not having any babies with him, are you?"

I laughed, "No, Mother Nature is giving me a helping hand there. I doubt I can have any more children, and that is a blessing. Someone should help raise his children and mine. They now have two parents again."

I picked up a kernel of corn which had fallen on the table from our meal. "You see this picayune piece of corn, Dear? You were no bigger than this when I starting growing you inside me, and I grew you to be a full-size baby, and I raised you to be a strong young man who is bigger than I am now. Your father did everything he could to teach you in his lifetime. And we loved you to pieces, but you are not going to tell me what to do with my money, my farm, my body, or my heart. You understand, Son? Now, you go on home to your wife and baby."

He held my gaze, slowly put his hat back on, and walked out

the door.

We finally got around to having the wedding on January 25, 1917, at the Emmanuel Lutheran Church. It was mostly our children in attendance. We thought we had handled the blending of our families about as well as we could. But one evening, in early February, something happened we had not anticipated.

My third son, Herman, asked if he could speak to William and me alone after dinner, so we told him to come into our bedroom. Herman was twenty years old, and I guessed he may be making plans to move out. William and I were already seated in the bedroom when Herman peeked around the door and then entered, pulling William's daughter, nineteen-year-old Johanna, or Hanna, by the hand. They both stood there, holding hands.

Herman tried to find his voice. "We are getting married."

William gaped at me and then at Herman and Hanna. "You mean to each other?"

"Yes, Papa," Hanna confirmed in a shaky voice like she was expecting the sky to fall.

"How long has this been going on?" William asked reproachfully. I put a hand on his arm to try to keep him calm.

"Nothing is going on, I swear," Herman said quickly. "We've known each other for some time, and now that we are living in the same place, we have gotten close. I mean we want to be together. You two didn't even know each other very well, and you got married."

William started to retort, but I interjected.

"Are you having a baby?" I asked bluntly.

"No! God no, I knew they would think that," Herman said,

turning to Hanna and blushing. "The hell with this. We are old enough to get married without your approval."

I faced William. "If Hanna wanted to marry some other nice twenty-year-old man, what would you say to them?"

"I guess I would want to know about his family. *Hmmm*, I guess I do know about his family, don't I?"

He didn't say anything more, but got up from the bed and gave Hanna a hug. She was starting to cry. Then he shook Herman's hand and ended up hugging him too. I waited until he was done, then hugged them both.

They were married in March, and it was another celebration combining our two families. By the time William's sons Reinhardt and August married my daughters Margaret and Frauka years later, it didn't seem so unusual. William and I had somehow reinvented the family as we knew it before. Even though we didn't have children together, we would have grandchildren in common. I can't say I didn't miss Hicke every day, but I learned to appreciate all he had given me when I looked at his offspring and was fortunate enough to see a whole new generation born.

I lost William after six years of marriage, but I was able to stay on my farm. For a few years, I lived in Beatrice, then my children convinced me to go live with my youngest daughter, Anna. I begged to return to my home farm, and after a year they let me. That is where the memories of my Momma and Daddy lived, and I could imagine I was still in the arms of my beloved Hicke. Little Lady Katie was back home again.

FREESE/ BAUMFALK FAMILY

ALMA MEINTS----------------------------------FOLKERT CROSS
             CHILDREN:
             JOHANN FOLKERTS CROSS
             ANTJE CROSS
             KLASS CROSS
             MAREKA FOKERTS CROSS
             TRINTJE FOLKERTS CROSS
             MARGRETHA FOLKERTS CROSS

ALMA MEINTS------------------------JURGEN HANSEN FREESE
             CHILDREN:
             FRAUKE JURGENS FREESE "KATIE"

FOLKA FREESE-----------------------DIRK HIKKEN BAUMFALK
             CHILDREN:
             GUSTAV GERHART BAUMFALK
             GRETJE BAUMFALK
             HICKE WELTS BAUMFALK
             WILT H. BAUMFALK
             ANTJE BAUMFALK
             HERMAN BAUMFALK
             (FULKE)LENA BAUMFALK
             MARTIN HIKKEN BAUMFALK
             DENA F. BAUMFALK
             FRIEDERICH DIRKS BAUMFALK
             DIEDRICH D. BAUMFALK

KATIE FREESE----------------------HICKE WELTS BAUMFALK
             CHILDREN:
             JURGEN HANSEN BAUMFALK
             DICK HICK BAUMFALK
             ALMT ELLA MARGARETHA BAUMFALK
             HERMAN FRIEDRICK BAUMFALK
             REKKA FRIEDERIKA BAUMFALK
             MARGARET J. BAUMFALK
             FRAUKA KATHERINA BAUMFALK
             MARTHA WILKELMINE BAUMFALK
             HICK JOHANNES BAUMFALK
             EMMA CLARA BAUMFALK
             TENA LENA BAUMFALK
             ANNA HILKA BAUMFALK

"Katie" Frauke Freese and Hicke Welts Baumfalk
Married February 21, 1889

AFTERWORD

It's been my experience that you only start to appreciate history when you become part of it. One day you wake up and realize that you are in the oldest generation of your family, and you can remember many years that other people cannot because they were not born yet. So this book, *HER Side of HIStory, Finding My Foremothers' Footprints* is an evolution of my newfound interest in family genealogy.

Initially, I rejected the notion that I was going to research my family tree. No, I was only interested in portraits of my direct ancestors and those of my husband. We had five generations of dead people hanging on the bedroom wall over our heads while we slept for ten years. When it was time to redecorate, and I decided to scan my historic photographs and put them in a place where other, younger family members would have access to them. Ancestry.com was one logical spot for that. To put the photos online, I had to add some details to the family trees. After that, it didn't take long before I caught the genealogy bug, and I was chasing down different branches in many directions.

Several members of different families had put together reports of our family history some thirty or forty years ago, and they were invaluable in getting started. However, I was able to find much more information now with the resources available to search and share on the internet. I also realized that I could search through some newspaper articles that were written over a hundred years ago to find out more about how my ancestors lived. I mean, who knew my great-grandmother gave demonstrations on how to caponize a chicken? I suppose this was the precursor to Tupperware or jewelry parties.

I dutifully created the family trees in various views and sent copies to relatives. I even included a brief profile of what I had learned about each person. But that seemed too limited. I wanted to provide a sense of how these people lived in previous times. Biographers tell the tales of famous people, why couldn't I create a fictionalized version of ordinary ancestors?

Thus began the idea of writing a historical novel about different women in my family tree. It is always easier to find information on the men in the family because they are more often in the newspapers. You can find their occupations in the historical census reports. You might find information about what they did in the war. They are sometimes profiled in books talking about pioneers of the county. With the ladies, it just looked like they stayed home and had babies. Often many babies by today's standards, but then birth control was mostly non-existent.

Most of the historical accounts of women in these times assumed they were powerless and subservient to their husbands. It seemed like they had a choice between staying in their father's household and taking care of him or marrying and subjecting themselves to the unfamiliar will of a husband, sometimes hampered by lack of education or not knowing English as new immigrants.

But I wanted to give them all a voice, sometimes in opposition, but often in support of their husbands and other family members. So I took the settings, demographics, and other factual and historical information I had on these women, and gave them fictional personalities to create compelling stories. Despite living many decades ago, they would have thought about many of the same issues facing women today: love, sex, pregnancy, family, food, shelter, money, war, occupations, relocation, and death. They may not have spoken as openly about some things as you find today, but that doesn't mean they didn't have to deal with them privately. I tried to use some timely expressions, but I didn't want to write in the style of a bygone era.

For anyone who wants more information about what sources I used, or what parts of these stories are factual, please consult my Ancestry.com pages, or visit https://claudiaseverin.net.

—Claudia Johnson Severin

ABOUT THE AUTHOR

Claudia Johnson Severin lives with her husband, Roger, on a southeastern Nebraska farm that was homesteaded in 1869 by her husband's great-grandparents, a setting for a portion of her anthology. She grew up and worked in Lincoln, Nebraska before beginning a second chapter writing historical fiction, using her ancestors as semi-fictional characters. She is a graduate of the University of Nebraska College of Journalism. Her three children and three grandchildren keep her entertained and inspired.

Thank you for reading my book. I would be happy to have you leave a review at Amazon.com, by searching the site for my name, clicking on the book, and scrolling down to the reviews. You can also review it at Goodreads.com in a similar way, or adding comments on my website.